The 7th Miracle of O.C. Merriweather

By: January Joyce

The 7th Miracle of O.C. Merriweather

ISBN: 9781728618807

ADDITIONAL WORKS BY THIS AUTHOR:

ANATOMY OF A FELON

ANATOMY OF A FELON II - TAKEOVER

HUNT FOR THE KERN RIVER KILLER
MURDER IN THE 6TH

SHAMEFUL BEINGS

DEDICATION

THIS BOOK IS DEDICATED TO MY SON, HIS WIFE, MY GRANDBABIES, MY SISTER, MY CRAZY COUSIN, AND ANYONE ELSE WHO HAS BEEN PATIENT WITH ME, SUPPORTED ME OR GUIDED ME THROUGHOUT THIS JOURNEY. I AM HUMBLY AND ETERNALLY FOREVER GRATEFUL.

SPECIAL THANKS: TRACY KELLY

"I believe in a passion for inclusion."

Lady Gaga

TABLE OF CONTENTS

PROLOGUE

You can do this, I told myself. *Don't be nervous. Follow his lead.* My heart pounded in avalanches and waves, flooding my nervous system with an infusion of fire, focus, and fear. Yeah, definitely fear. Riley took lead as we cautiously approached the suspect vehicle. My index finger glided along the smooth metal cylinder of the gun barrel, poised to pull the trigger at a moment's notice. The gun melded into an extension of my being. It became me. *Gotta make it home. Remember your training. Don't want to go out like Schwartz! Watch your partner! Cover Riley! You know he's got you covered in return!*

My shoes felt tight. Made from some new-fangled scratchproof synthetic, they shined like glass but afforded no give. Wondering why they hadn't broken in, I regretted my decision in trusting the salesperson and not going with my gut on the leather ones. With each step and then stride, I felt the sharp, splintered pinpricks of blisters beginning to form within their unrelenting death grip. Disregarding the pain, I continued my advance towards the unknown.

The day: February 4th. The year: 1993. The area: an unremarkable yet dangerous nook of Bakersfield, California, where we initiated the stop. The vehicle pulled to the side of the road one-and-a-half blocks from East Planz and South H, in a residential neighborhood across from Planz Park. The small community nook wasn't necessarily known for its tenderly-manicured lawn, stately trees, barbeque grills, and block-shaped cement picnic tables as it was for being a hotbed of criminal activity and street gangs, predominantly the Eastside Crip Disciples. The Disciples weren't your average ordinary gang of killers and thugs: they were law enforcement's worst nightmare. The Disciples had a reputation for assaulting police officers and resisting arrest. They had a blood-in, blood-out, shoot-a-cop-and-don't-go-to-jail mentality.

Dispatch was slow that day. Deserie called in sick, and her fill-in garbled half the ten codes then took her sweet time relaying the simplest communiqué. We had already exited the cruiser when the registered owner's name and vital information transmitted over the airway. "Registration's current. Owners name is Otis Cleveland Merriweather. DOB 3/5/48. 6'4". 330 lbs. Ocean. Tom. Ida. Sam."

Otis Cleveland Merriweather – the name in itself provided a wealth of information. The guy had to be Black, African American, Negro, or whatever they called themselves or was politically correct in them days. Besides race, I took into account his automobile, size, stature, the surrounding neighborhood, and all of my inner bells and alarms rang threat.

Police are supposed to epitomize bravery; I can't recall what I felt. All I can dredge up is the thundering roar of my heart's heed, cautioning me not to rush in or overlook clues. Time slowed and stole each breath for ransom. *Slow down*, I reminded myself. *Don't rush in! Don't go too fast!*

Sidling alongside the vehicle's freshly-polished exterior, I tried to get a look at the inside compartment; however, my vision failed to permeate the heavily-tinted windows, leaving me clueless as to how many people – or suspects – were in the car. *If he's Disciple, we'll call for backup. If I smell marijuana or see drugs, we'll pull him out of the vehicle and cite him for DUI and possession. If I see a gun or anything construed as a weapon…*

Riley had already reached the passenger side window. Whatever he saw had him alerted; he raised his Glock in front of himself in a stern, fire-ready position. Following suit, I raised my firearm as well. *Watch for a gun! Watch for a gun! Don't get shot!*

The driver's side window rolled down. The moment I saw him, my breath coddled. My heart skidded on a beat while my trigger finger steeled. The guy was a beast! He was as big as they come with the darkest skin I had ever seen. He had these wide-brimmed, almost snout-like nostrils that flared like a bull's when he breathed, but it was his disfigurement that set me on edge. A scar of mutilated skin traversed his left temple in a five and a half-inch fissure of flesh that glowed ghoulishly under the moon's incandescent beams.

Two-point five seconds later, I arrived at the driver's side door, parallel to Riley positioned on the opposite side of the car. We had our guns drawn as we shouted, "Roll down your window!" "Don't move!" "Place your hands on the wheel!" "Stay where you are!" "Don't move!"

The man turned out to be the sole occupant in the front seat. Besides the radio playing an old jazz tune (an annoying shrill mimicking alley cats in heat trumpeting their battle cry), the inside cab appeared to be immaculate with the exception of a small paper bag precariously perched by his right hip. *Watch the bag! Watch the bag! There could be a gun*!

Riley must have been thinking the same thing because that is when he snapped, "Stay away from the bag! Don't move! "Don't touch a fuckin' thing!"

Terror welded in the man's eyes. His lids shadowed. His chest brokered then broke with borrowed breathing. Everything about the man, his car, and the way he had driven screamed suspicion. *Watch his hands! Watch his hands!*

"Sir, your license and registration."

My heartbeat coddled as a thousand deadly spiders slithered inside my veins. And then the man looked down, and his shoulder flinched in a manner that suggested he was reaching for the bag. And *BOOM! BOOM! BOOM! BOOM*! I pulled the trigger and shot him. I shot him four times in quick succession. It was a split-second, life-and-death decision to administer force. I don't even remember thinking about it; it was more or less an instinctual, fight-or-flight reaction. Each shot cracked deafeningly loud as all four bullets penetrated the suspect's upper abdomen. Time slowed in the aftermath, and there was a strange, almost dreamlike sequence after the ringing in my ears subsided. It was then that I heard four distinct sounds.

The man grunting and groaning as he tried to hold on.

Dispatch reciting the owner's address.

Riley shouting, "Shots fired! Shots fired! Officer needs assistance!" into his microphone.

And then the last and most harrowing thing of all was what I heard coming from the backseat. I leaned in and saw the most horrific sight imaginable. A little girl. A baby, really. Buckled into a child's safety seat, she had furry pink boots and tiny little braids in her hair embellished with tiny pink bows. She started sobbing as she screamed, "Pawpaw! Pawpaw!"

The pain in my feet dissipated as my entire world went numb. *Oh, my God! Oh, my God!* I braced myself so that I wouldn't fall over. *I shot a man! I actually shot a man! What have I done!?!*

INTRODUCTION

FEBRUARY 4th, 1993

CHAPTER ONE
FOURTEEN HOURS EARLIER

My story begins with me being a patrolman. Yep, that was me back then – badge, boots, pressed uniform, and all. I was a brand new beat cop, a little shy of three months under my belt. In the previous weeks alone, I busted a meth addict, a couple of prostitutes, a spousal abuser, a couple of drunk drivers, and a crazed-faced skitzo who needed a ride to St. Ann's for a diaper change and bottle duty; that's observation to you. I accomplished all that with no glitches, no drama, no problems, and most importantly, no supervisory reviews. It didn't come naturally; nothing about police work comes naturally. Yeah, I had the inevitable awkward moment or two (such as the time I pulled over the mayor's mistress for a faulty tail light), but I learned more about what it takes to be a police officer with each new day on the job. Being a police officer meant everything back then. It was my father's dream.

February 4th began like any other workday: in bed next to my wife, awakened by the infuriating blare of her alarm clock. Liz liked to wake before dawn so she could prepare something for me to eat before I ventured out to the station. I didn't necessarily want all that fuss, especially not that early in the morning. Geez, I would've been happy with a Pop-Tart and soda; the sugar high alone would have wired me into a feel-good frenzy. But I wasn't allowed to have soda for breakfast, or packaged foods, or candy bars. Those days were long gone as well as pretty much everything else from my time as a bachelor, thanks to the onset of marriage.

Liz and I met in Advanced Statistics at Bakersfield College. I don't remember anything about the class. Statistical methods and the best way to calculate a coefficient evaporated from my brain a long time ago as well as most of the other course knowledge I acquired back then. Besides the piece of paper with my name on it verifying I earned a degree, I'd say the most relevant thing I got out of college was my crazy beautiful redhead, Miss Elizabeth Sue Doyle. Within the first week of class, I fell spell to the lass of her charms, her alabaster skin, her long vibrant-red hair, and warmhearted grin. Liz and I dated for five weeks and two days before we tied the knot in Vegas in a spur-of-the-moment escapade that changed my life for the better. In the years since we got married, Liz earned her Bachelor's degree and went on to teaching while I got me a sweet little gig in retail. I obtained the prestigious position of manager at Blockbuster 174 when the internet took off, the video rental business tanked, and I found myself searching for a new job.

I tried car sales after that; customers liked the way I looked and continuously flirted with me. Managed a grocery store, a pet store, and then I made the ingenious decision of trying my hand at vacuum cleaner sales. All the time I bumbled at all of those jobs, I had Liz's full support but not my father's. And as more time passed, I slipped further and further into the depths of his disappointment.

The only reason I applied to become a police officer was to make him happy. He had entered his third round of dialysis and had pretty much given up; fighting liver disease can take a lot out of a man, even a man as hardheaded as Bobby-the-Boxer Walsh. Liz always said that applying to the academy gave him that extra time. My father lived long enough to make it to my academy graduation, where he had this strange, goofy grin at my badge pinning. He still had that same goofy grin that Independence Day, although by then he needed a portable oxygen system to get around. My father died fifteen days after that, and I found myself grieving a great loss and feeling triumphant at the same time.

"Billy Bear, time to get out of bed!" Liz sang in her happy Liz voice, which could be (to be honest here) as cheerful as threadworms in my brain when you stayed up late the night before, and it was four forty-five in the morning. "Come on, one more day till your weekend. You can sleep in then!"

For a second, I considered taking her in my arms and holding her instead of indulging in breakfast, but the scents of hickory-smoked turkey bacon and organic coffee summoned me to the table. Sitting in my usual seat, I ate my tofu egg-white feast with unsweetened juice and liquid caffeine, trying to ignore her cheery disposition.

"Don't forget about next Wednesday!" she chirped while slicing vegetables for my healthy, diabetes-resistant snack. "You gotta arrange time off so we can make it to our appointment. It's a long process; we have to start soon if we wanna adopt by next year."

No! No, no, no, no, no. She's harping about adoption again. Don't upset her! Don't set her off. Eat your food. Just shake your head and agree. You don't want to endure another one of her tirades. Just agree, agree with whatever she says. "We'll talk about it when I get home. It's too early for that now."

Her expression waned. Panic in her pupils pleaded for me to say something that would stop the break in her heart, but I remained silent and aloof. She stood there for a few seconds, and I could literally see her brain sift with worry. *Please, Billy, please! I want a baby so bad! I want to be a mother! I need to be a mother. It's all I've ever wanted. My entire life is about children. I'm a teacher. I'm inundated with children. Children, children everywhere, and not one of my own to love. Please let us adopt. You would make such a great dad!*

She didn't say any of that though because Liz knew pleading would never work with me. Casting her hopes to the side, she evaporated into the back part of our house. A minute or so later, the water heater ignited, indicating she had completed the task of making the bed and prepared to hop into the shower.

After breakfast, I slipped into a pair of sweats that I liked to wear to the station. Shortly before I walked out the door, Liz exited the bathroom in her pink terry robe with eyes simmered in layers of sadness and strength. Walking up to me, she pressed her body against mine as she hugged me.

"Please be safe," she whispered into my ear. "I love you and couldn't last a day without my beautiful Ken doll!"

"Knock it off with that Ken doll stuff," I chuckled embarrassingly. "What have I told you?"

"Okay, Billy Bear," she sighed. "Just be safe!"

CHAPTER TWO
SIXES

Radio voices vetted conservative opinions as I drove to the station, enjoying my favorite news-talk program. Political hype always seemed to put me in the right frame of mind for policing. Patriotism fueled my drive, warming my ego with valor and pride.

Like usual, traffic along the 99 comprised of the occasional oilfield worker and truckers headed through town. When I got into downtown, the streets bustled to life with a conglomeration of business people, homeless people, and this one crazed-faced bicyclist who stood atop his pedal straps, cycling through town. Edging my Toyota to the side of the road, I flipped him the bird as I passed Riley in my usual morning hijinks.

An hour and thirty-five minutes later, Riley and I had already worked out, showered, and suited up as we headed into our 8:00 a.m. briefing.

"Aww," Commander Bennett chided from the speakers' podium at the head of the room. "Look who decided to grace us with their beauty."

The whole crew knew he was talking about Riley and me. We were both around six feet tall, had blonde hair and blue eyes, and were in great shape. The pair of us drove all the female officers and dispatchers crazy, although I would say that Riley (being that he had dimples, loved to flirt, and was actually single) was a little more dangerous in the swooning department.

"Thanks, Cap! I'll take that as a compliment," Riley chirped. And then he had the audacity of winking at our gray-haired round-bellied supervisor who brandished freshly-shined Commander's bars on his shirt collar and a left shirt sleeve tallied with thirty years of hash marks. "If I recall, your wife said the same thing!"

"Leave my wife out of this!" Commander Bennett snapped. "And by the way, Charlene wanted to invite you to dinner this next--"

And the whole room erupted with a series of heckles and sneers.

"Off the leg, Riley!" "He ain't that good looking!" "He's too pretty to be a cop; he should be selling hair shampoo or tampons on television." "Shoot, my old lady said his pretty-boy mug could come over to our house anytime!"

Riley leaned back, interlocked his fingers behind his head, and beamed as he bathed in the adulation. That's one thing about my partner: he had grown used to being complimented. As a matter of fact, I'm pretty sure he reveled in it.

"Knock it off," Commander Bennett cut in, and then he directed his attention to Sergeant Morrey. "Let's get down to matters at hand."

And with that, Sergeant Morrey took over the briefing by calling out roll and verifying our assignments. "Walsh," he addressed me individually.

Everyone rotated in their seats.

"This's your last week of OJT (on the job training); after that, you're on your own. Soak up 'em skills, rookie. Riley's a hell of a cop and one of our best examples. But I gotta say it wouldn't hurt you to learn something besides trying to be pretty."

And the crew erupted in laughter again.

Morrey shuffled his paperwork as he scanned the room, and the laughter and heckling subsided. Then our sergeant and first-line supervisor proceeded to spiel his same lecture of showing up on time, documenting reports accurately, watching our Ps & Qs around reporters, and continuing to remain vigilant about public perception. Before they excused us, we were provided a breakdown of occurrences from the previous shift, including a high-profile arrest and the names of a couple of perps who made it onto the hot sheet. And, lastly, they reminded us about Schwartz (an officer from a neighboring community, gunned down while responding to a domestic disturbance).

"Watch your sixes, guys and gals!" Morrey reminded us. "Whatever you do today, I want to ensure each and every one of you makes it home."

CHAPTER THREE
EVERYDAY ROUTINE

When we got to the car, Riley stowed his lunch pail in the trunk before taking reign of the driver's seat. As my senior partner and FTO (field training officer), it was a given he would get the spot behind the wheel. That is the spot of seniority and prestige, but if you ask any cop out there, they'll tell you that's the spot where all the action happens. Who wouldn't want to speed through town with the siren blasting, weaving in and out of traffic, chasing down perps and rushing in to save people? With all the bells and whistles associated with driving a police car, there is nothing workish about the spot behind the wheel. No, the workish position is in the passenger seat. That was me.

In all reality, it didn't matter because we had a lot of fun. Riley and I were the cornfed duo of policing. We were two towheads who wanted to make a difference in the world. We liked wearing the badge, helping people, and responding to trouble. And, man, did we get down to business. We hadn't even been in the car but a minute when the first call came in about a hit-and-run off South Chester. Riley hit the lights and gas while I relayed our response over the radio.

It took us a few minutes to get there because the reporting party accidentally transposed the numerical address. She gave us 2300 Chester Avenue when it should have been 3200. By the time we arrived on scene, the "long blue car with pointy tail lights" (that crashed into the Honda, causing it to careen into a utility pole) had already taken off behind a mobile home park and long since fled the scene.

Riley and I interviewed the driver as she lay on the stretcher, awaiting transport to Saint Ann's. Unfortunately (as frequently the case in collisions resulting in a gross bodily injury or fatality), obtaining the information became challenging, to say the least. The twenty-six-year-old victim kept crying and screaming because her only passenger in the car, her fiancée of five months, incurred a TBI & SCI and was DOA at the scene. The driver claimed that while she headed north on Chester Avenue in her 1986 Honda Accord, she had been struck in the left rear panel of her car, forcing her automobile into a pole.

"Raffi's face! Oh, God! Raffi's face! I love him! I love him so much! I don't know how I can go on without him! How am I supposed to tell his parents? It's my Dad's car; how am I supposed to tell my Dad? What am I supposed to do with his dog? What about our venue? I put everything we had in the down payment."

I felt terrible for the girl. She endured something unimaginable. One minute they were lawfully driving down the street in the early morning hours after sunrise, and the next thing she knew her car had been thrust into a light pole, resulting in the unintentional manslaughter of someone she loved.

To make matters worse, the negligent driver didn't take responsibility for the accident. He or she didn't get out of their car and take accountability. No, once the collision occurred, the other driver took off from the scene.

"He's dead! I can't believe he's dead! How can someone do that? How can someone drive off like that? Don't they have a conscious? How can they live with what they've done? How can people be so cruel? Oh, God, he's dead! He's dead! He's dead!"

As she lay on the gurney with her face and the front of her blouse covered in blood spatter, Riley provided her tissues to wipe away tears. I had never witnessed or heard of a police officer act with so much compassion. He stood by her side and patiently listened while she described her bridesmaid's dresses, how obnoxious her fiancée's dog was, and how they had met in a bookstore as he gathered information for our report.

At first, she couldn't remember anything about the car that hit them. She remained angry and hysterical, lost in a world of confusion. But after the calming effect of Riley's tender-hearted support, she was able to provide the car's description and the distinctive feature with the taillights. The victim even handed Riley her phone so that he could notify her father. Riley just had a gift of helping people.

After the accident, we responded to a theft in apartment 12C of the Park Villa Apartments off White Lane, where we met the mother of the victim who spoke Punjabi-influenced English. The mother indicated her son's bike had been secured inside their patio the night before and discovered missing when he went to perform his newspaper job. They didn't have any other form of transportation, and she worried he would lose his paper route, which happened to be their primary source of income. Riley and I took the report and then left.

For a second there, I thought it unusual that he headed down Stein and continued north because it infringed upon another unit's assigned territory. But when Riley pulled into the parking lot of Sander's Bicycles, I quickly surmised what he had in mind. Thirty-five minutes later, we returned to the apartment and delivered a brand new bicycle decked-out with headlights, state-of-the-art reflectors, and a newfangled lock that was purported to be unbreakable.

The mother became so overwhelmed with the generous gesture that she began to ramble her life's story. She told us how she met her husband, how he got a job in this country, how they left their families and traveled here, and how he died shortly after their arrival, leaving her and her son stranded and alone. Then she started to ramble about her son's ventures in school and with his paper route. Fortunately, we didn't have to endure the remainder of that narrative because we received our next call.

"10-70. 3952 Cypress Glen Court. Caller, Maria Torrez. Barricaded in master bath. Indicates three males, unknown description. Doesn't know age or race. No info on weapons."

Responding Code 1 (lights and sirens), we traveled west on White Lane to Dovewood, to Beachwood, to Cypress Glen, arriving within three and a half minutes of the dispatch. At the location, we found no cars stationed along the street out front, only a late model Volvo in the driveway.

Riley ran up to the front door with his firearm in a ready position, giving me the all-clear to peer through the adjacent window. Inside, I spotted two male juveniles rummaging through an entertainment console in the living room. The door wouldn't budge, so I kicked it open, immediately confronting the subjects. The shorter one froze in place while the tall, lanky one made a beeline out the sliding glass door that led to the side yard. Taking off after him, I was fortunate enough to tackle him to the ground before he made it over the fence. We detained the pair of them and were in the process of escorting them to the police cruiser when Sergeant Morrey and Officers Bettencourt and Doyle arrived upon scene. Bettencourt and Doyle took custody of the pair as Riley and I returned to the domicile to locate the caller.

Didn't take us long to find her because the house encompassed thirteen hundred square feet at the most. We found the woman, terrified and distraught, hiding behind the shower curtain in the locked master bath. She appeared to be in her mid-20s with dark brown eyes, long dark hair, and a pumpkin-sized baby belly.

"We already got two, found them in the living room," Riley informed her. "One tried to cut out the back door, but my partner here, Officer Walsh, apprehended the suspect before he could get very far."

The woman looked at me and nodded appreciatively.

"Before we go any further, I need to know if you're sure there were three of them. When the call came in, you indicated to dispatch there may have been three."

"I. Ahh... Yeah." She grabbed onto her big round belly and grimaced. "I'm pretty sure."

"Are you okay?" I cut in, concerned for her child. "Is everything okay with your pregnancy?"

"*What*?! she gasped. "What are you talking about? I'm not pregnant! Why would you say that? What is this? Are you calling me fat!?!"

There was a pause – a terrible, disturbing lull in our conversation – while my brain raced to find a polite, politically-correct response that would remediate my awkward assumption.

"His bad," Riley placated politely. "Walsh's wife has been trying to get knocked up for years. They've been having trouble; you see. Apparently, he's shooting blanks because they keep coming up empty."

"Oh," she sympathetically shook her head, "poor thing." She looked over at me and smiled with pity-sopped eyes. "Must be--"

"Anyhow, we're gonna ask you to step outside with our sergeant and a couple of other officers, so we can take a look around and ascertain the place's clear."

A few seconds after she joined them outside, we overheard Sergeant Morrey inquire about her pregnancy, and all we could do was burst into laughter as she yelled and shouted and screeched in return.

We didn't find anyone hiding underneath the beds, in the shower, inside any of the closets, or in the cranny behind the couch. The foundation had no basement while the dust coating the crawlspace into the attic hadn't been disturbed. We were almost ready to leave when Riley spotted a pair of sneakered toes sticking out from beneath the hem of the draperies in the back bedroom. The last suspect (a skinny, fourteen-year-old, African American male) wasn't necessarily happy at being caught.

"Forget you, you raggedy, dumb, limp dick, Aryan-lookalike pigs," he carped as we patted him down for weapons and contraband. Smiling voraciously, he snickered as he turned towards me. "At least I ain't shooting no rotten stuff!"

Once we brought him to the transportation cruiser, we secured him inside the caged-in compartment. Upon joining his disgruntled companions, he complained, "They kicked me in the nuts and stepped on my face. I think they even tried to break my nose."

The kid was not only a juvenile delinquent; he was a liar. I wanted to call him out and say something about his sharp mouth and erroneous ramblings, but that is when Riley intervened with, "Your nose was already smashed in when we found you. It's the same monkey-plug you had when you were born."

I stood taken aback for a second, and then Riley clarified with,

"The only thing uglier than your nose is that smell!"

"Damn!" moaned the teen who had run into the backyard. "I think I stepped in something!" He made a stink face as he held up his foot. "I got dog turd all over my shoe!"

Riley rolled up the window, leaving a tiny cracked opening. Then he shut the door, securing the three of them inside the compartment. We left them like that for twenty minutes or so as we joked around and bullshitted with Bettencourt and Doyle.

An hour from the end of our shift, Sergeant Fleckman let us know we had been assigned extra duty. Riley took the news eagerly in that he liked the concept of eight hours at time-and-a-half while I looked at my shoes, winced, and vehemently regretted the decision to purchase them. They looked good. No, they looked great. They shined like glass and had style. They looked professional and made me look professional, but they hadn't stretched out. As a matter of fact, they felt as though they shrank a size with every hour that passed. If that were the case, then by the end of the day, I would have sported elf feet. I didn't want to bellyache about it because I didn't want to be one of those whiney new people who cried about everything, but, by then, my heals spawned an infestation of sores.

My feet had to wait because we received a transmission relaying a disturbance of the peace call about a naked woman sprawled out on the sidewalk in front of Rock & Rodeo, a popular bar and dancehall that packed-in the hotties on any given night. We headed north up Gosford and had just taken a right onto Rosedale when the radio transmission indicated the woman was a 10-96 in route to St. Ann's.

"You could have waited until we got there," Riley grumbled. "Damn, we're only a mile out!"

"You didn't want to see or smell that!" Officer Tinoco grumbled back. "She hadn't showered in months, was full of bugs, had no teeth, and breath so bad, it'd layout a sasquatch. As soon as we got her onto the gurney, she sh—"

"Watch it," Sergeant Fleckman broke in. "Radios are for emergency codes, not banter. Remain professional."

Riley's face squelched in that I knew he wanted to say something comedic, but he didn't want to defy his supervisor and tarnish his reputation.

"Damn." He turned and faced me. "I wanted to introduce you to Dirty Marcy!"

"What?" I gasped.

"She does that every couple of months to get cleaned up at St. Ann's."

Scavenging through the lunch Liz had prepared, I munched on three granola bars and a packet of raisins, still feeling starved. By six, darkness descended, shrouding the sky in a billowing blanket of blithe.

"Almost done with your training," Riley announced. We were headed down Ashe, looking for anything that struck our interest. "Just know that I'll be around to answer questions and give advice. All you gotta do is call."

"Thanks, Riley. Thanks for the training and advice. Appreciate it. Appreciate everything you've shown me."

"You've got it down. You'll do fine!" He turned to face me for a second, brandishing his million-dollar smile that actually was disgustingly perfect. "You'll see; being a police officer is a lot more then they showed you in the academy. It's more than they fabricate on movies and TV. Protecting and serving encompasses a lot of things. It isn't just busting people as fun as that is. It's about change. It's making a difference. It's helping people and making our community a safer place to live. It's improving--"

Brrrrreeeeep, Riley was interrupted by the dull monotone droll of dispatch announcing a drunk and disorderly at The Bennington (a bar frequented by rabble-rousers and rowdy oilfield hands) located on the corner of Wible and Wilson.

"And for the record," Riley went on as we made our way towards

The Bennington, "I agree about the whole adoption thing. You never know what you're gonna get with those kids. Someone already cast them aside; why would you want someone else's junk? Anyone who does that is taking a chance with what they're bringing into their home. Just keep…"

He slowed to a stop in front of the entrance as I announced our arrival with the proper 10-code.

"…trying. Miracles can happen. I'm telling you, miracles happen all the time."

The moment we entered the dimly lit bar, patrons greeted us with a mixture of hesitancy and relief.

"He's over there," the bartender pointed out the tanked-up guy hunkered over the counter, wearing a baseball cap, beer jersey, and Hawaiian-themed shorts. "Hate to have to call you guys, but he's ruining business. He won't stop with the waterworks."

"Are you here to arrest meee?" a man who appeared to be in his late sixties or early seventies theatrically drawled. "I'm sorry! Sorry, Dave! I, I, I--"

"Let's go, old-timer," Riley summoned. "Let's get out of here so these fine drunks can poison their livers without you."

The bartender's brows furrowed. He didn't know if he should have felt insulted or relieved.

The guy appeared to be heavily intoxicated yet able to walk. Actually, it was more of a drunken stumble, but he made it to the cruiser without falling to the ground or breaking anything. Getting ahold of his license, I found that he resided just a few blocks away.

"Why are you drinking like that," Riley questioned. "At your age, you should know better."

"I do. I do. I'm sorry. I messed up. It's just been a bad day."

As I radioed in his information, Riley continued his exchange. "We all have bad days; that doesn't mean you can go to The Bennington, get smashed, and bother everyone. It's disturbing the peace, and it's illegal."

"Sooooory, officers." His head scanned back and forth between the both of us. "Had to put my dog down today. Vet sssaid he's ssssuffering too much and 'ad no hope. It was harrrd, harrrdest thing I had to do. Damn Rocket was a gooood dog. Loyal. Had him for ssseventeen years. Seveeeenteen, can you believe that? Loved him like family. He's, he's…"

The guy started bawling, resulting in a stew of snot and tears streaming down his face. Six minutes of snot fountaining later, dispatch finally announced the guy was clean with no wants or warrants.

"Okay. Okay, old man. We're gonna take you home and drop you off. You just gotta promise you won't come back here and bother those good drunks."

"I proooomise!" He blew his nose onto his shirt sleeve. "I proooomise!"

The man's wife met us at the driveway and aided him inside. They were both grateful we didn't arrest him and take him down to the station.

"Wouldn't have done any good," Riley said. "Poor guy's been through enough."

CHAPTER FOUR
THE ENCOUNTER

It had been a crazy, bizarre, left-field kind of day that can only be described as ordinary by police standards. We pulled over a late model BMW with a broken tail light. When the young female driver began to cry, Riley let her off with a warning. We pulled over a black Chevy Malibu for a California stop. When the soccer dad told us a rib-cracking joke, Riley let him off with a warning. Then we pulled over a Dodge Ram doing 70 in a 40, and the obstinate city manager threatened to file a complaint if we didn't let her off as a professional courtesy. Riley issued her a citation for excessive speed and expired tags. There had been a couple of situations that took a lot of time because every single detail needed to be documented while there was an encounter or two filed under "no documentation necessary." And I really felt like I was getting it. I was getting the hang of police officering. I began to understand that everything I read and studied in the academy was merely a blueprint of how to handle the job. Policing encompassed so much more than rules and wherefores; it incorporated this vast, unimaginable realm where lives, livelihoods, reputations, and personal liberties were always at stake. Riley was right when he said, "Anything could happen at any time. In a moment's notice, someone can pull a trigger, and someone can get shot," because that is precisely what happened next.

By then the only thing left in my lunch pail was the sliced carrots Liz had prepared, but to me, rabbit food felt as appealing as, well, rabbit food. I needed real food. I needed a turkey sandwich. That is why, ten hours and thirty-seven minutes into our shift, we headed to a fast food cafe with a halfway decent menu.

"Don't fret," Riley exclaimed, "I gotta feeling tonight's gonna be off the hook. Sometimes the wildest things can happen on Tuesdays."

No sooner had the words strutted off his tongue then we rolled by a powder-blue sedan. In the split-second we crisscrossed paths, I got a glimpse of the massively-large dark-skinned driver. Following the automobile with my gaze, I saw how the taillights lit in an unusual pattern that some may describe as being "pointy."

"That car," I anxiously announced. "The blue Lincoln we just passed had pointed taillights. It's a Continental, so it's long and blue. And there's something about the driver. Maybe we--"

I didn't even have to finish. Riley had already slowed and initiated a U-turn. Tipped tail lights weren't that unusual in late model cars; however, Riley and I knew it could have been a lead to the hit-and-run suspect that absconded earlier. Once we completed the turn, we followed the car as it went through the intersections of Dracena Street, then Palm, past a couple of car lots that looked like they were going out of business, then past a gas station where transients were known to panhandle poor people for money. At the corner where Oak turned into Wible, the Continental stopped for a traffic signal at which time our headlights illuminated the back window enough for us to spot the driver turn and say something to the occupant or occupants in the back seat.

"He spotted us," Riley declared. "Something doesn't feel right."

"It is definitely a long blue sedan with tipped lights. The guy definitely looks shady, and he's definitely in the right neighborhood."

"A lot of definitely's," Riley agreed.

We continued to follow the Lincoln as it timorously made a right onto South H. That is when Riley activated the overhead emergency beams and the tail end of the automobile bathed in flashes of blue, white, and red.

"I don't like this," Riley proclaimed with an edged tone. We were sitting in the cruiser, waiting for dispatch to provide us with the necessary information. "Deserie's not in and whoever's filling in is taking too long. He's probably still talking to whoever's in the back seat. He looks Disciple. If he's Disciple, you never know how this can end up."

"Rings like a bad dude," I confirmed. "Did you get a look at his size? He's Black as hell and seems like trouble."

"Let's go," Riley prompted as he reached for his door handle. "I'm not waiting any longer."

You can do this, I told myself as I cautiously approached the driver's side of the Lincoln, realizing this stop was different from the others we initiated that day. *Don't be nervous! Follow his lead!* My heart pounded in avalanches and waves, flooding my system with an infusion of fire, focus, and fear. Yeah, definitely fear. My index finger glided against the smooth metal cylinder of the gun barrel, poised to pull the trigger at a moment's notice. *Gotta make it home. Don't want to get shot! Don't want to go out like Schwartz! Watch Riley! Cover Riley! You know he's got you covered in return!*

My shoes felt tight. Damn cheap shoes strangled my feet with every step. We had already approached the Lincoln when the registered owner's name and vital information broadcast over the airway. "Registration's current. Owners name is Otis Cleveland Merriweather. DOB 3/5/48. 6'4". 330 lbs. Ocean. Tom. Ida. Sam."

Otis Cleveland Merriweather. He was a Black man, with a Black name, in a Black car, in a Black neighborhood. All of my inner bells and whistles rang threat. *Be careful! Watch his hands! Watch for movement!* I said to myself as Riley approached the passenger side window with his gun raised in a combat / fire-ready position. Following suit, I raised my gun and directed it at the driver who had to be the darkest shade of Black I had ever seen.

Not gonna lie here, at that point I was scared. The guy was a beast, and something about his long gnarled scar sent my pulse into a frenzy. I may have been a police officer. I may have been the one with the gun, but I kept thinking about Schwartz and the dozens of ambushed cops I had seen in training videos. None of them expected to get shot as they did. None of them expected to die.

"Roll down your window!" we barked. "Don't move!" "Put your hands up!" "Stay where you are! Don't move!"

And that is when I noticed the bag by his right hip and thought, *Oh, shit!*

Riley must have been thinking the same thing, because that is when he shouted, "Hands Up! Freeze! Stay away from the bag! Don't move! I said don't touch a fuckin' thing!"

The man sat frozen with his hands in the air.

Be careful! Watch his hands! Watch his hands!

"License and registration," I commanded as I struggled to maintain control of competing circumstances. And then the man looked down and moved. I saw him move! *He's going for it! He's going for his gun!* And *BOOM! BOOM! BOOM! BOOM*! I pulled the trigger and shot him. I shot him four times in quick succession. It was a split-second life-and-death decision to administer force. I don't even remember thinking about it; it was more or less an instinctual, fight-or-flight reaction. Time slowed in the aftermath, and there was a strange, almost dreamlike sequence after the ringing in my ears subsided. It was then that I heard four indistinguishable sounds.

The man grunting and groaning as he tried to hold on.

Dispatch reciting the registered owner's address.

Riley shouting, "Shots fired! Shots fired! Officer needs assistance!" over the airway.

And then the last and most haunting thing of all was what I heard coming from the backseat. I leaned in and saw the most horrific sight imaginable. It was a little girl – a baby, really. My entire body and world went numb. *Oh, my God! Oh, my God! I shot a man! I actually shot a man! What have I done!?!*

CHAPTER FIVE
AFTERMATH

"Shit! Shit! Shit!" Riley shouted. "What'd you see? What'd you see?"

"I don't know," I snapped. "He moved! He flinched. It looked like he was…"

Disregarding the man's grunts and groans, Riley leaned through the passenger side window, retrieved the bag, and immediately looked inside.

"It's an inhaler!" he spat.

The baby frantically coughed and cried from the back seat.

"A goddamn inhaler!"

"Shit!" I shouted! "What have I done? What the hell have I done!?!" My mind flooded with a torrent of thoughts, so many grim, godawful thoughts. *This is the end of my career. I've let my father down! He must have a gun! Just look at him! He has to have a gun!*

Riley opened the passenger door then slid onto the cushioned seat cover so he could detain the suspect by handcuffing his wrists to the steering wheel. The guy fell into a state of semi-consciousness as he remained slumped against the backrest, gasping for breath; nevertheless, the application of shackling his wrists had been protocol. Riley then frantically combed through the inside compartment, looking for anything construed as a weapon to substantiate what I had done.

"Don't move," he cautioned me over the driver. "Remain calm. Holster your firearm and compose yourself." As he searched under both seats, in the glove box, and the tray under the center console, he clarified. "We're on film. The cruiser's camera is recording everything. They'll go over the tape at the station. Don't freak out. Don't do anything dumb. Just stand there and let me figure this out!"

"But!?!" I began to say. I didn't want to lose it. I didn't want to breakdown and start crying; however, I couldn't help but think that this meant the end of my career. It suddenly transformed into a life-changing, unimaginably-horrific situation that seemed to get worse with each groan of the driver and the wails of the baby in the back seat.

"Shit!" Riley snapped. "There's nothing here! Suspect's clean. There's no gun, nothing to substantiate…" Riley paused, shaking his head as he knelt on the passenger side, looking distraught.

Time warped and stewed as the driver grunted, the baby cried, and our police radios blew up with traffic from a dozen responders.

Riley looked up at me. "All hell's about to break loose!"

"My life's over!" I proclaimed. "This is it! My career! My reputation! Everything! Oh, God, everything! I hope I don't get arrested. I could go to jail over this! I could--"

Off in the distance, the barks and screams of sirens approached from every direction.

"I'm in this too! I'm your partner and FTO. All this could come back on me." Riley began to lose it; I had never seen him flustered like that. "Shit!" he snapped again, and then he grimaced as he gaged me dead in the eye. "Hold on!"

Without saying anything else or explaining himself, Riley returned to the back of the cruiser. I didn't know what he was going to do. Melting into the wheel well with my elbows on my knees, I waited for my life to end. *What have I done? My life's over. My career's gone. Liz will be so disappointed. If my Dad knew, he would be disappointed too. I messed up! I messed up! Oh, God! I messed up so bad!*

Then arose the squall of responding police cars. Lights and sirens of five or six units flooded the scene, bathing me in an incantation of blood reds and bruised blues. They screeched to a stop alongside the Lincoln at exactly the precise time Riley returned to the doorframe. As they opened their doors and rushed out of their cars, Riley reached underneath his shirt and quickly discarded something onto the passenger side floor mat. Everything happened so fast. The sounds of sirens were screaming, the baby was screaming, my brain was screaming, and I think I may have blacked out for a second or two. Within an instant, I found myself surrounded by officers, paramedics, Sergeant Brad Allen Fleckman, and Fire Captain Cal Akeman of the Bakersfield River Fire

Department.

"We're good!" Riley said to Sergeant Fleckman. "It's justified. It's justified. From the position I maintained on the passenger side, I saw the whole thing. My partner here, Officer Walsh, had just approached the driver's window when the suspect reached for his gun. Walsh shot to stop the threat, and then I reached in and knocked the piece down to the passenger side floor mat. Look, it's right there!" He pointed to the gun he discarded onto the mat. "It's right there in plain sight. No one's touched it. Looks like an old .38."

As he spoke – as he said this made-up story, this fabrication of what happened, this lie – I became bewildered and confused. I felt lost, stunned even. And then my breath released as a tremendous wave of relief washed over me; ease that felt cleansing as if the salvation of my career didn't come from a lie but someplace sacred and holy. Riley nodded towards me for confirmation.

"Yeah, ahh," I said without even thinking about it, "the second I realized, I reacted."

Sergeant Fleckman's fret lines dissipated while his shoulders relaxed.

"He had no choice," Riley went on, "he…"

As Riley explained the story from the point of time when we first observed the Lincoln, ambulance technicians removed Mr. Otis Cleveland Merriweather from the driver's seat while a grandmotherly-type medic tended to the little girl. By then, bystanders appeared from out of nowhere. I didn't know if they had driven there or all come out of their homes, but once an angry mob amassed, the entire street had to be cleared and cordoned off with police caution tape.

When Riley gave his third and final step-by-step account of the incident, I relinquished my firearm to Sergeant Fleckman so that it would be processed into evidence. Part of me always knew I could tell the truth (I could explain how I had panicked and shot the guy for no apparent reason), but I didn't do that. I couldn't do it to Riley, and I couldn't do it to myself. So I did what any other blue-blooded law enforcement officer would do when pitted against such overwhelming circumstances: I backed my partner. I lied. I repeated everything Riley had said. I repeated his story, verbatim.

"Sounds good!" Fleckman vetted. "For now, we gotta get you out of here. The press is sniffing around. We don't want to give them a field day with another White on Black police shooting—"

"But—" Riley cut in.

"Yeah," Fleckman conceded, "I know it's good. Don't worry about that. Just fill out your reports the same way you explained it, and everything will be fine. But the douchebag paparazzi have spy cameras that have the ability to pick up everything we're saying, so I need the both of you to get to the station and fill out your reports. I don't need you here; the scene's hot. I don't want any retaliation. The Disciples could show up, and all hell could break loose."

"Okay," Riley agreed.

"You'll both be suspended with pay for a few days while this thing blows over. It'll be like a paid vacation."

"Yes, sir," Riley confirmed. "We'll head over there right now."

The moment we returned to our cruiser, we were met by Fire Captain Akeman and four or five of his firefighters.

"Officer Walsh," he greeted as he extended his hand for me to shake it. "What you did right there's damn right heroic. You probably saved the lives of two officers and who knows how many innocent civilians. In my book that makes you a bonafide American hero!"

CHAPTER SIX
WEIGHTLESS

"Shit! Shit! Shit! Shit!" I raged as we headed east on Planz towards the station. I was so mad at myself; I couldn't believe what I had done. "SHIT!" I punched the passenger side dash so hard that it nearly dislocated my finger. And once again my vocabulary tapered to a parochial litany of fecal expletives.

"DON'T! Don't freak out! Don't beat yourself up! What's done is done. Don't worry about it. I've got your back. I'm telling you, I've got your back. Everything's handled. I cleaned it up. We'll go to the station, fill out our reports, get our paid time off, and things will return to normal."

Images of being under the microscope and having to undergo an internal review weighed heavily on my mind, and I immediately dreaded the next phase of my life.

"The most important thing is that neither of us says anything different. You can't change your story, William. You're gonna be asked a dozen times what happened, and you've gotta stick with the script. Don't veer from the scenario. Don't change a word. I stuck my neck out for you; you can't hang me out to dry in return."

"I won't." And then I thought about it and added, "Thanks. You saved my life. I hate it. I hate the situation. I hate what I did. But, thank God, you were there. Thank God, you had my back."

"Don't worry about it," Riley quipped, and then he turned to me with his perfect face and his perfect, pristine smile. "That's what friends are for. And don't worry about that guy. He's slime; I can feel it. If he wasn't carrying this time, it was probably the first. Scum like him are dirty. Who knows how many people he's killed."

I didn't know if Riley meant Black people or gangsters. We found nothing on the guy, no tats, and nothing in the car to identify him as being Disciple.

"While stationed in the Navy, this one obnoxious kitchen staff worker constantly accused me of being a racist." He paused and then clarified, "I'm *not.* I have friends who are Black. I've worked with Cobbs and Gentry and never had a problem. Shoot, I've even had my share of Latin girlfriends. It's just different when you get these big, buffalo-headed Negroids because you know they're a threat. Can't trust them; they were born and bred for trouble. They're..."

As Riley spoke, my stomach stirred with a strange, eerie dread. I didn't know if it was the turmoil I experienced, the unsaid guilt from the cover-up, or the echoes of the gasping and crying that churned in my bowels, but it all became too much for me. As we traveled east on Planz, I had my first inclination of an ulcer.

"... change your report; that is the most important thing." Riley had completed his story about the guy stationed in the Navy and was in the process of preparing me for our reception at the station. "Whatever you do, don't change a word. Not One Word. Explain everything the same way you explained it to Fleckman, and that is the way you put it in your report. Don't change a thing. Don't edit it. Don't take anything out. And, God forbid, don't add anything. Adding details can conflict with the original statement. Elaborating anything else will only make you look suspicious and could be considered false testimony and--"

It was then, at that precise moment (as we passed an open juncture on Belle Terrace and South P while Riley spieled warnings of not changing our reports), that everything happened. That is when a black-and-gray semi blew through a red light at the intersection, ramming into the side of our police car. The semi T-boned the driver's side of the sedan in a tremendous, ear-piercing explosion that almost knocked me out of my seatbelt. And the next thing I knew, the automobile propelled into a series of pitches and turns. Becoming weightless against the backrest, I felt the cruiser roll over again and again.

CHAPTER SEVEN
CLAWS

Coming to, I realized I had been in a rollover accident and that the cruiser had been catapulted into the air, whirling and twirling – what two, maybe three times – then came down hard on its carriage in a loud walloping *CLOP*. Time warped. Everything came back to me in bits and pieces. Breath entered my lungs, and I ascertained that I made it. I was injured but alive. I still sat in the cab (still strapped into the seatbelt of the passenger seat) as my body lay limp against the dash.

My head hurts. Oh, God, my head hurts. I'm injured. It's bad. I know its bad. So many sounds swam in my head. Echos from the shooting. The man gasping and groaning as he tried to hold on. The baby crying in the back seat. Riley stating, "I've got your back." An explosion of metal slamming into asphalt. My own screams. And there was this other noise. This strange, eerie noise. This stream of screeches that seemed to emanate from all around me.

My eyes flickered open, and I caught sight of Riley's lifeless form as he remained sunken in the driver's seat. The impact had crushed the entire left side of his body while a shard of door frame shredded the flesh off his face, leaving behind the grotesque carnage of the gore that lay beneath the drapery of skin. His neck kinked to the side at an intense degree while his right eyeball dangled from his socket by a wobbling strand of optic nerve. The accident had taken him. Riley was dead! My partner, my friend – the guy who had just risked everything to cover for me – had died in the collision.

My head hurt. My thoughts riddled with turmoil. I felt sick. Then, to make matters worse, I discovered I couldn't move. *I don't want to die! I don't want to die! Oh, God, please save me! Please don't let me…*

As I floated in and out of consciousness, a river of warmth flowed into my eyes. I wasn't sure how bad my injury was but remembered the *snap* my forehead made when it shattered the dash. *It's fractured. I'm sure it's fractured. I could hear it. I heard my bones break when my skull cracked. It's bad. It's bad.*

Within the moment and within the pain came a dark, desperate screeching that seemed to emanate from the bowels of all around me. It was eerie and elusive, something I had never heard before. It sounded like the battle cry of a thousand tortured souls announcing their arrival. I couldn't understand it, but I knew it couldn't have been me. *It's not in my head, not me screaming.*

Nevertheless, I still heard these bone-chilling screams and echoes of screams as they began to brew louder. Suddenly, the inside cab became a vacuum of evil, almost demonic like howling. These things (I don't know what they were or where they came from), but they rapidly appeared from out of nowhere. They surrounded Riley in eerily ghostlike apparitions of swirling entities. They encapsulated him and gored into his lifeless body, and then they began to carve away at his life force. And I realized they were taking him. They were stealing his soul. Was this my injury? *I don't know.* Was I imagining it? *I don't know.* Did it really happen? *I don't know.* I don't know if I was awake, asleep, living, or dead, but I do know what I remember. I remember the shapes and shadows of demons. I saw them, and I heard them, and I felt them as they collected Riley's spirit from his dead, disheveled form.

And then I saw the most frightening thing of all. I saw Riley resist. I heard his spirit screaming. I heard the ache of his fractured life as he was pulled deeper into the earth. Riley tried to fight them off, but they pulled him down, down into the ground, deeper and deeper until he was no more.

SECTION I

ADVENT

CHAPTER EIGHT
AWAKENING

Drifting in and out of consciousness, a small part of me held onto the accident, but it was far, far away as if it happened a long time ago, as if it were a distant memory or something that occurred in another lifetime. I didn't know what day it was or how much time had elapsed. I didn't even know where I was or exactly what happened. I just knew that I lay in a hospital bed at the back end of a long sterile room with a door numbered 242 and two draperied windows. On the ceiling above me, dozens of square-shaped ceiling panels contained thousands of decorative dots. Gazing up at them, I imagined they formed a galaxy in another dimension. Connecting the dots into constellations, I found a Little Dipper, a Big Dipper, and a stick figure clown with spry sinewy arms and stubbed fingers.

Blankets tucked me in so tightly that I felt trapped. I became a burrito in a bed with barred rails and a concrete slab for a mattress. An IV fed into my vein while a contraption made a loud, repetitive commotion of hammering, hacking, and this God-awful *whooshing* sound. And there was my wife, my lovely redhead. My eyelids parted enough to find her sitting in a blue upholstered armchair with her head propped against the wall. She looked tired yet still strikingly beautiful in a turquoise pantsuit that she loved to wear because the hue of anything blue contrasted with her hair. Her shoes had been cast aside under her seat, leaving her barefoot and unabashed.

"Hey, Babe!" I managed to utter. "Geez, that looks uncomfortable. How can you sleep like that? Why don't we leave this place and go home? We can crawl into bed together and cuddle."

The thought enveloped me and took me to another place, a place of lovers and honeymoons, a place of happiness and peace and the muggy, unabashed tone of my wife's nighttime whisper.

I awoke again, finding myself in the hospital, still in a bed at the back of the room. The Big Dipper and Little Dipper imprinted the ceiling panels above me, and my mattress remained a rock hard slab of concrete. Once again, I didn't know how much time had elapsed. I didn't know anything, really. All I knew was that my beautiful wife remained by my side. Liz occupied the same seat next to my bed. This time she donned jeans and a frilly red blouse with gold seams and a forward point collar. She looked good. No, beautiful. Just like usual, the color of her shirt accentuated the hue of her hair, which I knew she selected with forethought. Liz was like that. Everything she wore intentionally highlighted or contrasted with her hair in a way that made her appear even more attractive. She sat there, reading a magazine with her lovely locks braided into a ribbon.

"Wow, Babe!" I gushed. "You look beautiful. Sooo beautiful! I love your hair like that. It is so…"

♪

A doctor hovered over me. I awoke when she lifted my lids then gazed into my eyes with a penlight.

"Hey! Watch it, doc!"

She stood over me with her fancy doctors' smock and her fancy doctors' stethoscope and shook her head despondently.

"You shouldn't just do that without saying anything. It ain't right; you could blind someone like that. It's not good to…"

♪

The next time I came around, it felt as though a little more time had elapsed, although I wasn't exactly sure how to measure the construct of time or if time truly existed. While I was out, I rested in a place with no police cars, hospital beds, people, or thinking. It had been a retreat from all brain functions as if I had checked-out from my own life, as if I ceased to exist.

Peering over the barred bed rail, I found Liz in her usual seat stationed next to my bed; however, she wasn't alone. Sergeant Morrey and Officers Bettencourt and Doyle sat alongside her. Sergeant Morrey had his Goliath-sized sergeant's hand wrapped around her pretty pristine fingers. And then he said something that withered her gleam with sadness.

"What the hell?" I goaded. "Why are you here? Why are you holding my wife's hand? What did you say to make her cry?"

Sergeant Morrey didn't respond. Disregarding my questions, he continued to grasp Liz's pretty pristine fingers.

"What the hell's going on?" I snapped. "Why are you ignoring me? Why won't you answer?"

Some sort of machine encompassed the spot at the head of my bed. I couldn't turn around and see it, but I could tell it must have been enormous by the vibration of its bellows, clanks, swishing, and chimes. A nurse entered the room and approached it in an ominous manner.

"Nurse!" I called out. "What are you doing?"

She dismissed me.

"Can you please turn it off? That machine's making too much noise! No one can hear me. They're sitting there *not* responding. That disrespectful jerk is holding my wife's hand. It's ridiculous! I told him to stop and either he's pretending not to hear me or the machine's drowning me out!"

The nurse ignored me, as well. Rather than assist me, she flipped chart pages that I suspected had something to do with the machine. Then she refilled a canister, making an additional ruckus of *clanking* and *clicking* while adjusting the diodes.

"Turn it off!" I pleaded. "Come on! Please turn it off! The thing's giving me a headache, and I can't hear a fricken thing!"

Once she completed her task with the machine, she shuffled to the side of my gurney. That is when I noticed her unique Mediterranean beauty, although there was something about her no-nonsense expression and how she seemed undaunted by her task at hand. No-nonsense continued to ignore me as she rotated my forearm to inspect the patchwork of adhesive where the IV fed into my vein.

"Where am I? Which hospital is this?"

She *had* to hear me! She stood directly next to me! She stood right there, inspecting the tape on my arm! I felt infuriated! This nurse person ignored my repeated requests. Her ear hovered inches from my head, yet she still didn't respond to anything I said. Instead, she went about her duties as if I were a department store mannequin or human shell.

"Hello? Can you hear me? Open your ears! You've got to be the worst nurse, I've ever seen! This is terrible! Are you proud of yourself? Are you proud of the way you treat people?"

No-nonsense turned towards the chairs, and then she had the audacity to ask them to leave. She said something I could barely hear because the deep throttled kicks of the machine drowned out their voices. All I knew was that whatever she said resulted in Liz, Sergeant grabby-hands Morrey, and Officers Bettencourt and Doyle getting up from their seats and proceeding to file out of the room. And I noticed Sergeant Morrey wore a black business suit with a pin-striped tie while Bettencourt and Doyle were in their dress blues.

"What the hell? Why are you in your dress blues? Did you just come back from a funeral? Who died?"

And then it came back to me. Tiny threads of memories worked their way inside my brain, and my mind weaved together the events of the accident. I remembered the impact. *What kind of truck was it? What were the make and model? What was the color? I need this for my report!!!!* And then I remembered the feeling of being on an amusement park ride as the cruiser overturned again and again in a series of loud, voracious flips and impacts. I remembered my head hitting the dashboard and hearing the snap. And I remembered coming-to in the demolished cruiser and how I found Riley.

One little thread of memories brought about others, and pretty soon a tapestry of recollections became clear. Riley, with his perfect teeth, his perfect face. The women. God, how they loved him and fawned over him. Even when he issued them tickets, they would flirt and become mesmerized by his boyish beautifulness. I remembered the young woman who cried herself out of a ticket. And then I remembered the speeding city councilwoman, who threatened to file a report on us even though her driving record showed twenty-six citations for the same offense. I remembered the bicycle and the woman whose fiancée perished in an accident. I remembered granola bars and how my uniform would always be coated in a confectionary of crumbs no matter how hard I tried to keep it clean. *Riley, what a good guy, what a great friend; he was such a stand-up kind of person.* And then my memories played a cruel, evil trick on me as an image of Riley laughing and flirting morphed into his freshly-skinned face with his eyeball dangling from a noodle of ocular nerve. A flood of anguish consumed me. *He's dead! Riley died in the accident! He's dead! My friend's dead!*

♪

I awoke again. *Tired of this. Tired of waking up and passing out for unknown durations.* Still didn't know the day, which hospital I was in, or exactly what happened. Then I ascertained the continuous pounding and the strange huffs and beeps of the machine no longer throttled at a level of mindboggling torture. The machine still *raged, clanked, beeped*, and *whooshed,* but the racket almost seemed tolerable. Either they turned it down to a bearable frequency, or I had become accustomed to the noise.

More people flooded into the room; I sensed them before I opened my eyes. I somehow knew that the room overflowed with family, friends, and coworkers. Peeking out from my position on the mattress, I found an array of my fellow police officers. There must have been fifteen or twenty of them squeezed in there. They were in their dress blues, and I noticed some of them adorned paper hospital jumpsuits over their uniforms. Liz remained by my side (still in the turquoise pantsuit) in her spot next to my bed.

"Hey, Babe," I greeted again. "Babe, I'm awake. I'm right here."

She ignored me as she listened to Commander Bennett. *Wow, it must be bad! Look at his face! Look at her face.* I had never seen my wife's face seem so distressed, at least not since my father's funeral. It must be bad for the commander of the department to leave the station, come down here, and sit in my room like that. I tried my best to listen to them, but the racket of the machine, although bearable, drowned out most of what they said. In-between the clanks and beeps, I overheard a couple of words and phrases. "Shocked when I got the call." "It's sad." "Attended." "Newspaper." "The family's devastated." "Wake." I took it in and surmised they had just returned from Riley's funeral. That is *why they're dressed up. That is why they're all together. I'm gonna miss you, my friend. You were a great FTO and an excellent partner.*

Layered within my thoughts of Riley and his perfect smile and how he liked to help people, I recounted events of the accident: the reverberations of rupturing metal, the windshield shattering, the sounds of us screaming, and the force and *crack* when my forehead hit the dash. And then I recounted what happened in the eerie, spooky-like seconds afterward when I awakened in a state of semi-consciousness, slumped against the dash with my head turned in his direction. How I heard the sounds and screeches of evil, demon-like visions as they reached through the car, collected his soul, and stole him away. I remembered Riley's spirit pitching and wailing as he vanished into the ground, and then all that remained of him was an echo of silence.

It couldn't be what I thought. I must have imagined it. I must have imagined the whole thing. It must have been a delusion or maybe a bad dream, or probably a result of my injury.

♪

No-nonsense scurried into the room and over to the machine. I couldn't see her, but I knew she was there. She said something about there being too many people as she propped the door open, and then she offered her condolences while they all shuffled out.

"Goodbye!" I called to them. "Thanks for visiting!" "Doyle, you cheap, penny-pinching fool, you need to get some new uniform pants. The ones you got on are three sizes too small and showcase your mangina!" "Thanks for coming out here, Commander Bennett. Thanks for talking to my wife and making her feel better." "Later, Gonzalez!" "Later, Pullen, Slater, Brinks, and Donnelly. Later, everyone!" "Oh, and goodbye, Sergeant Morrey. Can't wait to have a word with you when I make it out, you handsy two-bit wannabe!"

I wasn't disappointed when they didn't respond. By then, I understood they couldn't hear a thing I said. No one heard anything over that darned machine.

"For the umpteenth time, could you please turn it off!" I asked

No-nonsense once everyone had filed out.

She ignored my pleas as she directed her attention to the foot of my bed.

What's she doing?

Grabbing ahold of the lower hemline, she brought my blanket to my midsection.

"What the hell?" I gasped when she lifted my hospital gown. "Lady, why are you there? I'm married! I'm a married man! What are you doing?"

By then, she had me exposed. *What? I have a catheter? Is that what that is? When did they do that? How long has it been there? How long have I been impaled like that?*

She worked so gently I barely felt a thing, and then I realized I *didn't* feel a thing. As she changed out my catheter, I had no feeling at all.

Nooooo! No, no, no, no, no! Something happened to Mr. Pickle! Mr. Pickle's dead! He's dead! No-nonsense must have done something horrible when she inserted the catheter tube! She must have killed him!

Lost in the tangle of worry, I began to grieve the loss of my manhood when an even scarier realization came to light: I had no feeling anywhere. While she checked my legs, my arms, readjusted my blood pressure band, and changed out my IV, I had no sense of touch. It was my first indication that my life would never be the same.

CHAPTER NINE
THE FIRST TIME

I was out again. This time I entered a dream. I was in a car, listening to music, driving in my neighborhood. It wasn't my neighborhood in real life; it was my neighborhood in the dream. I had just turned a corner when the crisp reds and blues of police lights lit up my rearview mirror.

"It's okay, Charlotte! Don't worry, beanie. Pawpaw's here. Everything's gonna be fine."

But as I expressed those empty reassurances, a stony sensation of dread curdled my belly. My veins went cold. My blood pressure froze to a standstill.

"Mabel," I said to my wife's photo on the dash, "I swear I wasn't doing nuthin'! Just driving down this here street, not asking for no trouble. I wasn't doing nuthin' wrong so you can stop with the yammering."

Things became hazy. The next thing I knew, I had parked on the side of the road. Two police officers got out of their cruiser and proceeded to approach my car.

"Charlotte, little string bean, it's okay." I adjusted the rearview mirror so I could see her. "Don't you fuss now. Pawpaw'll take care of you. Pawpaw's right here. We're just gonna talk to these nice policemen then Pawpaw will take you inside and give you your medicine. Don't be afraid, beany. Breathe slowly. Relax. Please don't cry. I got your favorite Charlie Parker tape playing. Just listen to Charlie and remember Pawpaw loves you!"

They approached simultaneously with their hands on their guns. The taller of the two appeared at my passenger side window. He had his firearm in his hand with his finger on the trigger. He remained calm, cool, collected, and predictably smug.

The other one neared my driver's side window. He grimaced when he saw the side of my face; when he discerned what I looked like, what color I was, and the cauldron of mangled scar tissue that beguiled my brow. Tightening his grip on the backstrap, he nervously directed his gun barrel at my face. He didn't seem calm, nor cool, nor smug in his approach. No, this one seemed scared shitless.

They barked contrasting orders, and I found myself remaining motionless with both hands in the air, unmoving, unblinking, trying my best not to breathe. They yelled at me, shouting about the pharmacy bag on the seat. Something about the situation had them unnerved. I had seen it before, that level of fear, that level of tenseness. I had seen it in Korea and Vietnam. *They're gonna panic! They're gonna panic and shoot me! They're gonna kill me for no reason!*

I subconsciously reached for the bag to show them the inhaler when four gunshots blasted through me. Four pinpoint reminders that I would never see Charlotte again. The heartbreak I experienced became an endless torrent of pain, and I'm startled awake.

It's not real! It's not real! I told myself. *That is not why I'm here! I wasn't shot; I was in an accident! It didn't happen.*

Then, like little bees, threads of memories infiltrated my mind. I remembered being in the police cruiser. *Yes, I remember being there.* I remembered relaying the license plate information into dispatch. *Yes, that was me.* And then my mind swarmed with more and more memories as it all came back to me. *I'm the one who approached the driver. I'm the one disgusted by his face. I'm the one scared shitless! I pulled the trigger! Oh, God! What have I done? I killed a man! I killed him in front of a baby! I killed an innocent man! I killed him for no reason! I made a mistake, a terrible mistake, and I can't take it away or change what happened!*

SECTION II

INFANCY

CHAPTER TEN
THE PETTICOAT PRINCESS

I awoke again. This time, I didn't see anyone in the room, not No-nonsense, not the nurse with the heart-shaped necklace, not the nurse with the fuzzy grey mustache and ear hair, not even Liz. I was alone and couldn't be sure if I had been awakened by the clanks, beeps, and huffs of the machine or some other kind of disturbance in the room.

"Hello?" I ventured hesitantly. "Is someone there? Can you hear me?"

No one responded, so I returned to my predicament. *What's going on? Why am I here? What's happened to my body? Am I going to die?*

And then I heard the soft, subtle rustle of footsteps. I wasn't alone; I was sure of it! Someone was there. A presence I couldn't explain. Someone or something I couldn't see. Whoever it was, they waited behind the machine, and I had a strange, eerie feeling that I was being watched.

♪

I awoke to the sound of Liz crying while a new doctor occupied the adjoining chair. He began to explain something to her, and I immediately surmised he was filling her in on my condition.

"Doc, I'm right here! What's wrong with me? Is it something you gave me? Have you sedated me with tranquilizers, so I can recover and go home?"

Once again, the doctor and Liz ignored my statements.

"Can you, for the life of me, please turn off that God-forsaken machine!" I snapped. "I'd like to know what the hell's going on!"

And, still, nothing. No one said anything. No one answered my questions. No one volunteered to help. No one told me what was going on.

♪

The tangy bittersweet aroma of Kung Pao chicken infused my

senses, and I awoke long enough to discover Liz and Amanda Doyle holding take-out canisters from a local trending hotspot. *When did they meet? Are they friends now? Doyle's a doofus who's always carping about his wife, but she seems like a nice person. The way she's talking to Liz and supporting her seems so compassionate and kind.*

♪

A sudden sharp stab startled me awake. It felt as if someone walked up and punched me in the gut. "What the!"

Opening my eyes, I suspected it must have been late at night. Liz slept soundly on the foldout, crumpled into a crescent moon with an assortment of blankets burrowed into her chin. In the moon's crook, I saw the most astonishing sight. A girl! A little girl with pigtails and petticoat pajamas. Cozying herself next to Liz, she used the corner of my wife's blanket to keep warm. She couldn't have been much more than eight or nine. I had never seen her before and couldn't understand why she was there.

"Wasn't me!" she exclaimed from the spot she had infiltrated. And then she smiled to herself before hiding underneath the blankets.

At that point, I didn't know what to think. I couldn't understand what was happening. *Why do I feel trapped to the bed? Why can't they hear me? Who would mess with me by standing over my bed and hurling punches? And who is the little girl? It's not making sense! Nothing makes sense! What's happening?*

♪

The next time I awoke, they were back. Liz took over her usual seat. This time she had on a cashmere turtleneck and jeans with a wide-buckled belt cinched around her waistline. Doyle's wife accompanied her. She sat next to Liz and appeared to be keeping her company. Fuzzy-ear hair stood by my arm, checking my circulation while the little girl sat precociously perched on the lower rail of my bed with her ankles crossed and her shoes on my blanket.

"What are you doing?" I snapped. "Get your feet off my bed! That's not right! They're not supposed to be there!"

"Says who?" she giggled. "I've been sitting here, waiting for you to flip a lid! Geeze, took you boocoo time!"

"What do you mean? Who are you? How come you're the only one who can hear me?"

"I'm Ruby Josephine," she introduced herself while reaching out her dainty, delicate hand for me to shake it.

I couldn't move. I was trapped in the bed and couldn't understand what she was doing.

"Anyhow," she quipped, withdrawing her hand, "I'm bored of being here."

She hopped off the bed, and I noticed she wore old-fashioned lace boots and an old-timey poufy dress over her petticoats.

"And you should be too. Whenever you're ready, we'll be in the corridor waiting for you. That's where me an' the big cheese hunker down and shoot the breeze."

"What?" I gasped. "Who are you talking about? What cheese? What do you mean?"

♪

I had checked out again. I was asleep, and my thought process ceased to exist. I wasn't dreaming. I couldn't even feel my breath as it flowed in and out of my lungs. I was nowhere and nothing. And then a sudden sharp blow to my gut startled me awake to an overwhelming emergence of pain. I didn't know if I should welcome the sensation or curse it at the top of my lungs.

Shit, I groaned, *that freaken' hurt!* And then I saw it. In the billionth of a second that it took my lids to flutter open, I saw the fainting trace of a shadow slithering towards the back wall. The shadow disappeared into the recesses of clanks and beeps behind the machine.

"Who's there?" I called out. "Who are you, and why are you doing this? Why the hell did you hit me? Can't you see that I'm injured? Can't you see I'm in a hospital bed?"

No one responded. No noise could be heard over the brain-wracking commotion of the machine beating and breathing and beeping on end. I waited for it to return, *nothing.* I closed my eyes and pretended to sleep, *nothing.* I lay there and waited for an hour, then two (through Liz's arrival from the cafeteria with a fresh cup of coffee, through the doctor's visit, through three IV changes) and still *nothing*. No shadows. No little girls. No sudden sharp wallops of pain. The experience in that room had me baffled.

"Babe!" I called to my wife even though I didn't think she would respond. "Please answer me! Please let me know you can hear me! For God's sake, please tell me what's going on!"

She looked over at me, and I had a flicker of hope that she would giggle and say something like, "Of course, I hear you, Billy Bear. Everything's okay! The doctor said we could go home."

But she said nothing. Liz took a sip of coffee, set the cup down, and sat there as tears spontaneously rained from her eyes.

"Babe, why are you crying? Did something happen? Did someone say something to make you cry?"

She didn't respond. No one responded: not the doctor, not Fuzzy-ear hair, not the nurse with the orthopedic shoes, not No-nonsense, not the janitorial staff, not even the round-faced clergyman with bad breath and a boulder-sized blackhead in the crease of his nose. With the exception of the little girl, no one responded to any of my questions. No one heard anything I said. And I discerned there must have been a lot more going on in that room then I could possibly imagine. Somehow, something was happening that was far beyond common sense, logic, or reason.

No-nonsense returned. I hadn't seen her in a while and wondered if she had been assigned somewhere else or had just given up on me. When she entered the room, Liz greeted her as if they were longtime friends or college roommates.

"Hey," Liz volleyed, "I'm glad you're back. Hope you had a nice weekend."

"Yeah," No-nonsense volleyed back as she scanned dials and diodes on the machine. "Spent it with my family. We went to a jazz fest in Los Angeles. Great music and perfect weather. Did you get a chance to make it outside?"

"No," Liz sighed, "Didn't want to leave him. I'm hoping and

praying he comes out of it. I just…"

What does she mean 'comes out of it?' Am I in a coma? Am I paralyzed and in a coma? How can I be in a coma if I'm right here? How can I be in a coma if I can hear them? Wait a minute, how come I can suddenly hear what they say over the machine?

As a dozen questions emerged in my mind, I saw something disturbing that took my breath away but didn't take my breath away because I couldn't feel myself breathing. As No-nonsense changed out my catheter and replaced my filled urine bag, I observed her remove the old bag and saw that it contained blood.

What the hell? I'm bleeding internally? Not only am I paralyzed and in a coma – with a busted pickle and a voice nobody can hear, – but I'm bleeding internally? What else can go wrong? The thought terrified me as I laid in wait. Hour by hour, I waited for something to happen. I waited for the doctors to fix me, the girl to return, or the shadows of death to come and take my soul.

♪

This time, I wasn't completely checked-out. *I'm asleep, but I'm here. I can feel this! I'm floating! I'm floating!* My body felt weightless as my limbs reached out, expanded, and embraced a newfound independence. *I'm free! I'm free! I'm free of the shackles, free of the bed, and I'm rising, rising into the air. This feels too good to be true. This is awesome! This is fricken awesome! This is unbelievable!*

Opening my eyes, I found myself soaring toward the ceiling of my hospital room. *I'm floating! I'm floating! This feels amazing. It's unbelievable!* The Big Dipper and Little Dipper were just within reach, so I stretched out my arm, allowing my fingertips to caress the grooved ceiling tiles. Their mundane texture felt amazing. They were just ceiling tiles – average, ordinary ceiling tiles that had no stars or galaxies molded into them, – yet levitating to the ceiling and experiencing their sensation while being weightless felt deliriously fantastic.

And then, without thinking about it or realizing what I had done, I looked down and automatically overturned. I still hovered in the same spot, but instead of facing my beloved ceiling tiles, I faced something less beloved, less beautiful, and much less heartwarming. I faced me.

In my hospital bed below me, I saw my sad, pathetic body. Blankets bared my chest just enough to expose a grotesquely bloated form. The parts of me that weren't bruised had paled into an unusual pasty color. I lay unconscious and appeared half-dead. But it was the machine by my head that sent shivers down my spine. *NO! I'm on life support. That machine – that terrible, loud, insidious machine – has been breathing for me and pumping my oxygen. It's keeping me alive!*

Descending closer to myself, I began to inspect what I could of my injury. Bandages obstructed most of the damage, but my poor pathetic face had become bruised and swollen while traces of blood had soaked through the gauze. *I wonder how bad it is. I heard a crack; I wonder if I'll ever awaken.*

"Pretty gross, huh?" I looked over and saw that Ruby Josephine had entered the room and found me floating above myself, inspecting my injury. "Betcha blood and gook spurted all over the place when you broke it! Betcha it was icky! Geeze Louise, I get the hebbie-jeebies just thinkin' about it!

"Yeah," I agreed, and then I found myself gliding back to the ground. I completed a wobbly, clumsy, unintentional descent until I landed on the floor and awkwardly stumbled. As soon as my feet made contact with the smooth linoleum surface, I had to steady myself so that I wouldn't fall.

Ruby Josephine giggled. "Not bad for a first-timer," she proudly proclaimed. "Just takes practice. You'll get the hang of it!"

I felt confused and confounded and a bit woozy. "What? What takes time? What's happening? What are you talking about?"

"Why leaving your body, William Walsh." Clutching onto her belly, she giggled with childlike vibrato. "It's always hard the first time, but you did pretty well. Just stand there for a moment or two, and you'll catch your bearings."

"What's going on? Am I dreaming? How come you're the only one who can hear me? How come…"

An overwhelming wave of confusion enveloped me, consuming

the thought. I became dizzy and felt as though I would keel over.

"Don't worry," she assured confidently. "If you pass out, you'll just fall back into your body."

"I'll what?"

The room swirled. My eyelids became heavy, and I found myself getting sleepier and sleepier.

"Your soul!" she responded.

And I was out.

CHAPTER ELEVEN THE SECOND TIME

The scent of something rich and hickory infused my senses. *Is that bacon? Cookies? No, but I know that smell. It's something I like but haven't had for a very long time, something cakey and salty and mouth-wateringly good. And sweet! Yeah, it's something sweet, something that smells like my mother's cooking, something reminding me of my early childhood home.*

Even though a portion of my brain understood I lay in the same hospital room (on the same concrete-hard mattress with my body attached to that same machine that clanked and rattled and made that unbearable *whooshing* sound as it kept me alive), a rollover in my semi-consciousness brought me to another place and time. I awoke not in the hospital room but in a quaint, simple abode on a quaint, simple bed that felt strange but, somehow, seemed familiar.

How did I get here? What kind of bed is this? Is this a day bed or trundle? It was like no bed I had ever seen, nothing manufactured or sold from any department store. This twin-sized custom fit Cherrywood frame appeared to have been carved by hand. Someone tenderly sanded, stained, and constructed each slat of wood in a way that exposed the burls and grains within the timber's imperfections. But it was the mattress in which I instantaneously fell in love.

It wasn't the rock-hard slab of concrete in the hospital room. It wasn't the mattress of my childhood with lumpy padding. And it wasn't the foam-topped monstrosity from my home with Liz, made to be synthetically-comfortable yet retained heat to the extent I roasted alive. No, this time, I nestled upon a pillowy-soft feather-filled mattress that cradled my body as a heavenly cloud. And that scent. *What is that delicious smell? Is it cookies?* No. *Pancakes?* No. *I know what it is but can't--*

"Otis!" the musical drawl of a female voice originated from another room. "Baby, it's time to getcha up! It's a beautiful day! You better believe it. Beautiful!'

What's going on? Where am I, and who is this person calling me?

The door to the room opened, and a strange woman that I had never seen before stood in the threshold, wearing a long-sleeved black dress smocked with an oversized apron. Her hair had been tightly gathered and collected into a meticulous bun while her black leather shoes shined like matching rain puddles.

"Honey child," she greeted with a magnificent grin.

What the hell! Who is this person? Who are you?

"You needs to get outta bed an' get yourself ready. First day of schools today, an' I'm mad crazy excited for you on this big day for your big adventure. Now gets that beady little behind out of bed and gets dressed!"

I didn't exactly know this woman, and I couldn't understand what was happening. I didn't know what to do. Remaining sunken into the padding that fit my body to a T, my brain scrambled to make sense of it all. *I'm awake!?!* I muddled. *I'm awake, right??? I feel awake! I feel like this is happening, or could I be hallucinating again?*

I didn't know if this could have been a dream or something to do with my injury, but I didn't move. I just lay there. This woman – this peculiar woman who spoke so colorfully and looked so strange but somehow seemed familiar, – I couldn't understand how I knew her.

"Dear sweet Jesus," she declared in a huff from the door's threshold. Her dark eyes wouldn't stop staring at me as she collected patience by brushing invisible dust off her apron.

I couldn't comprehend how I had gotten to this unusual place with this unusual person who was not my mother but seemed so maternal. And then she strode across the room in my direction. *Wake up! Wake up!* I told myself. *This can't be real! I don't know this person and don't know why I'm here!*

With each step, her shoes clattered the old hardwood floor, producing crisp *clacks* that reverberated throughout the room. The reverberations stopped when she bent down and gently placed a kiss upon my forehead.

"Pudden' child, I do loves to see you getten' your sleep. You's a growen' and needs your rest, but not today, my little man. Today, you kin gets that spindly little bony body of yours out of this here bed and join me for some fixings before school!"

Gathering ahold of the covers, she whisked them to the foot of the bed in one swift gesture, and then her eyes flared with astonishment. "Oh, my goodness, boy child," she gasped, "what have we gots here?"

On the side of the mattress, I saw a funny-looking musical instrument of some sort.

Her dark black eyes smoldered with dismay. "Wha'd I tell yous about playin' with pawpaw's sax! Didn't I tell you, you weren't supposed to be play'n with that? Who gave you permission, and why the dickens you got that thing in your bed?"

Without another word, she carefully collected the bright shiny saxophone and walked it out of the room as if it were a prized heirloom.

I had no clue what I should say or do. I didn't know this woman. At least I didn't think I knew her. But I had somehow transformed into a kid around the age of seven or eight, maybe a little younger. Everything happened so fast. One moment I had been a police officer involved in an accident. And the next, I lay in a coma having unusual dreams that took me to a place that felt real and unusual and extraordinarily surreal.

In this dream (or whatever it was) this woman thought I was her son, and to tell you the truth, it felt true. However, one thing drastically stood awry with the scenario, and it wasn't the little insignificant circumstance like the simple, unusual room with the strangely-familiar mattress that felt foreign and fantastic at the same time. It was this woman. This peculiar woman felt like a stranger and my mother at the same time. But she couldn't be. She couldn't be my mother. My mother had blonde hair and porcelain skin. My mother stood petite with a mellow disposition. My mother spoke proper English and always used appropriate grammatical tenses; she didn't use words like *Lord Jesus, Pawpaw, boy child,* or *playin'*. No, this woman was something completely different. This female person stood taller and thicker and bigger-boned than my mother. Her voice crooned rich and buttery-smooth while her clothes were something from another era. But the most significant difference between this woman and my mother was unmistakable. This woman was Black.

♪

After she left the room, I lay there for a moment or two, trying to muster my bearings. *This is crazy. Should I go out there, or should I stay here and try to go back to sleep? If I go back to sleep, will I return to my real life? Will I go back to being a voiceless zombie, trapped in my body on a rock-hard mattress in the hospital, attached to that Godforsaken machine?* And then I recalled the sight of me as a patient as I hovered above myself and decided wherever I was and whoever this person was, it had to be better than teetering upon the brink of death. So I sat up from the bed and placed my feet upon the floor, and I realized I was Black also. I was African American, Negro, dark-skinned, and – somehow – it didn't feel terrifying or unusual or wrong. It felt comfortable. I felt like me.

♪

The room was sparsely furnished. Besides the bed, I found a chest of drawers, a rickety handmaid chair made of nothing more than four one-by-ones attached to a small wooden plank, and a set of shelves that contained a collection of oddly-shaped minerals, a rusted firetruck with mismatched wheels, and a decorative Bible. I don't know why (I was a grown man with a college degree and an occupation as a civil servant) but for some reason, I got up, crept over to the toy box, and peeked inside.

Within the contents, I discovered a treasure of my beloved possessions. Actually, they weren't my possessions, but they somehow seemed familiar. First, I recognized the baseball glove that had been Uncle Thaddeus's hand-me-down he had given me when I was nothing more than knee-high to a grasshopper. I remembered playing ball with Ethan. And then a rush of memories came to me at once. I remembered how Ethan and I were best friends and how we had skipped out on chores to meet up at the spot by the river where we would go fishing and rock skipping. We spent many lazy afternoons, pretending we were Babe Ruth and Jackie Robinson, practicing our home runs, choppers, and dastardly duck snouts.

"Otis!" she impatiently paged from the other room. "Hurry up and gets yourself dressed. This here cornbread ain't gonna stay warm just sittin' here. Move your britches!"

Inside the dresser's third drawer, I selected a pair of hand-stitched black pants and a white button-down shirt. Once I slid them on and fastened each button, I headed into the adjacent room that appeared to be a living room, family room, and kitchen combined into a common living area. And then the aroma of *real* food infused me. If the scent that roused me into consciousness had been heaven-sent, the smell of cornbread with bacon and eggs swooned with delicious divinity, and I remembered that it had been days (maybe even a week) since I had eaten.

"What!?! Lord Jesus child, now you is try'n my patience!" She walked up to me, clasped her hand across the back of my neck, and shepherded me back into my room, spouting, "Why'd you put on your good church clothes? Who are you try'n to impress? Is it that *Ethan,* I know you been hanging around? Listen, I done told you that that boy ain't gonna be associating with you nows that it's time for school. It's not your fault; you've done nunthin' wrong. But I told you them White folk don't take a liken' to none of their kind play'n with the likes of ours."

Pulling open the bottom drawer, she selected a raggedy pair of jeans with patched knees and a stitched zipper, and an old brown shirt with tapered sleeves, and handed them to me.

"Here you go, child." She smiled voraciously, and I noticed her teeth had a small gap in the front while a couple of them were uneven; nevertheless, that smile lit up the room with unfettered happiness. The way she looked at me and spoke to me made me feel grounded and wanted and safe.

"Now gimme dem good church clothes so I can fold 'em for Sunday, and then you need to hurry an' get ready! Today's not just any other day. Today's your first day in your new education!"

Once I redressed myself and combed my hair, I arrived at the table where I found two bowls filled with whatever produced that delicious aroma. Sitting in the smaller of the chairs, I looked into my bowl, discovering an unusual feast of cornbread and egg topped with fresh bacon and a funny crumbly substance.

"What's that white stuff?" I asked as if I were an eight-year-old. And then I saw the saxophone (previously located in my bed) displayed on a wall mount adjacent to an old-fashioned stove.

"It's Mrs. Washington's good goat cheese. She shared some with you on account of it's your first day in your new school. You have to remember that you won't be there alone; there's a lotta us Colored folk that'll be behind you, hopen' and prayen' things go well. Look at that there egg, that comes from Ben Blackwood's hen house. He brought it over just for you. He's a good man; I'm telling you!" She nodded her head as if trying to convince me. "Good man."

As she spoke, I had my first bite of soul food breakfast and actually felt my toes bend and burrow inside the brown boot-like shoes. The aroma may have been divine, but that was nothing compared to the combination of flavors and crunch that tantalized my taste buds in a heaven-sent soirée of unfettered deliciousness.

"Otis, baby, you gots to remember that some of dem White folk won't take a liken to you going to their school. They wanna keep it divided. They don't want you minglen' with their childrens. They'd rather you worked the fields as if we was still slaves. It feels like it sometimes, but we ain't." She chuckled to herself. "Now that the courts desegregated things, you're gonna be one of the first of us to goes to their school."

"Why me? Why do I have to be the one to change schools? Why can't they just--"

"Baby, we don't have no time for that now. Just know that the courts are behind you, and so's our people. This's a blessin,' don't you see? The school that I went to only had one raggedy ole' book for all of us to share. We didn't have no paper or pencils for practicing. Our roof leaked when it rained while our playground was nothen' more than a dirt patch so bitty it couldn't keep a five-legged billygoat confined. In fact, my teacher worked at the school part-time then went to her real job healen' and deliveren' babies! But the place you's gonna go, now that's a real school with real teachers who've been to college. You's gonna be educated right!"

♪

She twisted the knob then pushed the cumbersome door open, revealing a neighborhood like nothing I had ever seen. The houses in this place were rundown tiny bungalows with cracked walls, boarded over windows, and fenced in earthen beds for yards. They weren't architectural or pretty. To be honest, I would describe them as weathered and dreary and bleak. *Do people really live like this? Is this a mind trick or poverty infomercial? Something I've seen on television and am reliving in my dreams?*

The roadway that connected the properties was merely a dirt path. No raised trucks or sports cars waited in the driveways. There were no extended parking areas for their ATVs; in fact, there were no ATV's, nor boats, nor motorhomes. It was just an alcove of rundown, stamp-sized bungalows spaced alongside a narrow dirt-laden path. Then I saw a tire swing dangling from a gigantic maple tree and mud tire tracks in one of the yards, detailing imaginative voyages of tiny bicycles. And, three or four bungalows over, I saw a vegetable garden where I imagined people from around the area worked as a community, tending to their harvest.

Following the path that led east, the sun's early morning rays sauntered my skin, reminding me that the body I possessed wasn't my own. *This is so real. I actually feel the sun's warmth; it's like nothing I have ever experienced in a dream. Why is this happening? Why am I dreaming about this? I'm Black! I don't want to be Black. Why can't I dream about normal things such as beating up bad guys and winning the lottery? Is it normal to become another person in your dreams?*

As I grappled the circumstances of my "dream," my mother person walked alongside me, spieling her advice. "Listen to me," she preached in her buoyantly baritone drawl. By then, we had passed three or four bungalows and were halfway along a field of strawberries. "Just ignore 'em if they say anything to scare you, but doncha let 'em be callen' you no names. If they start with their Klan talk, you remind 'em you gots a right to be there. Remind 'em of the court case. Just don't lose your temper none. They already talk about us folk as if our men's itching for a reason to knock knuckles. You is our example. You prove we's gots a right to be there, and that we's good church goin' people."

She smiled at me, and even though I didn't know this woman from a stranger on the street, I could tell that she preached to mask her worry. It didn't take a police officer's instinct to see that. She loved this kid and generally cared for his well-being.

So I remained silent. I listened to her maternal campaign as we traversed the dirt path that seemed to become more familiar with each step. And, for some reason, I grew to care for this strange woman. I cared about her and wanted to reassure her. I wanted to tell her that nothing was going to happen to me because I wasn't her eight-year-old son; I was actually a twenty-eight-year-old police officer who was positively, absolutely not at all intimidated at the prospect of going to a school to face a bunch of whiny little kids, especially not whiney little Caucasian kids. After all, I had a lifetime of experience as one of them. I belonged to their club.

The road dead-ended at the gully beneath a weed-infested hill. We didn't veer or head off in a different direction; we simply foraged into the softly-sloped thicket of dried grass and dandelions towards the top of the mound. Every couple of steps my floppy heal stuck into the thick, murky patches of earth, and I fretted it would break off, causing me to fall. Nothing like that happened though. The heel remained intact as we made it to the top just in time to see a train gliding along the tracks in our direction.

"Hurry, now," my mother person implored, "we gots to beat this here train!" And then she grabbed ahold of my forearm and hastened her pace as we neared a "No Trespassing" sign. I took five, six, ten steps towards the tracks with my heal sticking into the mud while the train quickly headed in our direction. The moment I saw the conductor's profile, every basic instinct I had screamed to stand still, but she remained strong and agile as she effortlessly leaped over the tracks, ushering me alongside her.

Moments after we made it to the other side, the train sped by, producing a voracious whirlwind of pebbles and sand grains that pelted my backside in tiny cannonballs. Mother person ignored it. Pulling me by the hand, she brought me to an overlook at the top of the mound where I gazed down upon a large subdivision with sprawling lots adorned in a mosaic of rooftops with differently-shaped chimneys. There must have been three hundred houses (if not four) laid-out in pretty pristine rows with perfectly-manicured lawns and shiny windows decorated with flower boxes and colorful vinyl coverings. And driveways. The place had lots and lots of driveways filled with an array of children's bicycles basking freely amongst an assortment of baseball bats, wagons, and other toys.

"I can't be late, pudden'," she said. "You know I have to be at work on time. If I'm even a minute late, Mrs. Anderson told me I might as well finds me another job. You know the way." She pointed to the sparkling-clean street that led towards the northeastern portion of the subdivision. "Just follow this here road until it takes you to that there school."

Regardless of the fact that I was actually a grown man, a part of me felt like a little kid. I felt like *her* kid. And even though I wanted to resist the urge to be kind to her, that son part of me wrapped my arms around this mother person and hugged her tightly before taking off down the hill. And it didn't matter that she wasn't my birth mother, was a different color, or that she spoke funny by using a lot of mixed-up words and discombobulated tenses; that hug felt like something special. It felt like chocolate chip cookies straight out of the oven when the chips were still gooey. It felt like the cool squishy sensation of beach sand between my toes on a warm summer day. It felt like riding on a Ferris wheel, gliding between galaxies of sparkling lights. And it felt like puppies – like lots and lots of puppies – as if I were hugging a litter of cuddly puppies with fur so soft that my arms sank into her motherly midsection. And for a second there the little boy in me – whose mother died of cancer when he was a mere eight years young – felt the unmeasurable joy and nurturing he had ached for every single moment of his life.

Halfway through the neighborhood, I heard the impatient trill of a school bell. "Hurry, child," she had said. "You mustn't be late on this here first day. Go on now, run!"

So I took off as fast as I could into the strangely familiar neighborhood in my strangely familiar delusion, dream, or whatever it was. And somewhere along my way (as my muscles acclimated to the pace of gliding through air and time, as I steeled to the gate, and as I could feel myself breathing), I came to life. *This is phenomenal! My heartbeat, the wind, my blood pumping through my veins, and every muscle in my body can feel each and every inkling of being alive. This doesn't feel like any dream I've ever had. It feels real, deliriously deliciously real!* And I realized running like that felt more like racing down the field in a game-winning touchdown then being stuck in a bed, having a delusion. Every ounce of my body invigorated with power, strength, and vitality. *I'm alive! I'm alive! I'm alive! I'm alive!* After being trapped to a bed – unable to move an arm, a leg, or even the tip of my pinkie finger, – running like that became a dream come true. It became total and complete freedom. Floating across the earth top with unbridled joy, I became invincible.

A minute or two later, I reached the school's blacktop. From outward appearances, John Adams Elementary resembled any other ordinary school. Actually, it seemed remarkably similar to the grade school I attended twenty or so years in my past. As I traversed the pristine concrete sidewalk that led to the corrugated brick entrance, I observed hundreds of children in the playground engaging in hopscotch, shooting baskets, jumping rope, hanging upside down from pullup bars, and pretty much milling about, enjoying the beginning of their day.

As I neared the massively-large, sparkling-clean expanse of blacktop, all of the children stopped jumping and hopping and tether balling as if time suddenly stalled. They all paused what they were doing and stared at me, the new guy, the Colored boy who invaded their school.

Luckily for me, that was pretty much the extent of the protest. Bands of irate parents had not gathered at the front of the school. The National Guard had not been called in, and no angry mobs of protesters carried signs, ranting racist epithets, threatening to lynch or skin me alive. And even though I was either a little kid or a grown police officer in a coma in some faraway hospital, I ascertained this dream or projected experience happened sometime after *Brown vs. Board of Education*, after the great protests of "Black Monday," and all the movements spurned by The White Citizens Council in Mississippi.

Whatever school this is, it has been forced to comply with the infamous ruling. This kid is probably one of the tens of thousands of nameless African American children who had to endure the degradation of being the first to go to White people schools where they were not welcomed, wanted, or received well. Instead of being the pretty boy whom everyone cherished and adored; I'm receiving an ugly little taste of discrimination.

"Boy!" a petite, pink-faced woman called from the center of the blacktop. She wore a navy-blue pleated skirt that billowed around her calves, brown saddle shoes, and a white button-down blouse topped with a beige cashmere sweater with pearl buttons. And a whistle – I will never forget about that part. A large metal pea whistle dangled from a stainless steel chain around her neck. "Otis!" she called again.

Otis, I thought. *Somehow that name rings a bell. I know I should know it. It's so oddly familiar. My mother person had called me Otis. I know that I know it from somewhere.* I couldn't get it, and I couldn't let it go. Although I knew my body languished somewhere in the hospital, part of my brain waded in and out of a thick fortuitous fog of uncertainty.

Some of the pieces of my real life were clear. I was married. I loved Liz. She wanted a baby while I preferred to wait. Riley had died, and then my memories became murky. *What happened to that man? Did he shoot me? Did he die? Why is this happening? Somehow the name Otis seems familiar.* I sensed that I someway knew the answer. It felt like it wandered around in my head and had become lost. It seemed if I searched hard enough, I could find it and put the puzzle together, and then *FWEET*!!!!! The shrill shriek of her whistle announced the end of recess. All of the children immediately mustered into a staging area where they assembled into lines.

"Otis Cleveland!" she called out again, and I noticed they were staring at me. The children stood in formation, waiting for me while this pink-faced woman scowled. That is when it dawned on me that *I* was

Otis Cleveland. More and more recollections tumbled into my mind. The accident. The man. He was Otis Cleveland Merriweather! I was the childhood version of that man!

♪

"Now children…"

It was *her,* the perky woman from the playground. Same pretty face. Same coifed hair. Same pools of trust for eyes. Smiling graciously, she stood poised in front of the chalkboard.

"Take your seats," she greeted as we strode inside her classroom. "My name is Miss Mercy, and I am your teacher. There's folded placards on everyone's desktop with your names on them, as well as a brand new pencil box of pencils, erasers, and other supplies. Everyone take your seats and quiet down. Please quiet down. We have a lot to go over."

As the other children swiftly found their assigned seats, I stood befuddled in that I didn't see a placard with the name "Otis Cleveland Merriweather," and I certainly didn't see one with "William Walsh" on it either. I became the sole straggler who stood in place while all of my classmates shuffled about the room, located their placards, and then slid into their assigned desks. And then – in that split-second of chaos and commotion – I saw him. My friend! I recognized him even though I had never met him or seen his picture. But, somehow, I immediately knew his coppery hair, freckles, and that swashbuckling, bucktoothed grin.

Ethan. My friend Ethan had the same class. Ethan was there with me. And even though I was actually an adult male stuck inside some sort of weird, bizarre dream, a part of my belly warmed with well-being because I knew with Ethan there that everything would be fine. I looked over at Ethan and smiled, and his eyes immediately skirted to the side.

He probably didn't see me, so I called to him. "Hey Ethan, it's me! Can you believe it? We're in the same class!"

By then, most of the children had settled into their seats.

Waving my arm, I tried a little louder. "Ethan, can you hear me?"

He didn't move. He didn't look up and acknowledge me. He just sat there with stooped shoulders and offset eyes. By then, everyone in the room looked his way, including Miss Mercy.

"Quiet children," she admonished. "This isn't the time to be socializing."

And then she directed her attention to me. "Otis," Miss Mercy explained in her nicest teachers' voice, "there aren't enough seats. I didn't want to cause a commotion, so I've arranged a special place for you in the extra little chair we have." She pointed to the northeast corner of the room. "Right over there."

She didn't point to a desk with a seat and a brand new pencil box and decorative name placard. It wasn't even a rundown desk with a cracked backrest or missing leg. It was a stool, a backless three-legged stool set up in the back corner of the room. Part of me wanted to fight her. Part of me wanted to protest by saying something like, "This is wrong! This is wrong! It isn't fair!" But it wasn't my life, and it wasn't my problem. I didn't know how long I would be there or how much longer this delusion would take place, so I compliantly lumbered down the narrow row of perfectly-placed desks.

I shuffled by Ethan whose face cast down in angst, by three or four girls who leaned as far away from me as they could (as if having dark skin was akin to having cooties), and was just about to pass a pudgy tow-headed boy when he stuck his foot into the aisle and intentionally tripped me. I fell hard, flopping onto the pristine clean linoleum, while students around the classroom broke out in a chorus of laughter and jeers.

Time slowed and stewed as I remained on the floor for a moment or two, trying to regain my composure.

"Mr. Anderson," Miss Mercy directed in her tender yet firm teachers' voice, "That's not appropriate. I know you don't want him here." She snickered politely. "In fact, I'm not sure anyone here wants him. But that doesn't mean we can misbehave. Keep your hands and feet to yourself! According to Principal Mumford, Otis will stay in our class until the courts come to their senses and make things right!"

Maybe his brain has a buildup, or he's got plugs in his ears so he can't hear me. As I sat in my stool, I tried to rationalize Ethan's continued cold shoulder. *It doesn't make sense. Ethan's my best friend. Maybe he doesn't*

recognize me and thinks I'm another Colored boy. Maybe alien creatures beamed down and lasered his eyes, so he can't see anything but blue people or green people or people with two heads and snail antennae. Or maybe my mother person was right. Maybe back in this period, it would have stirred "a heap of trouble" if he associated with someone like me.

"Otis," Miss Mercy called to me. "Turn to page four. I don't know if you can read *real words*, but the least you could do is follow along by looking at the pictures."

"I can read," I responded insolently. *I've only been this Black person for an hour or two, and I'm not liking it. I don't like the way I'm treated. I don't like her insinuations of ignorance. And I especially don't like the way my fellow students turn and scoff at me every time she calls me out or says something that suggests I'm stupid.* "I already know this."

"What do you mean by you 'already know this'?" she snickered in her sweet teacher way. "Colored people can't read big words. This is the Preamble to the Constitution of the United States, not some silly comic strip."

"I realize that," I shrugged. "I know it."

A rumble of voices percolated throughout the room as my classmates animatedly objected.

"This is absurd!" she declared, posturing herself arrogantly. "This is exactly what I was talking about when I told them I didn't want any Colored segregates in my class. It's a distraction; I'm telling you. It's a distraction."

"Miss Mercy!" Jimmy-John raised his hand. "Miss Mercy!"

"Yes, Mr. Anderson."

"Miss Mercy! I know his mother. His mother's our maid. She's been working for my family since before I was born." Jimmy-John twisted in his seat so that he faced me. "He's lying; I'm saying. He's lying. His mother can't read nor write none. She's about as dumb as dumb gets." Proudly smiling, he nodded his head in satisfaction. "She can't talk rights none either."

Miss Mercy wagered a smug sneer while crossing her arms in front of herself. "Well, class," she decreed. "It seems as if we have one of them lying little-Colored boys who likes to run their mouths and make up stories. Let's just disregard him and tend to our lesson." She smiled pleasingly. "Miss Bowers, I believe you will be first to start."

"We the p,p, pebble," a girl in the second row hesitantly began, "of U, U--"

"United States," I cut her off midsentence, "in order to form a more perfect Union, establish justice, insure domestic tranquility, provide for the common defense, promote the general welfare, and secure the Blessings of Liberty to ourselves and our posterity, do ordain and establish this Constitution for the United States of America."

As I spoke, Miss Mercy's eyeballs nearly popeyed from their sockets while her mouth gaped open in astonishment. And then I closed the book, reached over, and gingerly placed it on a neighboring shelf before I continued the Preamble from memorization. "Article I, Section 1. All legislative Powers herein granted shall be vested in a Congress of the United States, which shall consist of a Senate and House of Representatives."

"Enough!" Miss Mercy snapped. "That's enough!"

Ignoring her, I continued with, "The House of Representatives shall be composed of Members chosen every second year by the people of the several States, and the Electors in each State shall have—"

"ENOUGH!" Miss Mercy barked. "Otis Cleveland, you've just earned your first trip to the office for insubordination. It was Miss Bowers turn to read." She pursed her lips as she impatiently scribbled something on a pink pad of paper. "*Not* your opportunity to mock my class and put on a sideshow." After tearing the slip from the pad, she held it above her head for all to see. "Take this to Principal Mumford. You can sit in there and think about your actions and the disrespect you placed upon poor Sarah LeAnn."

"But I didn't get a chance to finish. I didn't get to explain in *real words* how no person shall be a representative who shall not have attained the age of twenty-five years and--"

"LEAVE!" she growled as she pointed to the door. "Get! Out!"

As I walked the dreaded path between desks to the front of the room, Miss Mercy continued with, "You can return after lunch. I'll be sure and go over a little early American history about the prestige and righteousness of the great Andrew Jackson, and his visionary for our country," she exclaimed in her politest teachers' tone. "It should make for a colorful afternoon!"

♪

Principal Mumford shook his head, dismissively waving me off as soon as I got to his door.

"No, no, no," he exclaimed, "you're not going to sit in here. Whatever you did to set off Miss Mercy is gonna have to be dealt with in the hallway. I'm not going to sit here and perform my duties with you cluttering up my workspace."

"But I didn't--" I started to say.

"Don't give me any lip! And don't talk back. Sit in the hallway until your detention is over. I have a school to educate."

♪

Three hours and twenty-six minutes later, a demure stilt-legged woman escorted me back to Miss Mercy's room to fetch my lunch for the midday break. But when I arrived at my stool, my lunch bag had disappeared. I looked around and couldn't find it anywhere, confused as to where it could have gone. By then, I was hungry and looking forward to the cornbread honey ham sandwich and peanut butter cookies my mother person had made.

"That's strange," said the escorting parent volunteer, "you probably should have brought it with you when you went to detention."

The student cafeteria was basically a carbon copy of the one I had in grade school. It was a sizeable rectangular-shaped room filled with rectangular-shaped tables surrounded by chairs. It also had a stage for school assemblies with a flagpole on the side. Next to the American flag hung a large print of Dwight D. "Ike" Eisenhower, and my brain racked trying to remember which year he held office.

"Not that table," the volunteer directed when I attempted to sit down. "Miss Mercy's class is assigned to the first row of tables, the one in front of the stage." She pointed to the row of students quietly eating their food under President Eisenhower. And I thought it ironic that all of these children with racist propensities and upbringings were sitting beneath a President who would go on to propose civil rights legislation that set forth the Civil Rights Act.

And then I saw Ethan look up and almost smile at me. *He wants to be my friend but is too embarrassed. Is he ashamed because I'm poor, because I'm Black, or because he's worried about what the others would think?*

"No way!" Jimmy-John scoffed, and all the kids looked up at me. "No flippin' way you're sitten' here. This is a *White* people school with *White* students. You need to go sit outside on the porch and eat like your mother does."

But his words didn't sear into me nearly as much as the sight of the brown paper bag that sat on the table in front of him. Jimmy-John had my lunch! My peanut butter cookies were laid out in front of him while my cornbread honey ham sandwich was in his hand!

"You stole my lunch!" I snapped. "I want it back. I want my lunch back!"

And *boom*! Silence. Everyone stopped talking and eating mid-bite.

"What'd you say?" Jimmy-John snarled as he slammed his fist upon the table. "Are you accusing me of--"

"Stealing! Yes, I am." I stood defiant. "That is my lunch. Those are my cookies, and that is my sandwich!"

Jimmy-John's face flushed into the shiniest shade of rage. He sat there, trembling for a moment, and then he jumped out of his seat and proceeded to attack me. I didn't have a choice, so I defended myself by attacking him back. We were going at it for a good couple of seconds when the parent volunteer grabbed each of us by a shirt collar and broke us up.

"What's going on?" she snapped. "Why are you boys fighting?"

"Ma'am," I explained as calmly as I could. "Jimmy-John stole my lunch. When I asked for it back, he attacked me!"

"He's a liar!" Jimmy-John spat.

By then, half the school had gotten up and clustered around us, including Miss Mercy and several of the other teachers.

"He's a troublemaker! Ask Miss Mercy. He's bad and doesn't deserve to be in our school. He doesn't belong. Huh, Miss Mercy?"

"He did disrupt my class," Miss Mercy attested in her sweetest teachers' voice. "He—"

"Check The Bag!" I cut her off.

"What," the parent volunteer asked.

"Check the bag," I repeated. "He rolled it down so no one would notice. Check the front of the bag, and you'll see *my* name on it."

As the parent volunteer began to reach for the lunch bag, Jimmy-John shot his arm out in an attempt to snatch it up. Intent on beating her, he tried to prevent the bag from being unfolded so that he could save face, get away with it, and make me look bad. Unfortunately for Jimmy-John, someone else got ahold of the bag before he did. Someone no one expected. Ethan. My friend, Ethan. And as Ethan unrolled the bag, the entire room became a vacuum. Nobody talked. Nobody ate. Nobody murmured even the slightest whisper.

With the entire school watching, Ethan unrolled the bag in front of himself careful not to tear into the thin brown paper material, and then he turned the bag around so everyone could see it. O T I S. My name had been scribbled in indelible ink. Everyone gasped and stared at Jimmy-John.

"I didn't see it," he lied. "I didn't notice it was there! I swear Mrs. Mumford! I swear!"

And it was then that I determined three things at once.

I wasn't going to get my lunch back.

Mrs. Mumford wasn't just any parent volunteer; she was the principal's wife and someone who took her position as school aficionado very seriously. As she pinched his ear, marching Jimmy-John out of the cafeteria, she ignored his yelps and squeals that he had been hungry.

And, most importantly, Ethan returned to being Ethan again. Once he saved the day with the lunch bag fiasco, he made a space for me by sliding to the side so that I could squeeze in next to him, and then he passed me half of his PB&J and three sections of an orange. He didn't apologize or explain why he had acted that way. Instead, and in front of the entire school, he draped his arm over my shoulder. Everyone started talking and eating again as if it were an average, ordinary school day. And it was then, in that tiny little crook of my dream, that I had the first inkling of the grace` of forgiveness and the peculiar predicaments that forge friendships that endure through time.

SECTION III

GROWTH

CHAPTER TWELVE
ROOM 242

Round and round, my thoughts whirled in confusion. Sometimes I remembered the exact details of my life while others everything remained lost. *Where am I now? Why's this happening? What happened to me? What happened to me, William Walsh? What happened to…* And then I heard the resounding clanks, beeps, clacks, and the insidious whorling sound of the machine. *I'm back! Back in Tomb 242. Back in my life where I belong!*

Every muscle gored in agony. *How can I hurt so much if I'm in a coma? Wait a minute, I can feel! I feel pain. I feel the pain of being attached to this machine.*

Then I sensed it. I somehow knew of his existence before I opened my eyes. The shadow person returned. Looming in the same spot behind the machine, he lurked over me so he could witness my suffering. *He's gonna hurt me again! He's gonna--*

Just as I had predicted, a sudden wallop of pain pummeled my gut. The onset of which was so sharp and excruciating that I felt my body lurch from the bed.

"What was that?" Liz cried out. "Nurse! Nurse! Did you see that? He moved! My husband moved! His whole body flinched! He's there! I know he's—"

"Mrs. Walsh," No-nonsense kindly placated. "That wasn't intentional. It's more or less a somatic response, what we call a reflex arc. It's just a reflex. These things happen. They're, they're… Listen, Dr. Baylor and Dr. Skeets have completed the tests. The team is going to be here later today. They'll fill you in and let you know more about what's going on. You can go over this flinch idea of yours then. Did Lucile tell you it's scheduled around six?"

"Yes," Liz muttered timidly. "But don't you think it could be something? The flinch, I mean! Don't you think it means…"

I needed to let her know I was there. "You're right, Liz! You're right! I'm here. I'm right here. Don't worry, babe. I'm coming back. I promise I'll figure this out."

Struggling and tussling, I tried to make my body work. I tried to sit up and open my eyes, but nothing happened. I tried to flinch again with no response. I couldn't even wiggle my toes. All I could do was lie motionless and listen as if a part of me remained in the place between lives.

"Relax," a childlike voice intervened, "you're trying too hard! How's you supposed to come an' meet us in the hallway if you're lying in here struggling with yourself?"

My eyes fluttered open and found the same little girl in my room. Once again, she perched herself on the railing at the end of my bed.

"That's better," she chirped. "You got's yer eyes open. Now all's you gots to do is sit up and follow me!" She wore the same poufy dress over her petticoats as she sat on my bed rail, and, just like the time before, her boots stamped an invisible indentation of floor grime on the blanket at the end of my bed.

Immediately infuriated, I decided to ignore her childish games and ways. Instead, I turned towards my wife and became shocked by what I saw. Liz wasn't Liz. She wasn't wearing one of her pantsuits that contrasted with her hair. Her hair hadn't been styled. Her makeup wasn't done. No, the Liz I found in the chair adjacent to my bed had become a weathered, worn, beaten version of my usually pristine wife. This time she had on jeans and a plain blue tee while most of her hair escaped from a messy bun so that it was halfway up, halfway all over the place.

"Yeah," the girl seemed to know what I had been thinking, "she's a wreck. Poor thing! She looks to me like she'd be a great mom. But you wouldn't… You didn't want those things. That is all she ever wanted, but you--"

"What the?" I gasped, and then the pain hit again.

"I'm bored," she declared. Stretching her arms as far as they could reach, she sighed exuberantly. "You can stay here and suffer by yourself and watch them fawn and doddle over you, or you can join us in the hallway. The Big Cheese is there. He's looking forward to making your acquaintance." Swiveling her boots over the railing, she hopped onto the floor. "Something's about to happen," she declared as she sauntered towards the door. "It's gonna be bodacious. Bigger than a parade! We're waiting for it to begin. Not sure when only that it could be any day now. It's supposed to be a jim-dandy good show!"

"Show? What are you talking about? How am I supposed to…"

And then I watched as the little girl in her elegant poufy dress and funny-looking shoes walked over to the door and passed right through it. She didn't reach for the knob and open the door; rather, she evaporated into the wood-planked surface as if it were merely an illusion.

Forty-five minutes passed with me lying there, doing absolutely nothing while a million worries besieged my brain.

"Nurse," I called to the medical professional who, like the others, didn't seem to have the wherewithal to hear what I said. "Can I have something to drink? This dehydration is killing me. And while you're at it, can you do something about the noise? Okay, so I know I need the machine to breathe for me and keep me alive, but can you do something about the constant beeping? The rings? The clacks? And what about the… You know what, screw it!"

Resting there for a moment or two, I exhaled, feeling defeated. And just like that, I slipped out of my body again. One second I had been lying there, fighting with myself and everyone else, and the next I stood beside myself, viewing my injury. *Shoot, I look awful. Damn, I don't know if I'll make it. This looks a lot worse than I thought. It looks bad, really bad.*

The blue chair sat empty. Liz's coat draped from a wall mount while the foldout held a men's jacket and ball cap. *Whose jacket is that? Whose hat? That team? Who likes that team? The logo's vaguely familiar. Where did she go? Where did Liz and this person go?* As I stood next to myself – wondering where Liz went and if I would wake up or remain in a permanent state of slumber – one of the nurses entered the room, walked over to the wall chart, and scribbled: 6:30 P.M. MEETING WITH DR.'S

BAYLOR, SKEETS, AND FLEMING.

Dr. Fleming is my regular doctor, but who are Dr. Baylor and Dr. Skeets? What's the meeting about? And what are they going to tell Liz?

Just then, the door to the hallway opened, and Liz entered the room, looking exhausted and spent. She didn't say anything, but I could tell she had been crying. She seemed to have aged five or six years in the past couple of days. Instead of returning to her chair, she walked over to my bedside and delicately clasped onto my fingers.

"Please wake up, Billy Bear!" she pleaded. "Please, I love you so much! I miss you. God, I don't know if I can do this without you. This is hard, really hard. Please come back to me! Please open your eyes and show me you're alive! Please! Move your hand! Move a foot! Move anything. I need to know you're in there. I saw you flinch that one time. I saw--"

"Mrs. Walsh, you mustn't put yourself through this," the nurse interjected. "We already told you the preliminary results show nothing. We've called in specialists, and they've performed an array of tests and scans. The doctors will go over everything with you this evening, but for all intents and purposes, there are no brain waves. Dr. Skeets performed the test himself. There's no brain activity, no neurotransmitter activity, no signs of life. He can't hear you. His brain stopped functioning. Your husband is officially brain dead."

CHAPTER THIRTEEN
THE THIRD TIME

Drifting inside an endless haze, I floated between worlds again when the epiphany arose that the noise had evaporated and I felt comfortable. I actually felt comfortable. My back, legs, and head cradled on a nest of pure perfection, and I knew where I was before I opened my eyes. *I'm back*, I told myself, *back on the down-filled mattress on the homemade Cherrywood bed, somewhere in another time in another person's life.*

Opening my eyes, I saw that the Little Dipper and Big Dipper weren't on the ceiling, confirming my suspicion. I wasn't attached to the ominous machine that buzzed, rattled, and beeped as it kept me alive, and for a fleeting moment, I felt grateful for the transition. In this life, I can drink water. My dehydration will be quenched, my lips won't be parched, and my throat won't feel as dry as a fossil in the desert. I'll drink homemade lemonade and strawberry water, and I'll be able to eat again. I can have food, real food, soul food cuisines with flavors and scents that curl my toes and satisfy my belly. And I will be able to run. I'll actually run. I'll run again, welcoming the wind on my face as my muscles galvanize to the gate of streaming steps, and the invigorating infusion of endorphins as they flood my system with power. I'll feel alive.

"No brain activity," the nurse had indicated. "We've performed every neurological test out there, and it's the same. There's no brain waves, no neurotransmitter activity, no signs of life. His brain has stopped functioning. Your husband is officially brain dead."

How can she say that? How can they say that? How many tests did they do? Who performed these tests and where did they get their credentials?

"I'm here!" I wanted to shout when I heard that. "I'm right here. I can hear you. I can hear what you're telling my wife."

"Time to get up, sleepyhead," she called from the doorway. "I see 'em lil' possum curls peeking out from under dem covers. Get on up, now! It's a beautiful day; I'm telling you! Beautiful! Mite bit cold though, so make sure you put on your warm shirt and britches before mosying in here. Hurry up now, you know I've got's to get to the factory!"

As I got out of bed and shuffled to the dresser, I immediately noticed the difference. I had become taller and, somehow, more mature. Gazing down at my feet and how much they had grown, I guessed my age to be somewhere around ten or eleven. *I don't want to be here. This is absurd. If I'm going to time travel into someone else's life, why not a rich person or a king. Why not a famous historian? Why not someone who propagates change? I don't want to be this person, and I especially don't want to be Black.*

Three minutes later, I seated myself at the kitchen table, summoned into the chair by the buttery-sweet harmony of her voice and the rich, flavorful aroma of buckwheat pancakes with real Maple syrup. Indulging in my first bite of paradise, I practically inhaled the entire feast. *Butter! Real butter! How long has it been since I've had real butter or something this good? It feels good to eat! It feels good to be alive!*

"Child," she gushed, "what's gotten into you? Why's you eatin' like that?" She looked perturbed for a half-second, and then her face flourished into a sly grin. My mother person lifted the stack of pancakes from her plate and slid them onto mine. "You must be in one of 'em growth spurts. You need this here food more than me."

I should have rejected the gesture, but I didn't know how many days it had been since I had eaten. My stomach felt famished, so I sat there and indulged in food paradise, wolfing down one delectable maple-soaked forkful after the next.

When she stood to clear the dishes, I saw that she donned thick raggedy jeans, a knit turtleneck, and brown leather work boots. My mother person wore work boots!

"Why are you dressed like that?"

"Dressed like what?" she quipped confused. Leaning over the enameled cast iron sink, she meticulously washed and rinsed each piece of tableware.

"In jeans and boots. What about your black dress?"

"Sugarpie," she shook her head, despondently, "you already know the answer to that. I done gotta job at the factory. It's a good job. I already told you not to worry none about how dangerous it is. I'll be safe. I'm telling you; I'll be safe. Now, stop your fretting and finish getten' ready!"

While brushing my teeth in front of the old antique mirror, I couldn't quite place it, but – somehow – it seemed as if the true Otis person wanted to tell me something; a message I couldn't decipher gleamed in his eyes. Some of my haze lingered, so I had trouble putting everything together. And then I recalled the events that happened the last time I was in his life, including the disaster with Jimmy-John and determined it precipitated his mother's job change. *What I did altered the course of my mother person's journey. Is that what you're trying to tell me? Are you trying to warn me that my actions have an impact on your life?*

Once I ventured back into the common living area, she took one look at my expression. "Now, don't you feel bad none. I already done told you it's not your fault! I was ready for a change. Ready to leave that job and start something new. You gotta look at it this way: I's the first female worker at the factory. I's the first one they's trusten' with that job! It's an honor; I'm tellen' you. An honor."

Once she retrieved my coat from the closet, my mother person held it open so that I could slide my arms into the sleeves. And then she dotingly buttoned the front panel.

"You and I's a part of this here change. I knows you thinks it's dangerous, but I'm safe. The only thing I don't like are dem long days an' late hours. But I don't gotta worry none cause I know Mr. Blackwood's gonna look in on you. You haven't given me no flap, so I guess it's working out between Mr. Blackwood and you. Right?"

I stood stumped. This was a lot for me to take in. I didn't know this Blackwood character from a stranger on the street. For all I knew, he could have been some weird pedophile freak who used kindness as a ploy to immerse himself into the lives of children. I didn't know what else to do, so I shrugged my shoulders and said nothing.

"Wha'cha doing? Why's you just standing there collecting dust like that? What's gotten into you, Otis? We gotta leave. Go gets to steppen' and gets' your cap."

While I made my way to the wall rack and collected a gray tweed Newsboy with a bent brim, she scurried around the place with the house key in her hand. After performing a safety check of the burner, she turned the lights off and opened the door.

"We got the whole day awaitin'! Don't want to let one crazy God-given minute to get away from us!"

Right about then – immediately before I stepped out the door – I caught sight of something unusual. Something that might have been insignificant to the untrained eye; however, as a trained police officer (who had undergone weeks of instruction honing attentiveness and looking for clues) I thought it strange. The saxophone. The saxophone on the wall adjacent to the potbelly stove. Its sparkle caught my eye, and I immediately determined it wasn't the same instrument that had been burrowed under my covers the last time I had been in this life. But I didn't have time to say or do anything as a brisk wave of early morning dew assaulted my senses. She smiled at me as I stepped outside.

"It's gonna be a good one," she exclaimed with a hearty laugh. "I can feel it. Lord's gonna bless us with another beautiful day!"

My mother person headed west along the rock-laden path while I ventured towards the train tracks and the rising sun. *Has it been a year, two, or three since the last time I was here? What grade should I be in? How will I know which classroom to go to? Is Jimmy-John still in the school? What about Ethan?*

"Hey pork face!" someone called to me from fifty or so yards back along the road.

I turned around and saw another Black kid like me, who appeared to be around the same age. He was the same height and approximate weight, while his hair had been cut so short that his scalp gleamed clean between tiny tuffs of curled coils.

"What's you doin'?" he groused. "Why didn't you wait?" By then, he had caught up and walked alongside me as we traipsed by a vegetable garden. "What's your hurry for anyway? Is it to see that new girl?" He elbowed my ribcage.

I was so skinny that it actually stung a little. "What new girl?"

"Don't play no games with me! I knows you's sweet on her. Ain't got no chance on account of she's taken' a liken to Big LeRoy Billings. Heard they was caught necken' by old man Cranston's property. Heard they was locking lips behind the old Cypress. Heard old man Cranston sent 'em skit scatting in a dead dash, had a switch in his hand and all!"

"I didn't hear that," I replied. I didn't know why, but I suddenly felt my blood stop short while my insides puttied.

"On the lips, if you can believe that! They was kissin' on the lips! That's gross if you ask me! Gross-a-rony!"

"Knock it off," I snapped. And then I heard the low-rumbled grumbling in the distance. "We gotta hurry, gotta beat the train."

"Ain't no big deal, I's…" He looked back and paused midsentence with his face furrowed in a rancid-milk gag.

Following his stare, I saw what had him stumped and almost keeled over from a heart attack. Her! She was there, right there. Directly behind us appeared the prettiest girl I had ever seen, and I immediately recognized my beloved Mabel. In that one-tenth of a second, my heart fluttered with so much happiness that I felt my feet lighten and lift a little from the ground.

"We wasn't talken' about you!" Rodney said a little too eagerly, and I began to suspect that he, too, had a crush on my Mabel. "We was talken' about someone else. Someone new. There's this new girl, and—"

"We don't have time for that," Mabel cut in. She caught up alongside us, wearing a gray pleated skirt and white blouse accessorized by a pastel pink sweater. And shoes. I can't forget about the shoes because she had on a brand new pair of Mary Janes, which was indeed quite something because not many of us Colored kids had brand new shoes back in them days. "We have to beat the train, or we'll be late."

The three of us tore off in a dead run as our six little legs hurdled gofer holes, sticker bushes, and coyote landmines. Halfway up the hill, the conductor's cabin could be seen gliding along the tracks atop of the long bowing cow pusher, and I suddenly ascertained the trajectory of speed between the train and us rushing up the hill didn't look right.

"Wait!" I attempted to warn them. Every ounce of my intuition sensed the wrath of impending danger. "I don't think this is a good idea. The train looks as if…"

Disregarding my heed, the pair of them made it to the top of the hill and proceeded to scurry across the tracks. However, before she made it to the other side, the left heel of Mabel's Mary Jane momentarily wedged beneath a wooden rail tie. She stumbled and then fell face down onto the patch of pebbly ballast between tracks. Time warped as everything happened at once. Rodney made it to the other side. The train whistled a deafening shrill that reverberated within the hollow of my bones. And then I saw the terror on Mable's face, and all of my instincts took over (or it may have been the instincts of the person whose life I occupied). A half-second before the train passed, I whisked Mabel into my short, spindly arms and carried her to the other side. Death slithered past the lower hem of my coattails.

As I knelt upon the thick dewy soil – trying to think of what I would say, – Rodney assisted Mabel into a stand. Nervously swiping his hands, he struggled to brush dried grass and leaves from her pretty pink sweater.

"I swear it was another girl," he tried to assure her. "I'd never talk about you that way. You're too pretty and too much of a good church girl."

As Rodney placated, Mabel looked my way and smiled. A gesture so magnificent, it felt as though the heavens opened and delivered me an angel to love; a beautiful angel with caramel-coated eyes, soft ebony skin, and dimples. Mabel had the cutest dimples I had ever seen.

It was then, out of the blue, without reason or warning and at the worst possible time that the most disgusting thing happened. I do not know if it originated from the near-death experience or the fact that I had wolfed down two enormous stacks of pancakes drenched in a vat of thick buttery real maple syrup, but instead of checking on Mabel or telling her what I wanted to say, I opened my mouth and vomited. I didn't throw up into the grass or onto the tracks. No, I threw up in the worst possible place. My barf came out in a smelly gross batter of pancake-sludge, drenching the top of Mabel's white frilly ankle socks and all over her pristine Mary Jane shoes.

Mabel looked at my barf, looked at me, and then stormed off towards the school without saying a thing. She didn't thank me for saving her life. She didn't yell at me for ruining her brand new shoes. And she didn't say goodbye. Folding her arms across her chest, Mabel trudged off in an embittered yet brazen huff. And I knew then and there she was the girl this Otis person would eventually marry.

I had no difficulty finding my class; Rodney led me straight to it. "Of course, we're in the same class, pancake chucker. Why'd you think anything different?"

When the bell rang, our remaining classmates scurried in, quickly sliding into their seats to avoid being late. Sometime along the scurrying and sliding, I ascertained the vines of tolerance were still a bit slow in that Rodney and I were the only Colored kids there.

"Now children," Miss Roust proclaimed from behind the teachers' podium at the head of the room, "find your seats and be quiet. We have a lot to cover."

As she began to take roll, I attempted to get Rodney's attention, but he hunched furtively in his seat with his hand in his pocket.

"Abigale."

"Here," a blonde-haired girl in the front row answered.

"Abby-Mae."

"Here," another blonde-haired girl in the front row answered.

In between names, I still tried to get Rodney's attention, but he just sat there with whatever he had in his pocket. I had no clue what it could have been in that his scrawny, meddlesome fingers obstructed my view. But, I swear, I thought I saw a leg move.

"Cynthia Marie."

"Here," another blonde-haired girl in the second row answered.

Leaning not so subtly in Rodney's direction, I secretively whispered, "What is it?" trying my best not to be caught.

Rodney squinted his mad-scientist gleam as he shissed me; he actually shissed me. Then I saw it again! Something moved, something wiggly and slimy and green.

"Henrietta."

"Here," another blonde-haired girl answered. Her hair wasn't necessarily blonde as a very light brown.

"What is it?"

Rodney looked to the right then to the left, and then (once he assured no one could see what he was about to show me) he furtively slid his hand out of his pocket, revealing an enormous American bullfrog covered in ugly brown blotches and bullfrog warts.

"Name's Beauregard," he whispered proudly.

"Keep it down!" Miss Roust snapped from behind her podium. I'm calling out roll here!" The class quieted for a few seconds, and she continued with, "Jake."

"Here," replied a brown-haired boy in the second row.

"Jimmy-John."

When no one said anything, she scanned the room to confirm Jimmy-John's absenteeism before recording it on her roll sheet. Unfortunately, when she made her notation, Rodney inadvertently squeezed Beauregard's middle, and the alarmed little guy produced a hideous frog bawl that bellowed throughout the classroom.

"What was that?" Miss Roust snapped.

No one said anything, but the entire herd of little blonde heads turned towards Rodney and me. Miss Roust shook her head despondently then continued with, "Lawrence."

"Here," a blonde-haired boy answered from the third row.

As Rodney clasped Beauregard on his lap, I started to question why this was happening. *Why am I here? Why am I in this person's life? I don't want to be a different race. I've never wanted to be a different race. This must have something to do with that man, that Black man we pulled over. I don't under--*

Someone poked my right shoulder, and I realized Rodney prodded me with his frog cootie fingers.

"*Otis*!" she snapped. "Why didn't you answer? Why do I have to call your name several times? What is it about you people? You want to be here, but you—"

"Sorry," Rodney placated on my behalf. "It's just a little hard to hear you all the way back here in the Colored people section."

She groaned as her eyes bowled into hard-boiled eggs. "There's no *Colored section* in my class," she quipped curtly. "I accommodated both you boys back there so you would be more comfortable because you have so much in common."

"Oh," Rodney sighed dramatically. "It's not the Colored people section. It's where Colored people are segregated to keep us happy. Now I see. Thank you for explaining *accommodation* to me." Rodney smiled as he leaned back in his seat with his pet frog.

"Otis and Rodney, you both just earned marks for insubordination."

And then her face morphed back to a polite-hearted production of sincerity as she directed her attention to the freckled-faced kid in the fourth row. "Brett."

"Here," Brett jovially responded.

Thirty-three minutes later, we were in trouble again. We, meaning Rodney and me. And I suspected it wouldn't be a rare occasion that the troublesome twosome disrupted her class. Miss Roust sat prudently behind her desk as we took turns reading from our books on American Civilization. Lawrence stumbled with the vocabulary as he read from a passage while Rodney seemed to have difficulty comprehending the text.

"Miss Roust! Miss Roust!" Rodney summoned excitedly, waving his hand in the air. "I don't understand something. Can you explain it?"

"What?" she groaned. "What is so important that you think it's acceptable to disrupt my class and interrupt Lawrence's reading?"

"I don't understand why the Indian people were so happy when the colonists arrived. In this here picture, they're smiling and waving while all them White people are getting off the boat, wearing fake wigs and funny-looken' clothes. Look at this here Indian baby; he even has his arms stretched out. Why's they stretched out like that? You'd think they'd be running for them hills cause them Colonialists look like a bunch of pirate ghosts from another planet with their giant ships, ghastly-white skin color, and them funny-looking pants they is wearing."

"They were happy because they were grateful to receive visitors. They were tired of being alone and living as aboriginals. The natives indigenous to this country didn't have the amenities of a European education and etiquette."

"They didn't have no guns or smallpox either. Ain't that how them White people killed all the Indigenous people? They shot 'em with guns, and them that they didn't shoot, they infected with all them plagues and diseases."

"No, Rodney," she droned in an exasperated huff. "These Indians are the friendly ones. These are the ones who banded together in a mutual celebration of gratitude for the fruitful harvest."

"And then they killed them. The colonists shot 'em with their guns. They shot all them women folk, all them men, then they stole their kids and turned 'em into pets. And if they didn't steal this here little baby with his arms spread out and make him their pet, they slit his throat, killed his mom and dad, and then burned down their entire village."

Henrietta shrieked as Cynthia Marie slid out of her seat in a dead faint. She lay sprawled on the floor as Lawrence and another boy leaned over, trying to sneak a gander at her long underwear.

"Look what you did now," Miss Roust chastised crossly.

"I'm not the one who killed all them people. They was here first. Look at 'em. From all these pictures, they was a-livin' pretty fine. They was happy. They had fish and sweet potatoes and turkey and maze. I'm not the one who done killed all dem people so I can thieve their horses and take over their land."

Henrietta shrieked again, and then she joined Cynthia Marie on the floor in a faint. Lawrence practically hyperventilated as he dropped his pencil then reached to the floor to retrieve another gander.

"Enough!" Miss Roust spat. "Mr. Washington, you've got a lot of nerve spreading tales like that after all the things this country's done for you and your people."

"*To* my people," he snapped.

But it was too late. Miss Roust marched across the classroom and grabbed ahold of his earlobe.

"Ow!" Rodney cried out.

Twisting Rodney's earlobe, she brought him up to a stand.

"Ow! Ow! Ow! Ow!"

"You two can go sit in the principal's office for all I care. I'm teaching a lesson, and you won't stop with the constant interruptions!"

I didn't know what to say or do, so I followed Miss Roust and Rodney to the front of the room. We stood obediently as she filled out our detention slips, ranting, "I never! You boys should be grateful for the education we're providing, but what do you know, you with your *littler* brains are disrupting my class!"

She handed me my slip and started to give Rodney his when she noticed his hand tucked inside his coat pocket.

"Whacha got there?" she seethed accusatorily.

"It's nothing, Miss Roust. Nothing, I swear."

"No," her voice curdled. "There's something there. What is it? What did you steal?"

"Didn't steal nothing, Miss Roust." Rodney's eyes widened to the size of dinner plates. "I don't steal things, I…"

And it was then – as Rodney explained how he went to church and read the Bible – that a flash of memory came to me. In a split-second window of realization, I remembered accusing a young African-American kid of shoplifting at a convenience store. It happened on my fourth day of patrol, and I just knew he had something in his pocket. I felt sure of it. No one saw him take anything. Nothing, in particular, was missing. But, somehow, I knew he was a thief. After forcing him to turn his pockets out, I saw the only thing he had on him was his mother's shopping list.

"Let's just see what we have…"

My attention returned to the situation at hand just in time to see Miss Roust stick her long, intrusive fingers into Rodney's jacket pocket. It happened so fast that I didn't have time to warn her. Fishing inside the pocket, she immediately grabbed onto Beauregard, who let out a loud piercing frog scream from being squeezed. The bullfrog squeal – as well as the sight of the ugly green amphibian in her hand – startled Miss Roust. She shrieked and vomited a littlc before she, too, keeled down to the floor in a dead faint.

Beauregard, feeling perturbed by the injustice of it all, decided to leap onto a nice safe place where he could relax and preen his beautiful warty posterior, so he picked the top of Abigale's desk. Abigale screamed, and then a hysterical stampede of students frantically scurried out of the room.

The only people left were Rodney and me, and Lawrence, who crawled around on his hands and knees.

"What do you think we should do now?" I asked Rodney once Beauregard had been returned to the safety and security of his pocket.

"I don't rightly know." He shrugged. "But right now I feel like one of them Indigenous people when all them Whites was circling with all of dem guns."

"You know what, Rodney," I exclaimed. "I know what you mean."

The two of us decided to ditch the rest of school that day. There were so many cantankerous classmates and so much turmoil around the office that we easily slipped by Mr. Mumford's secretary's station into the storybook neighborhood with the perfectly manicured lawns and the perfectly-pruned trees. Hundreds of birdies serenaded our escape as we turned left at the train tracks then headed down the way to Pike's Creek.

We were there a good hour and a half (having a good time skipping stones and talking about make-believe flying cars and other imaginative fantasies) when the sound of crackling leaves alerted us of an impending approach, and we became alarmed. After all, two Colored boys in that part of town all by themselves wasn't exactly the best situation in which to be caught. So we took cover behind a thicket of brush, hoping and praying it was Ethan or one of our Colored friends.

Suddenly, two large able hands drew the brush open to a familiar face peering down at us with eyes lit in astonishment, and we immediately knew we were in trouble. The person staring down at us wasn't Jimmy-John or one of the other racist people from the community. No, it was someone much more formidable than that. It was Pastor Jeremiah Langston Washington. Pastor Washington, the lead preacher of our local church and (this is the terrifying part) Rodney's overbearing, overly-protective father and my overbearing, overly-protective church leader.

"Well, well, well now," he greeted in an overtly surprised tone as he assisted the two of us into a stand. "What's we got here. I do believe it's my beautiful, strong, churchgoing son and his dutiful churchgoing friend!"

As he looked back-and-forth between us, Pastor Washington's stature grated while his eyes shown into my soul.

"Now gentleman, I've got a problem here that's mighty unsettling, and I'm hoping you can help me out."

"What with, Dad?" Rodney stammered.

The two of us stood with jittered knees, looking up into the eyes of the towering community leader and dad.

"Good, good, good now. It's a mighty fine thing you asked, Son."

Guilt streamed into my veins, flooding my system with shame.

Rodney's father guided us to a clearing along the creekbed where we sat on sun-warmed rocks, gazing into the tide.

"Well," he started softly, "I got a phone call from your boys' school that was a mite bit distressing, so I set out to go down there and straighten things out, and – lo and behold – you boys wasn't anywhere in sight." He paused while staring down at the both of us. "Can you explain this?"

"Well, Dad. It… It started as sorta a bad morning. Miss Roust was talking a mighty bad game about racism and dem Indians, and she wasn't treating us right. She has us sitting in the back of the room, and—"

"Did she hit you? Did she threaten a lynching? Did she call you a coon or Niggard or some other offensive term?"

"Well, no, Dad, but—"

"And, you, Mr. Merriweather." His eyes shown down at me with a helping of warm chocolate chip cookies and warrant. "What do you have to say for yourself? I know your father was taken many years back because them hospital people neglected to help him, so I'd like to think of myself as a community mentor. Therefore, I'd like to know why you are sitting along this here creek when your mother's working hard at that ramshackle firetrap they call a factory. And if you're going to say anything about discrimination, then you better not even think about it. You couldn't imagine the conditions she's braved to keep you safe in that there home and put fixens on your plate."

My head bowed in disgrace.

"That place still has a backhouse for Negros. She's not allowed to use their facility, drink their water, or eat their food. In fact, she takes her breaks on an ole' wood crate behind the coal barn. Rain or shine she's out there, sitting by herself, enduring the struggle. *Not* quitting."

"Sorry," I grunted.

"I'm sorry, Dad," Rodney agreed.

"Listen here, boys. The Lord's been good to me in that I've seen many changes in my lifetime. It's not happening all at once, but He's shown us the way. Your mom got that there factory job. She's the first person of color out there, and she's a female. They've made it easier for us to qualify for loans so we can buy property; it has to be in a Colored neighborhood, but the change has begun. You boys are part of the change in that you've been granted the opportunity to go to their school, a real school, where you'll be educated and have the ability to do whatever you want with your lives. We's a breaking down the barriers, boys. We's a breaking down the barriers."

"Yes, Dad, that is what the—"

"But we can't give them the ammunition to put them walls back up and fence us in. Our community can't afford frogs in pockets, backtalk, or any form of disrespect. When you go there, you represent us. You represent every Colored person in this here community. You boys go there and get yourselves a decent education. You are our hope to lift us out of poverty and our chance for a brighter future. And while you're at it, take note of all the changes that need to be made. Then you'll earn the right to stand on the platform and propagate change. Your voices will be the ones to unshackle our kinfolk. Your voices will--"

"Okay, Dad," Rodney chirped, wrapping his arms around his father. "We'll go back. We won't like it, but we'll go to their school, keep our mouths shut, and learn everything we can to make a better world for our people. I'm gonna make you proud."

"You already have, Son."

Reaching his arm around my back, he pulled me into their embrace.

"The both of you have made me very proud."

Six O'clock that evening, someone knocked on the door. Looking out the peephole, I discovered a tall, lanky man carrying a rectangular-shaped brown leather case.

"Hey, O.C., heard you had a rough one," Ben grunted as he walked into the small humble abode. "Never mind that though, because we only got an hour or so before she gets here."

What's he talking about? I wondered as a pang of dread welled in my gut. *What's he sneaking? What am I supposed to do?*

Ben laid the case on the kitchen table where he meticulously unfastened the latches. The case creaked open, revealing an ornate, freshly-polished saxophone.

That's it! That's the one that is supposed to be on the wall. He must have switched them for some reason.

Ben turned and saw that I just stood there.

"Well," he perplexed, "Whatcha doin'? Go gets my sax off the wall, so we can trade back and get your practice in." He thought about it and added, "Oh, and by the way, I told you, she wouldn't notice. Not only did I fix that their stock rod you accidentally jammed, but I got her cleaned and tuned right. She's one purdy lady!"

A minute or so later, we sat side-by-side, facing a sheet of music with a set of shiny brass saxophones in our hands. And the realization flowed over me that I was expected to know how to read and play music. *I've never had a music lesson. I'm more of a talk radio, documentary type of person. How am I going to do this? This is…*

And then, out of the blue, without even thinking or concentrating, the strangest thing happened. As I sat stumped, looking at those peculiar little flags that sailed on that peculiar track of lines, my fingers somehow skillfully knew where to go, and I made my first note. *What the?? What's going on???*

That note was followed by the next and the next after that, and, before I knew it (without concentrating or knowing what the heck I was doing), I played the first few bars of *Mary had a Little Lamb. This feels real, weird, but real. It must have imprinted on his brain. I'm using his skills to play the sax. I'm playing music!*

Six songs later, Ben suddenly rose from his seat without saying a word. He strolled over to the kitchen window and peered through the curtains, gazing into the neighborhood.

"What's wrong?"

"It's, it's nothin'," he responded dismissively. He stood there for a second or two, not explaining himself. Then just as solemnly, he returned to his chair, sat down, and impatiently tapped the top of the music page I had been practicing.

A minute or so later, a dog barked from the cottage across the way. And then we heard the sound of footsteps trampling upon the old rickety decking of the front porch. Ben shot up and got to the door before he or she knocked. He opened it just in time to see a strange Caucasian person I had never seen before. Even though I didn't know the man, it was apparent from the way he presented himself that he was an authority figure of some sort. Before the man said anything, Ben turned to me.

"Go to your room," he directed. "Go to your room until I find out what's goin' on."

Even though I was a police officer living the life of this strange person, I heeded to his direction. *I don't know about this guy,* I told myself. *He made dinner, ensured I completed my homework, and is teaching me to play the saxophone. But why? What's his motive, and why's he doing this? Why is he going through all this effort to help this kid?*

A few minutes after hearing the front door close and the echoing thumps of the man's footsteps quietly dissipate, this Ben person tapped on my door then entered my room. *What's he gonna do? What's he gonna do to me? What happened?*

"O.C.," Ben began in a grave and gravelly tone as his long, lean legs started to pace back and forth. "That was Sheriff Jamison. There's been an explosion at the factory—"

"Mama!" I blurted without thinking.

"They don't know. There's been no word!" his voice choked. "So far, three bodies have been found. They don't know who they are because they've been burned so badly that--"

"But my mother? How will I???"

"Don't worry about you. I'll be here for you, no matter what. If something bad happened, I'll step in and raise you as my own. I'll do my best by you and your mama. You have my word on that."

Bowing my head, I couldn't respond. I don't know why I felt as sad as I did; it almost seemed as if his feelings for her had imprinted on this Otis person's heart. I felt his encompassing worry and concern.

"But for right now, let's get on our knees and say us a prayer. Let's pray for a miracle! Let's pray that your mother returns home safe and sound!"

And so the two of us (me and the tall, kind-hearted man who seemed to be an essential influence to the true Otis) slid down to our knees with our hands clasped in a prayer position. And even though it had been years since the police officer version of me had been to church or prayed, I recited this man's prayer that he seemed to make up as he went along.

Shortly before we finished, we heard the neighbor's dog barking again. Ben looked over at me, and I saw the weatherworn creases on his face had filled with tears. A pause of expectation settled, and then we heard the sound of the front door creak open and the distressed, delightful sound of my mother person's voice calling for us.

Running out of the room, I wrapped my arms around her, and then I cried into this strange woman's bosom. Even though I was a grown man and a police officer, the Otis part of me became overwhelmed by the miraculous reunion. Weaving her fingers into the nest of my curls, she pulled me into her as she planted a kiss on my crown.

"Sorry I's late," she exclaimed breathless and frazzled. "Went to Doc Booker's to gets stitched up." She lifted her coat sleeve, displaying a freshly-bandaged arm. "There was an explosion and—"

"Loddie Mae Merriweather," Ben interrupted. And then he paused for a second or two before he crouched down to a knee. "I loves you, and I loves this here boy. I don't want you worken' at no damn factory where's people are getten' burned. We almost lost you today, and I don't know if I can live without you!" Reaching into his pocket, he pulled out an old worn-down gold band marred with an assortment of scratches and dings. "This here's Mammy's."

My mother person gasped.

"I want to marry you, Loddie Mae. I want to be a father to O.C. I know you quit music when Daniel died, but music is a good thing. It's in his bones."

He looked over at me and nodded, beaming with pride. "He's good! He's good; I'm telling you. He's something special!"

"I, I, I…" my mother person was taken off guard.

"Please marry me, Loddie Mae. I want us to be a family. I want to fill our world with music! You can quit your job, and we can start our own band. I know it's something you've always dreamed of."

My mother person shook her head affirmatively with her mouth gaped open, happily not saying a word.

"It'll be amazing," he assured. Tenderly and lovingly, he glided the ring onto her finger. "O.C., you, and me will finally be a family. We'll have the best life!"

SECTION IV

DEVELOPMENT

CHAPTER FOURTEEN
BATTLE BELLY FLOP

I felt cold and realized I was someplace dreary, someplace beyond a conventional bed chill. And then I heard the familiar *clanking, huffing, beeping,* and *chimes*, and I knew where I was before I opened my eyes. *I'm back,* I welcomed myself. *Back in the hospital, back on the concrete rock hard slab of a mattress, back to a body that is artificially extant while it lies here attached to that godforsaken machine.*

And I determined something was different. This time, a bone-chilling detachment settled into the hollow of my bones. Besides the sharp stabs in my abdomen, I had not felt anything before, not even when the nurse redid my IV or exchanged my catheter. This time, though, it felt different, and I honestly didn't know which was worse: not feeling anything at all, or the shrill splintered pricks of death beginning to dwell.

God, I hate the smell of antiseptic! It reeks! This room stinks! They must have just cleaned it with an industrial-grade detergent that eviscerates my senses. Why can't I wake up to the sweet buttery-rich scent of pancakes or grits or--

A voice interrupted my thought – a mere utterance over the clanks, huffs, and beeps of the machine – and, in that fraction of an instant, I knew. I knew he was there before I opened my eyes. *God, why did he have to come? Who invited him? Why does he have to be here?*

Dread welled in my gut. I didn't want to look at him. I didn't want to see his face. I never wanted to see that face again but, still, my eyes slowly peered over the bedrail, confirming my suspicion. Jeremy was there. The infuriating failure of a son had settled himself in the chair next to Liz. Holding identical coffee containers, they perched forward in their seats as they watched me lay in the bed, withering away.

"No! No, no, no, no, no! I don't want this! I don't want you here!"

"Liz!" I turned to my wife. "Why'd you call him? You know how

I feel! Why's he here, and why did you invite him?"

They grasped hands and began to pray.

Could this get any worse? I don't want him praying over me! No one gave him that right! I don't want his prayers. I don't want his sympathy. I don't want anything to do with him. Not now, not ever!

I know it sounds ridiculous, but I couldn't take the degradation of being trapped to that bed, listening to *his* prayers. And the next thing I knew it happened again. Slipping out of my body, I made an effortless, almost graceful descent until my bare feet procured the pocket of cold linoleum between my brother and the trapped me.

"Why did you come!" I spewed in his face. "I'll never forgive you."

The door swished open, and No-nonsense entered the room, toting an empty urine bag and a fresh set of tubes.

"No," I groaned. Reaching my arm out, I attempted to block her from getting by and performing her duties. She simply passed through me and over to the me on the bed.

Can this get any worse? Can this get any fricken worse?

"This'll only take a sec," she explained to Liz and my brother. As if *he* deserved to be there. As if *he* deserved an explanation.

"Why weren't you at Dad's funeral? Why didn't you check on him when he became ill? What makes you think it's okay to miss out on seeing Dad on his deathbed? He called for you! He called for you when he was suffering, and you were… You were…"

Amid my outburst, I realized I might as well have been yelling at the doorknob or a light fixture for that matter. My body remained an empty shell while I encompassed a different place, a dream or dimension between time, as I stood beside myself riddled with rage. And then I determined I was wasting my time, putting on a show for… *For what? Why am I doing this?* One moment I raged with anger, and the next, I felt stupid and, oddly, alone.

Not knowing what else to do, I sat next to myself on the mattress's edge and glared at them. They sat there staring at my weak, decrepit body, so I took it upon myself and stared back.

Liz remained her beautiful self, a little frazzled, but just as breathtakingly beautiful as the day we met. My brother, Jeremy, however, now that was a different story. Jeremy *had* changed. I couldn't quite put my finger on it, but he had somehow gotten taller since the last time I had seen him, maybe even gained a few pounds. He still had the same flowing hair, same blue eyes like me, same scruffy beard, but a maturity emerged that I found undeniable.

"Time's catching up with you," I goaded. "You've aged. Not even the great Jeremy Walsh can escape the inescapable." And then a flurry of memories arose of us boys playing freeze tag, hide-and-seek, and the hundreds of hours we spent in our fort in the backyard. Us boys sitting at the kitchen table, stashing string beans under our placemats. Us boys diving into the swimming pool, taking turns at jackknifes, cannonballs, and seeing who could make the goofiest belly flop. Us boys racing our bikes to and from school. The time that I crashed and fractured my arm, and how Jeremy lay in the street with me, tending to my worry as one of the Albers brothers rode to the house to get Dad. And I remembered when I got the Chicken Pox and felt miserable with an infestation of sores, how Jeremy took a permanent marker and blotted red dots all over his face because he wanted to mimic my outbreak.

Stop that! I told myself. *I'm mad at him! I haven't forgiven him; in fact, I don't know if I'll ever forgive him! He should have been there for Dad!*

And it was then – as my heart clashed with memories of our childhood while I fumed with anger because he had missed our father's burial day, and as No-nonsense checked on me and changed out my bag – that the tiniest creak of the door adjusting to the pressure of the ventilation brought me back to the present.

I don't have to be here, I realized. *I can leave! The girl! That's what she said! The girl with the poufy dress and petticoat pant legs. She mentioned something about meeting them in the corridor. She mentioned something about hanging out with her and a "big cheese" and that they were waiting for something.*

So I hopped off the bed, walked over to my brother, and kicked him in the shin. I'm not sure why I did it (I wasn't in my body, so he didn't feel anything), but, somehow, it felt like the brotherly thing to do at the time. And then I turned towards the door, deciding to escape that dreadful, dreary, hospital room and get as far away as I could from the wretched smell of antiseptic and the even worse stench of my decay.

My first attempt at making it through the door failed miserably; nothing happened either than receiving a bump on my forehead. Positioning myself at the other end of the room, I attempted a running start. This time instead of bumping my forehead, I banged it pretty hard. It didn't make sense. None of it made sense. *What are the rules of this dream or out of body experience? How do I control going in and out of my body, levitating, and moving through objects?*

That is when (as I waited on the pristine antiseptically-clean floor, trying to figure a way to finagle myself out of the mess) No-nonsense concluded her duties and walked out of the room. So I did what any dumb lucky schmo would do: I got up and followed behind her. And for the first time in a little over seven and a half days, I found myself in someplace new. I made it to the sparkling-clean expanse of a hallway.

"Well, well, well now. See, Cheddar," she squealed with delight. "He made it! He made it! I knew he could do it! I told you! It just took the right amount of persistence and gumption."

Ruby Josephine sat in a cluster of chairs that lined the long narrow corridor. "About time, William Walsh!" Smiling voraciously, she patted the seat next to hers. "Didn't know if you'd make it in time to see the celebration or if you'd stay stuck in that room until you—"

"Hung Luu," the boy brought his hand out for me to shake it, "but you can call me 'Cheddar.'"

When we shook hands, I experienced an ordinary handshake. *Odd*, I thought, *this is the first normal contact of my out-of-body self.*

"Dude, I know it's ill, and you got like a zillion questions," Cheddar began as I slid into the seat between them, "but for right now, you gotta relax, bro. Sit back an' chill for a lil. We'll go over your questions in a bit. But for right now--"

"Ruby," he directed his attention to the girl, "could you hit up the supply closet and appropriate a pair of fuzzy wuzzys. His dogs gotta be killin' him."

Ruby Josephine got up and skedaddled down the corridor, hopping a few steps, skipping a few steps, dancing, leaping, and actually bopping. As soon as she arrived at the row of small symmetrical doors, Cheddar looked my way and gave me the up and down.

"Oh, and get him a robe or some jammies if you can find any, or we'll be adding his crack to the booty parade!"

Letting out a hearty laugh, he leaned in and explained. "Dude, you wouldn't believe some of the butts I've seen. I've seen pillow butts, ping pong ball butts, butts that sagged down to their knees, hairy butts, tattooed butts, pimply butts, butts missing cracks, and cracks missing butt cheeks! What we got here is a constant continuum of crack!"

"You live here?"

"Yeah, well, err, sort of," he chuckled. "If you wanna call it that."

"I don't understand. Why would you want to stay?"

"Some of us have no choice, that's people like you and me. I see you're in 242. That's a good room, nice and cush. You've been there, like, what, almost *eight* days now?"

"I think. I'm not—"

"It's okay, Bro. It's okay. I had the same confusatory at first. Had a lotta trouble understanding things." Pointing to the room two doors down from mine, he indicated the small grouping of people conglomerated outside the doorway. "See her with the red coat?"

"Yeah," I replied.

"That's my Granny Jin! She's the bomb. Comes here every afternoon and waits her turn to visit me. Not to brag or boast or anything, but it's usually standing-room-only in there. Got four younger brothers who drive the hospital staff crazy." He chuckled. "They don't like all us Asians muddling up their establishment, but they gotta put up with it on account of I'm sorta famous."

"What are you talking about?" I asked bewildered. One minute this guy was talking about the confusion, and the next he boasted a claim to fame. "I don't know you. Never heard of you." And then I thought about it and asked, "Is that why she calls you 'the Big Cheese?' Cause you call yourself 'Cheddar,' and you think you're famous?"

"Yeah, she's cra-cra like that!" He chuckled again, glancing up just in time to see Ruby bopping in our direction with her arms laden with supplies.

"Hit the Jackpot!" she declared excitedly. She handed me a powder-blue terrycloth robe and a pair of hospital slippers. "Haven't seen a robe this nice since…"

She looked at Cheddar, and they both winced.

"Since what?"

"Oh, ah, just never mind. Doesn't matter how the robe got there or who it came from; all that matters is that you're warm and your butt's covered. Right, Cheddar?"

"Right," the teenage cheese-lover chirped, nodding his head in agreement.

As soon as I slid into the slippers and robe, a wave of warmth encapsulated me. "Thanks. This is—"

"Nooooo!" Cheddar cut me off. "Look who's headed this way on her afternoon bender! It's Flapjack!"

"Oh, No!" Ruby agreed. "You're gonna wanna cover your eyes!" she said assuredly. "Cover 'em good!"

"Mrs. Kravitz is coming this way," Cheddar clarified. "Her hospital gown will be open, and she'll be flashing some major crack, flanked by two squashed cheeks so deflated they're wobbly pancakes flapping in the wind."

But it was too late. By the time they completed their warning, I had already seen the backside of Mrs. Kravitz's pancakes as she rolled her walker past us. I had already seen that her hospital gown gaped open and gotten a glimpse of her eerily deflated derriere.

"Too late," I rumbled with remorse. "Didn't close my eyes in time. It's bad! It's bad! It's an image I don't know if I'll ever be able to forget. It's branded on my mind."

"Bummer," Cheddar uttered.

"Yeah, bummer," Ruby agreed.

The moment Mrs. Kravitz negotiated her walker around the corner and out of my line of vision, the door to 233 swished open, and another patient strolled into the hallway. She was also in her 80s or 90s, but this woman lit up the corridor with her perfectly-coiffed purple beehive, lowcut burgundy nightdress, and full-on theatrical makeup. Coordinating her showy hair and makeup was something even showier: her Sexton Walker 396, which sported dual precision wheels on the front legs and flamingo-pink tennis balls on the back (for gripping), a wicker basket adorned with Papier-mâché flowers for carrying supplies, and a bedazzled bike bell.

"Looken' rad," Ms. Cunningham," Cheddar declared. "Bell's a sweet addition to your ride."

He turned to me and clarified. "I like Ms. Cunningham; she's got street cred. She ain't gonna let no broken hip cramp her style. No, she's banking the bling with that bedazzled bike bell and them faux leopard skin orthopedic slippers. When I get old like that…" He glanced over at Ruby and shrugged. "I mean *if* I get old like that, I wanna be like her. Don't wanna give up like a lot of these poor schmucks. I wanna Pimp Daddy these here halls. I wanna—"

And it was then (as Cheddar detailed his Pimp My Ride, Geriatric-Edition that included getting a scooter that could do whirls and wheelies, had a hydraulic hop, and a tectonic speaker system that could blast any old school song) that I caught sight of something that captured my attention, knocking me off guard. When Ms. Cunningham left the door to her room braced open for her impending return, she provided a clear line of sight into her room. On the television mounted on the back wall, I saw an image that had me captivated.

"Hold on," I uttered while I sullenly rose from my seat. I didn't say anything else or explain myself; I simply got up and proceeded across the hallway. Something about seeing the situation on the screen at that precise time intrigued me, almost as if being there had been preordained.

♫ ♪

The inside of Ms. Cunningham's room pervaded with scents of freshly-cut lilacs, tequila, and oddly enough, a faint hint of weed. Adorning the countertop, she displayed a collection of photographs and memorabilia. Next to the photo of her modeling cars at The World's Fair was one of her in a cockpit of an old Red Lockheed Vega. It surprised me and caught me off guard, but only for a fraction of an instant in that my attention remained drawn to the television.

"... of protesters banded on the front steps of the Bakersfield River Police Department," the reporter touted, "expressing outrage regarding a potential cover-up in last week's police-involved shooting. That man, fifty-five-year-old Otis Cleveland Merriweather, is currently in St. Ann's. Mr. Merriweather's expected to make a full recovery from being shot by Bakersfield River Police Officer William S. Walsh during a routine traffic stop on the corner of E. Planz and South H. The prognosis for Mr. Merriweather is good in that he sustained only moderate injuries as a result of the shooting. That, unfortunately, is not the case for Officer Walsh. Sadly, shortly after the shooting – as officers Walsh and Riley headed north on South P on their way to the police station – their cruiser was struck by an inattentive driver who some suspect may have been texting. The accident resulted in the immediate loss of life for Officer Todd Riley, an eight-year veteran of the force, while Officer Walsh has been hospitalized at St. Ann's. According to sources at the hospital, the prognosis is not good for Officer Walsh who remains on life support." Pausing a few seconds, he let that sink in as his eyes honed into the camera.

"As Officer Walsh's life rests on the brink of death, a band of protesters led by Dr. Rodney T. Washington of the All People Are Created Equal movement (who is famous for bringing attention to police misconduct in the Gerald Butler case in Cincinnati as well as representing the family of little Billie Joe Marigold, who won a thirty-six million dollar settlement in the unlawful death of a child by officers with the Miami Dade police department) has converged on the steps of the Bakersfield

River Police Department. Dr. Washington has petitioned the court for an outside review of the case.

"For the third time in a decade, the Bakersfield River Police Department has been named the deadliest in the nation," Dr. Washington orated to the crowd before him as well as into the camera. "Shooting innocent people isn't protecting and serving; it is a *crime*. The science and the math speak for themselves; the statistics are clear. Something is wrong! Why is this police force profiling and killing so many minorities? Why are they the most deadly? And how come they're getting away with it? As I stand before you, Commander Bennett and officials with the Bakersfield River Police Force Shooting Review Board have converged to determine the facts of this case. And we all know they're going to clear Officers Walsh and Riley because that is what they do. That is what they *always* do. They cleared gunning down a senior man with dementia who simply walked in front of his own house with his hand in his pocket, holding onto a small wooden crucifix. They cleared gunning down a young disabled boy who held a plastic toy plane in his hand while sitting in his wheelchair. They cleared gunning down a suspect in a car on Hotel Circle Drive when they purposely entrapped him there via the assistance of a police informant. And there are, unfortunately, dozens of other cases. What is the common denominator in these cases?"

The camera spanned the crowd of protesters holding candles, banners, and signs.

"That is easy! The common denominator is the police clear all of these cases because the police are policing themselves. And IF the police are policing themselves and consistently clear shootings that are questionable and shady then what in the Lord's name, would stop them from continuing to shoot whoever they want! I ask you what???? The way the laws are—

"William Walsh," she said from behind me, "you have to leave. Ms. Cunningham's on her way back, and it's not right for you to be here. It's an invasion. We don't do that. It's not part of our—"

"I'm sorry?" I asked, confused. "What?"

Ruby pointed to the corridor. "You have to leave. Staying in here and watching her would be sinning, and you ain't exactly in the best place in the sin department," she scoffed.

"What do you mean?"

"You're on the fence, William Walsh. *Not* a good place."

"What fence," I garbled as Ms. Cunningham strode through the doorway.

Ruby grabbed ahold of my arm and pulled me into the corridor. "H&H, William Walsh. H&H!"

"H&H?"

"Heaven and Hell. You're on the fence between Heaven and Hell, and it ain't looken' too good right now!" She shook her head while her eyes shown convincingly. "Man, I'd be boocoo nervous if I was you. In fact, I'd be—"

Ms. Cunningham released the doorstop. The door swung shut, releasing a gust of lilac-scented weed.

"I don't understand. You sit here and see people's backsides. What's the difference between that and watching television in her room?"

"A lot!" Ruby explained. "We're not here to check people's backsides. That happens, and it's funny, but that is not why we're here. We're here for healing."

"Healing?"

"Yeah," Cheddar chimed in. "As my body's laid up in the bed, recovering from the accident, I'm sitten' here, recovering from life."

"What accident?"

"Pro-Am Board Tour. Badly rad, bro. Badly rad. Had sponsors and a fat endorsement. Then I flubbed a flyboy. Didn't stick an under flip, busted cap, and broke brow."

"Huh?" I groaned. "Could you use real talk and not that slang skater gibberish. I can't under—"

"I fell out from under my board, slipped outta my helmet, and bumped my noggin."

"And?"

"And I ended up here, same as you, in the Neuro-Science Ward of St. Ann's."

"Neuro what?"

"Neuro-Science, dude, for people with busted brains. You know, brain cancer, congenital disability, or – as in our cases – bashed in from accidents."

"So, how are we able to sit here and be in our rooms?"

"Oh, that," Ruby cut in. "That's the marvels of the human spirit mixed with a little divine intervention."

"What?"

"Man, William Walsh. You still have a lot to--"

"Oh my gosh, *LOOK*!" Cheddar jumped out of his seat as he directed our attention to someone who had just turned into the corridor from the opposing side of the wing. "Booyah! We got another one! Dang! Wow! Chippity-chop! Can you believe it?" He turned to face Ruby with his eyes lit with expectancy. "Another newbie – that's two in one day!?!"

"Oh *my*!" Ruby gushed excitedly.

"What are you talking about?"

"HIM!" they answered, simultaneously pointing out the man at the other end of the corridor, who appeared to be making his way in our direction.

"Someone else left his body," Cheddar declared. "We got a new member to our little--"

"I'm not the same as you." Ruby cut in. "I'm more of a..."

But I lost track of what they were saying as my attention focused on the new person.

Approaching from down the corridor was someone surprising, somebody I never imagined. All of a sudden, I felt horrified, terrified, astounded, and (oddly) relieved. So many things happened at the same time from so many directions: my body, my brother, the newscast, and now *this*!

For some reason, I got the crazy idea of trying to hide from him.

Slipping down into my seat, I hoped he wouldn't recognize me. And then the man's eyes melded into mine as they made contact. His mouth gaped open in complete shock.

"YOU!" he snapped vibrantly, quick-stepping his approach.

"Damn!" Cheddar sang. "It's about to go down!"

Ruby patted my knee for reassurance. "H&H," she reminded me. "Remember William Walsh, what you do and what you say…"

Part of me wanted to go back to my hospital room, return to my body, and let nature take its course. Part of me wanted to find a way out of there and make a run for it, thinking I could make it home. I could sit in front of the television, drink craft beer, and watch a good movie. While part of me wanted to fall to my knees and beg for his forgiveness. I felt lost as my thoughts spun in a whirlwind of uncertainty. *Why's he here? Nothing makes sense! I'm in a coma. I'm out of a coma. I'm out of my body. I'm in a hallway. I'm in another life.*

Everything began to feel fuzzy again. I couldn't understand why this was happening. Was it a dream? Was it really him, or could it have been another hallucination? Things became hazy, then blurry, and then dim.

"Don't worry," Ruby exclaimed before I passed out. "We'll be right here, waiting for you. Come back soon, though. You don't wanna miss the big…"

The last fleeting image before I passed out was the strangely familiar face of the man whose life I snatched and then invaded. The face was unmistakable. It was the man I shot. It was Otis Cleveland Merriweather.

CHAPTER FIFTEEN
THE FOURTH TIME

In a sound sleep, I was far far away, floating in a sea of serene peace and tranquility, when I awoke to the squeaking and creaking of branches rustling upon a windowpane; their tiny stick slithers scratching along the glass. *I'm not imagining this. I hear the wind. I hear gusts and squalls of air streams strumming through brush and tree limbs, creating a symphony of snaps and creaks and whistles and screams.* And for the third time, I found myself safe and at peace on the comfortable bed. *I'm back,* I confirmed, *back to being him.*

But this time I wasn't alone. On my right side, a tiny warm body lay curled with his spine to me. And on my left, an upside-down kid lay haphazard with his foot smashed on the side of my head. *It's on my face! It's actually on my face!*

"Uggg," I grumbled as I sat up, finding myself in the same room with the same furnishings. However, this time, a mismatched panel of whiteboard replaced the third drawer of the dresser. The toy chest overflowed with an assortment of Tonka trucks, toys, and an old baseball bat. A row of instruments lined the front of the closet, including a trumpet, two saxophones, a six-string guitar, and a shiny new banjo still in a box. And underneath a framed drawing of a Black angel were three hand-painted prayer plaques. One crafted for Otis (me), the person whose life I kept going back, while the others belonged to a "Harley" and an "Emmitt." Looking down at the pair of skinny little, afro-headed, cover-stealing, bed hogs, I presumed a couple of things.

My mother person and Ben must have been busy in that they already procreated a couple more band members.

A few years must have passed in that the elder of the two, Mr. Stinky Foot, appeared to be around the age of eight or nine.

And even though I found myself cramped between the two of them, that mattress remained the same pillowy cloud from sleep paradise.

The smaller one rustled under the covers. "Bruther!" he greeted excitedly, glaring into my eyes in sheer panic. "I gotta pee! Gotta pee! Hurry! Hurry! Take me!"

In all actuality, this kid wasn't my blood relative. In fact, I wouldn't have known him from a stranger on the street. But something about not wanting to be drenched in urine and his cute cherub gleam sparked a brother-like sense of concern. Scooping him into my arms, I carefully brought him through the main living area (which still hosted a variety of mismatch furnishings and whimsical smells) over to the quaint closet-sized restroom that not so surprisingly looked the same.

Standing in the door's threshold not only granted him some privacy as he stood with his back to me, urinating mostly into the round porcelain bowl, it also allowed me to view myself in the olden day mirror above the vanity. The transformation had me astounded. What had once been chubby cheeks and a short stubby nose had taken on many of his characteristics. *It's you!* I said to my reflection. *You look like a thinner, younger, not so intimidating version of the man who had me rattled that day.*

The familiar flush of the toilet brought me back to the situation at hand, and I saw that the little guy had made it over to the stepstool and began to sing "Rudolph the Red-Nosed Reindeer" as he washed his hands, inadvertently neglecting to use hand soap. I thought about counseling him or mentioning something about the spread of germs, but discounted the notion in that I really wasn't this Otis person; therefore, he really wasn't my brother.

Reaching his chubby little hand onto the faucet, he turned the water off before spider-leaping into my arms. That is when (in that tiny little crook of a second) I knew this one was Emmitt, that he was four years old, hated prunes, was crazy about firetrucks and cinnamon toast, and was deathly afraid of Siberian Snow Tigers.

"Bruther!" he shuddered. "Hurry! Bring me back! My feet's cold, and I'm afraid there might be a, a, a…" Scanning side-to-side, he looked at me with tentative reluctance.

"A what," I asked even though I suspected what he would say.

"A tiger!"

"I already told you," which I seemed to recollect this Otis person telling him, "all of the Siberian Snow Tigers are in Siberia. You don't have to worry about them here."

"But," his eyes were giant caldrons of hot chocolate fudge, "there's one at the zoo. There's a Siberian Snow Tiger in the zoo, and with this here storm he might escape an'—"

"Who told you that?"

"Harley did! Harley told me they likes to eat little children's on account of we taste better!"

"Harley's messing with you," I declared assuringly. "The truth is Siberian Snow Tigers are very finicky eaters. They don't like the taste of children, especially not children with brown eyes and brown curly hair."

"Like mine?"

"Yes, just like yours. In fact, if I recall from my expertise in studying rare exotic animals, there's one thing that Siberian Snow Tigers are very much afraid of, so afraid that they will run away as fast as they can if they even smell the slightest hint of it!"

"Whaaat?"

"Something so powerful, it renders them incapacitated."

"Whaaat!" His eyes lit with excitement and intrigue. "What is it????"

"It's simple," I proclaimed in my best big brother voice. "They're deathly afraid of hand soap! Anything that looks like soap or, perhaps, smells like soap will send them running to the farthest reaches of the country."

"Really?" he chirped, eyeing me with keen skepticism. "Why's that?"

"Simple, soap messes with their olfaction and makes them woozy."

"What?"

"It's like a stink bomb in their face."

Pausing for a second with a stern expression and furrowed brows, he contemplated his decision. "Hold on!" he said, "I gots to do something!"

Rushing back to the sink, he soaped himself all the way up to his elbows then took the additional time to wash his face.

"I'm safe!" he boasted with a smug swagger. "Any of dem Snow Tigers come over here and try'n get me, and the stinky scent of clean will knock em' out!"

And then he grabbed ahold of me and held onto my neck as I toted him back to the room. After returning him to the bed, I made sure he rested comfortably and safe, before heading into the common area.

I can't understand why I'm acting like this, I puzzled. *I never had patience like this around kids. Never checked on Jeremy or tucked him in bed. I didn't care if he washed his hands or peed all over the wall for that matter. I loved Jeremy but never set his needs before my own. Somehow I think Otis's protectively paternal affection for his brother is influencing me. There's a part of him that's changing the way I am.*

"Otis!" my mother person clutched onto her chest and gasped when she found me sitting at the table. "What on God's green earth has gotten' into you! Why's you still here? Is that coffee? What in heaven's name? Since when do you like coffee?"

"I—"

Looking at the clock, she about had a heart attack. "Lord Child!" she sputtered. "It's almost six! You should have eaten and left already. You can't be late, not on a day like this. Not TODAY! Todays about the biggest day of your life. You've been working on this for months. You can't blow it now. Your entire future rests on how it goes. Hurry, child. Get dressed and gets! You need to be at the bus stop in twenty," she looked at the clock again and about screeched, "make that nineteen!!!!!"

"I—"

"Hurry now!" Shaking her head from side-to-side, she bustled about the kitchen. "I'll fix something you can take with you!"

After refilling my cup, I headed into the bedroom where I found both of my brother people snuggled back to back, presumably sound asleep. While I selected an outfit from the drawer with the replaced face board, my mind spieled with concern. *How am I going to do this? I don't know where I'm going, where this bus stop is, or how long I'm going to be here.*

"Boy oh boy," he chorused from the bed. "Can't believe you're running late on this here big day! Not after all that work!"

Glancing towards the bedcovers, I found Harley propped against the headboard with his arms crossed, his afro smashed on one side, and his expression not so much worried as self-satisfied.

"What do you mean?"

"You knows what I mean! Today's that stupid science presentation you've been harping about for months. You keep saying," Harley's voice morphed to a shrill screech, "'It's my whole grade! Gotta get an A so I can get that scholarship. Gotta get that scholarship so I can go to college next year. Gotta go to college so I can beat the draft. Gotta beat the draft 'cause they's been putting us on the front lines, and we be getten killed.'"

I had already dressed and collected my boots when Harley added, "You keep tellen' us how Big LeRoy Billings got drafted. He was over there, what, four months and got shot down. Same with Titus Adamson, Luther McDaniel, Alonzo Morris, Bobby Freeman, and fat Jay. Oh, and—"

The implications of what he conveyed hit hard, and I recognized the significance of this day to the real Otis. *I've already done enough damage; I can't screw this up. I have to be you and make it to the presentation on time so that you can make it to college.*

"So," I suggested while lacing my boots. "If I had a brain fart and forgot where the bus stop was, where would I—"

"A what?"

"A brain fart, like a forget spell."

"Weird." He produced a low, raspy chuckle in the pattern of a motorcycle. "I don't knows what they been teachen' you, but you already know the bus picks you up at the corner of 1st and Jay."

"Got it!" I quipped, bolting to the door. "And while I'm gone, no more messing with Emmitt with all them tiger stories. The kid's terrified in his own--"

"Don't know what you's talking about," Harley quipped back, and then he tugged on the covers so that he hoarded the majority of the blankets as well as most of the bed. "My brain's farting big time 'cause I don't know nuthen' about no Siberian Snow Tigers."

After closing the door and accepting my lunch from my mother person, I was just about to head out the front when Harley sarcastically added, "Or dem South African Jumping Spiders that spit poison!"

The bus trip to Farmington Springs made for some storybook sightseeing. Spanning the terrain outside my window, we passed long rolling fields of lush foliage, huge canopying trees, and quaint countryside cottages surrounded by white picket fences and an assortment of other fanciful barriers. Not knowing what state I was in, I became stunned when we passed a road sign for Illinois. *Illinois*, I perplexed. *How on earth did I get here? Never before have I dreamed or experienced anything like this. I'm not just in another timeline; I'm in another state!*

Along the journey – along the sixteen or seventeen stops the bus made to pick up additional passengers, – I opened Otis's science journal and perused his presentation on solar energy and became overwhelmed. *I can't believe it!* I marveled. *This guy's a genius! How'd he know so much about solar power in 1964? Was it popular then? Did they even know about solar energy? They didn't have computers, so how did he do this research?* With each page that I turned, I saw the hundreds of hours that must have gone into his assignment. *I wonder if this guy is one of the people who revolutionized solar energy.*

The brakes squealed a voracious objection as the bus pulled to a stop in front of the sprawling facility of Farmington Springs High. Exiting down the stairs, I followed the herd of students towards an elaborately constructed entrance flanked by matching rock-laden pillars. A brass sign embedded in one of the cornerstones displayed the school's motto, "We Shall Shine!" I can't recall if I thought anything about the slogan; I was too intent on locating the Science Lab. *I just got to get to my class and read off this information, so this Otis person can go to a good college and avoid the draft. This is the least I can—*

"Looksey here," a blonde-headed, broad-shouldered, angular-faced football player type taunted from his perch beside the sign pillar. "Here comes our token negro!"

The crowd around him looked away from me as they elbowed each other, sniggering with glee.

"Hey, nigger!" he called to me. "We don't want you here, nigger! Don't you hear me, nigger! We don't want any Negros in our school!"

I didn't respond. I didn't say anything. I simply kept walking. The way I saw it; this wasn't my battle. This was something between him and the real Otis.

Unfortunately, averting the situation only seemed to make matters worse. After hopping from his stoop, he crouched down to a squat and began to swing his arms, mimicking an ape. "Looksey here, everyone. I's an ape! I got's an ape nose and an ape brain. I'm gonna pretend I can read books!"

"That ain't right, Jimmy-John!" an attractive girl giggled.

What? That's Jimmy-John!?! That's the same bully who harassed this Otis person in elementary school, the one who stole my lunch and ate my sandwich. I can't believe it. He's grown so much. He's no longer the same short, pudgy kid that I remember.

The girl turned to Jimmy-John and smiled coyly before planting a kiss on his cheek, and then she skipped off to join her friends as they trekked the main throughway into the heart of the school.

Ignore them. I don't want to screw this up. I don't even care because I'm really not a Black person. None of this should bother me. Just go to 204, give your presentation, and before I know it, I'll be back to…

"Sorry about that," a skeletal-thin kid with a leg cast rambled as he caught up alongside me. He took two steps, stumbled, and almost fell. And then he took two more steps, stumbled, and almost fell again. "Not all of us are like that."

"Like what?"

"Racist. Not every white person's a racist," he said, and then he stumbled again. This time, his backpack slipped off his shoulder and onto the ground. Leaning over his crutches, he fumbled about, struggling to retrieve it.

I felt bad for the guy, so I picked it up and attempted to hand it to him.

"Can you carry it?" he asked out of the blue. "We're in the same class."

"Sure," I replied because I felt sorry for the guy.

Then it became weird. Every step I took and turn I made, I suddenly felt watched. Not because I was the only Black person in the school, I experienced this cold, clammy sensation of scorching eyeballs. *Something's not right. Desegregation's been around for a while now, but it's pretty clear this upper-class community doesn't like it. This is stupid. Being racist like this is crazy.* And then I experienced a faint realization of directing my firearm on the adult Otis.

"That's good." He paused to catch his breath in front of the restroom. "I'll take it from here. You can put it there," he directed, pointing to the pristine clean spot on the sidewalk next to the doorframe.

Once I leaned his backpack against the wall where he had indicated, I held the door open for the guy so that he could shuffle inside. That's when I noticed the door across the hallway labeled SCIENCE LAB. *I made it! Look, room 204 is right there. I made it! I made it in time. All I gotta do is head over there, do the presentation, and I'll probably return to my real--*

It was then – as I momentarily lost focus on the circumstances around me – that a pack of them rushed from behind. One grabbed ahold of my right arm while another grappled my left. And the next thing I knew, Jimmy-John positioned himself in the front of the pack, brandishing a kilowatt smile and a lasso made out of cattle rope. The door to room 204 stood a mere eleven feet away. I thought about jerking out of their arms and bolting into the classroom, but in the two-point-five seconds it took for the thought to filter into my mind, Jimmy-John had already slipped the noose around my neck.

"Get your black, nigger ass inside," he jeered excitedly "or die here!"

I sure as hell didn't cooperate; that part, I remember quite well. I tussled and struggled and fought as best I could. Nevertheless, the seven or eight of them strong-armed me into the sparkling, pristine-clean expanse of a restroom and over to the barrier that separated the stalls. As I kicked and yelled and screamed, Jimmy-John tossed the end of the rope over the upper partition of stall enclosures, pulling it taut until it brought me to my toes. I balanced there as his marionette, facing a rivalry of Jimmy-John and his white lookalike friends. And I knew that whatever happened next was gonna be bad.

"Thanks, Frankie," Jimmy-John chirped, and the skinny kid with the crutches sullenly turned and hobbled back outside.

Once the door closed behind him, all of their attention drew upon me. *I can do this! I know how to fight. I can kick, and I can fight! I'm not some wimpy kid; I'm an adult male police—*

I couldn't complete the thought. Jimmy-John passed the loose end of the rope to one of the lookalikes, and then he stepped in front of the angry mob with a baseball bat in his hands.

"Looksey here, nigger," he crooned while warming up his swing.

The mob hushed. They stood frozen with faces lit in excitement and expectancy. My blood drained from my heart. Then came the strike as Jimmy-John took aim at the crux of my left shoulder.

The bat slammed into my shoulder bone, fracturing Otis's hopes and dreams. Not wanting to give him the satisfaction of hearing my pain, I wailed inwardly, releasing only a slight guttural sigh.

The crowd roared and cheered with enthusiasm. "Get him, Jimmy-John!" "Get him!" "Get him good!"

The second strike pummeled the side of my thigh when I tried to kick him. The pain that set in became immeasurable and debilitating. My determination began to wane; it took everything I had not to scream and beg for mercy.

But it was the third and final blow that stopped everything while changing the course of my journey. The seven or eight of them cheered as if they were at a big-league game and Jimmy-John was their favorite slugger.

"Do it!" they chanted. "Get him good!" "Get him good!" "Swing for the bleachers!" "Get a home run!"

And then I felt the third and final strike smash into my left temple. It rattled my skull with so much intensity that it split open the side of my face, knocking me down. The pain hit hard, and I broke. I lay on the ground, wailing in agony as my blood flowed and wept into my eyes.

"Oh, *SHIT*!" Jimmy-John chortled.

And then I heard the mass exodus of a hundred shuffling footsteps.

As I lay on the cold, dank, concrete floor – watching the puddle of my blood bloom and flow down the drain – I realized I would never make the presentation.

I should have seen it coming! I scolded myself. *I should have known what they were going to do. I should have known how racist people like that are.* And then, just like so many times before, I blanked out.

SECTION V

CONTEMPLATION

CHAPTER SIXTEEN
MOCCASIN MADNESS

The next time I came to it wasn't to the rich, bountiful bouquet of chitlins and grits, sweet potato pie, fried chicken, or blueberry pancakes drenched in a delicious confectionery of rich buttery syrup. It wasn't even the pungent scent of disinfectant that disturbed me. No, the next time I awoke to the grating sensation of being attacked. Someone hit me. I didn't see him or even know he was there, but as I lay in my hospital bed (presumably in a coma and on life support), I experienced the same harrowing sensation of being punched. My eyes momentarily opened and saw the faint trace of a shadow fading into the recess behind the machine.

What the hell? I perplexed. *Who's messing with me? Is it Commander Bennett, Officer Bettencourt, Doyle, or is it Riley rising from the place beneath graves. It doesn't make sense. Why would someone want to hurt me? Why would someone want to infiltrate my hospital room and attack me when I'm hovering on the brink of my demise?* And then I heard Jeremy's voice and all of the negativity and animosity of being attacked immediately vanquished by the animosity of my brother's presence.

"No!" Jeremy bellowed.

Half asleep and half awake, I lay on my hospital bed with my eyes closed.

"I'm not having it! It's too early. Not yet! No fricken' way."

What the hell! I scoffed. *What gives HIM the right to come to Bakersfield and think he can meddle in my business? Go back to Texas, Jeremy! Go back to where you came from! You're not welcome here!*

"Mr. Walsh," a stately voice responded, "I understand your reluctance. This may seem like a difficult choice, but you must realize this decision has already been made. It isn't up to you. The matter has already been addressed by Officer Walsh, himself when he filled out his driver's license as well as when he discussed it with his wife.

See Jeremy; they don't need you. Whatever decision they're talking about has nothing to do with you, so you can hop on the next plane and fly your low-grade, non-funeral going self back to Texas.

"NO!" Jeremy's voice bellowed louder. "It's too soon. I'm not changing my mind. Liz, are you hearing this?"

"Mr. Walsh, we encounter family members all the time who have trouble grappling circumstances like this…"

Jeremy, Jeremy, Jeremy, they're about to tell you! They're about to tell you nothing you say counts, and you can shove your big fat opinion where the sun don't…

"…because it's a difficult time for everyone. But we assure you that we have the best neurological staff in the country. Dr. Baylor has been doing this for thirty-two – no, make that thirty-three years now. Dr. Baylor has an impeccable record dealing with hundreds of patients with traumatic brain injuries. Dr. Baylor and Dr. Skeets have consulted extensively on this matter, and both concur with the recommendation. In fact, Dr. Fleming – who's been your brother's physician for the past eight years – is also on board.

So, Jeremy, it's all the specialists against you. Whatcha gonna do now?

"Liz, listen to me!" Jeremy pleaded. "This is important! It's too…"

I snickered at Jeremy's persistence, and then *badda bing badda boom* found myself out of my body again. It seemed to be getting easier. All I did was think about it, and *poof* the next thing I knew, I found myself standing at the foot of my bed. I still didn't know if these were dreams, results of my accident, some sort of divine intervention, E.T. interference, or out of body experiences. All I knew was that my wife leaned into the railing with her hand tenderly clasped onto the forearm of the me on the bed. This time she wore a navy blue pantsuit and a tan blouse with mismatched buttons resulting in an off-kilter collar and rumpled neckline. But that wasn't the messy part. No, the messy part of Liz's attire was the fact that she sported two different shoes. On one foot she had on a low-heeled blue moccasin with a brass-finished buckle bridging the brim while on the other she donned an old house slipper. Liz, the queen of fashion and looking snazzy, wore a house slipper in the middle of the hospital!

She's losing it, I fretted. *Her buttons are off, and she's wearing two different shoes. She looks as though she's about to pass out or topple over.*

"Liz, what's going on? Are you tipsy? Did the doctors prescribe you something to help with your anxiety?"

While I checked on Liz, Jeremy continued his idiotic rant. "It's too early! This isn't right. I know they have a job to do. I know they say it's time-sensitive, but I'm looking out for my brother here. Liz, please! Please don't let them talk you into this. Please give it some time. This is—"

"I don't knooow," Liz drawled drowsily. "It's beeeen a week. They're saying they neeeeed to do it now because they're viable. They're saying they caaaaan't wait any--"

What is this? It suddenly dawned on me that my contempt for Jeremy may have overridden my common sense.

"In all actuality, this isn't *your* decision, Mr. Walsh, err, Jeremy," Dr. Skeets interjected. "Your brother signed the donor card. He already made the decision. It's not a question of *whether* the donation should occur; it's a matter of *when*."

And then I watched as Dr. Skeets walked over to Liz and placed his palms on her shoulders. "I'm sorry about your loss, but that is what it is. Your husband has already passed. He was technically dead when he arrived at the hospital. He's no longer with us. All the tests confirm it. He's been unresponsive for over a week now, and it's time. It's time to follow through with his wishes."

Liz's fingers trembled as she brought them to her face.

"It's time," Dr. Baylor confirmed.

"No, Liz!" I shouted frantically. "Don't do it! I'm alive! I'm right here!"

"This is what your husband wanted. He wanted to help people. He wanted to be a donor."

"Are you fricken' crazy? If you take my organs that *will* kill me! I'm not dead! I'm right here! How can they say my brain stopped functioning if I'm standing right here in front of you?"

"I'm sorry, Mrs. Walsh," Dr. Baylor pressed, "but you must understand that your husband wouldn't want to be like this. He wouldn't want to be attached to a machine indefinitely. Back in the day, we called it a 'vegetative state' because old-time doctors likened it to being a vegetable. It's an outdated term we no longer use, but the concept remains the same. Do you want him to linger like this with a dead brain? Like a carrot? No man, I mean no *police officer* would want that. No police officer would want to put that kind of burden on his family. His wishes were very explicit. He wouldn't want to be laid up like this. Nobody would want this. This is not what he—"

What the hell? What the hell?

Liz looked as though she was about to fall out or faint. No-nonsense and another nurse tended to her side as Dr. Skeets knelt in front of her, offering the clipboard so that the papers could be signed. Dr. Baylor then stooped on her other side, offering his pen.

"All you have to do is sign this, and--"

"Jeremey, do something!" I pleaded. "Please, Jeremy. Now I know why you were so adamant!" I walked over to him and attempted to grapple his arm, but my hand floated right through him. "You're right about this. Don't let them! Please don't let them do this! Take the pen, Jeremy. Don't let her sign it! I don't understand what's going on, but I'm standing right in front of you. I'm not dead, exactly. Not alive either."

Tears slipped from Jeremy's eyes, almost as if he could hear me. He sat there, trembling with rage when he suddenly reached over and snatched the pen out of Dr. Baylor's hand.

"Hold the pen, Jeremy. Don't let it go! Please don't let them kill me." Once again, I tried to reach for his arm and felt defeated when I couldn't make contact.

"Okay, okay, I admit it. I was hard on you. I shouldn't have sided with Dad and said what I said. I'm beginning to think that being a police officer may have gone to my head. Actually, I see a lot of things differently. I don't know what it's like to be gay or how much it hurt when Dad treated you like that. You didn't deserve it. You never deserved it. I'm sorry, Jeremy. I'm sorry I didn't stand up for you. Sorry I kept my mouth shut when I knew how much you hurt. Remaining silent was wrong. I shouldn't be mad at you for leaving us and staying away. I probably would have done the same thing if it were me."

Tears welled in my eyes as an overwhelming sensation of guilt consumed me. And it was then, in my moment of shame and remorse that I finally remembered the missing pieces of what happened that day. I remembered pulling the trigger and shooting that man. I remembered Riley tossing the throw-away to cover up my wrongdoing. I remembered lying to Sergeant Fleckman and Captain Akeman of the Bakersfield River Fire Department. The entire ordeal, everything, it all came back to me in a sudden, sharp wallop of pain.

Oh, God, what have I done! What have I done! I feel so horrible. I'm a lousy person. Here I've been given this enchanted life, and I've had it all wrong. I was a crummy brother. I should have protected Jeremy; instead, I remained silent when our father berated him with crude innuendoes and snide remarks. As a husband, I should have considered Liz's thoughts and feelings to be a mother. And as a police officer, I shot a man because of his race then helped Riley with the cover-up. That is a crime! I committed a crime! I'm a horrible, terrible person who's messed up everything.

Dr. Baylor handed Liz another pen. "Sign the form, Mrs. Walsh. It's the right thing to do. Your husband can help so many people. He can--"

"I'm sorry, Liz," I found myself saying. "Sorry that my actions led to this."

"Proud of you, William Walsh!"

Turning to the bedrail, I found Ruby Josephine in the usual spot on the foot rail with her feet crossed and her old fashioned shoes on my mattress.

"That right there's a big step."

"W,what?" I stuttered. "What are you talking about? Do you know what's going on? Do you know what's about to happen?"

"Of course I do, William Walsh!" she giggled. "I have eyes and ears too." And then she hopped off the railing, trotted over to the chair, and squeezed her skinny backside into the small gap between the arm of the chair and Liz's left hip.

"Poor, girl," Ruby pouted sympathetically. "Told you I like her, right? She's been here since day one, tending to you and saying like a bazillion prayers."

She held onto Liz's hand, and it almost seemed as if Liz's worry lines diminished.

"She's a good person, you know."

"Yeah, I know."

"Too bad, you didn't want a family. Self-centered, don't you think? Thinking about yourself first all the time. She would have been such a--"

Her attention became distracted when Liz accepted the clipboard from Dr. Skeets and the pen from Dr. Baylor. Liz sat poised with the pen juddered above the signature line.

"Ohhhhh!" Ruby Josephine gasped in astonishment. "This is it!!!! This is the big moment! They say your organs and tissue can help like *fifty* recipients. Don't know all the technical mumbo jumbo of how they chop you up and stuff your guts and gooey parts in other people, but I know that you'll be saving a lot of lives."

"Can you stop this?" I pleaded. "Can you do something to prevent her from signing?"

"Nope! No can do. It's against the rules, William Walsh. Rules are things that you swore to protect and serve but—"

"Jeremy," I said to my brother. "Do something! Please help me! Do something, Jeremy! I need you. You're the only person I can count on right now."

"Oh, not quite. But you're getting there, William Walsh. There's someone you can—"

Before I had a chance to fall to my knees and pray, and before Ruby Josephine completed her statement, Jeremy leaned over and snatched the clipboard out of Liz's hand.

"Two days!" Jeremy snapped angrily. "Give him two days!" Actually, he was beyond angry. I had never seen my brother so adamant.

"I don't agree with this, but at least give him another forty-eight hours. Liz, I told you that I don't feel as though he's gone. I'm his brother; you'd think I'd feel something. But I don't. He's a police officer and a fighter. I believe he's in there. Please don't give up on him! Not now! Not my brother! I'm just asking for forty-eight hours, and if he doesn't come out of this, then I'll support this, this euthanasia for harvest."

Liz looked up at Jeremy, and I swear I saw a hint of relief cross her brow.

"Forty-eight hours is good," Ruby Josephine said to me. "I think everything can be wrapped up by then."

"Mrs. Walsh, we have already discussed this," Dr. Baylor pressed. "Another forty-eight hours is too long. It would be ineffectual. He's not doing so well. The longest we can prolong the harvest is twenty, maybe twenty-two hours at the most. After that, several of his organs will no longer be viable for transplantation and it--"

"Twenty-two hours then," Liz cut in, in complete distress. And before anyone could agree or disagree, she retorted, "Don't argue with me, Dr. Skeets. Don't argue, Jeremy. I'm trying to do the right thing here. No one says another word!"

"Ohhh, William Walsh," Ruby Josephine gushed precipitously. "I guess that leaves you with twenty-two hours."

"Twenty-two hours to do what?"

"Produce a miracle, William Walsh, a real miracle. And it's gonna have to be a doozy on account of your unique little predicament."

I wanted to ask her what she meant but didn't have time because she grabbed ahold of my robe sleeve and carted me over to the bed rail so that I faced the disheveled mess of the me on the bed.

"How do I produce a--"

Before I could finish, two small, determined hands shoved me in the center of my back, and the next thing I knew, I had fallen back into myself, and everything went dim.

CHAPTER SEVENTEEN THE FIFTH TIME

If there's a horrible place to wake up – worse than awakening and finding yourself attached to an insidious machine – it would be coming to in a freezing cold rice field in the middle of a firestorm, twenty-one clicks (kilometers) from basecamp. We were on our way to an outpost near the U.S. Marine garrison at Khe Sanh, located in the northwest quadrant of South Vietnam, in a terrain that incurred a particularly hard hit and was under attack. But I didn't know any of that at the time. I didn't know where I was. I didn't know January 21, 1968, meant anything. And I sure as hell didn't know the hit we took in the field that day would be nothing compared to the bombardment that occurred twelve hours later at the Keh Sanh Combat Base (KSCB). All I knew was that I awoke in a mud-drenched water-soaked uniform and slushy boots, lying next to a couple of ripening bodies the way cucumbers clump next to each other on vines.

The guy on my right had a portion of his face blown off. I didn't know if he was Caucasian, Black, or Vietcong for that matter because the skin that remained had been burned beyond recognition, leaving behind the grisly carnage of charred human skull. The nauseating stench of cooked flesh caused me to retch, nearly spewing vomit all over myself and along the trench way.

No! I gasped. *How am I going to do this? How am I going to survive waking up in a hellhole like this? I don't know that much about war. I don't even know which war this is or what this Otis person is supposed to do for that matter. I need to get out! I need to get as far away from this situation as I can!*

Cautiously peering over the muddy trench ridge, I attempted to find my bearings when *Brakakakakakakaka Brakakakakakakaka* a flurry of bullets buzzed by my head. One grazed the lid of my helmet nearly hitting my ear.

"Shit!" I cursed as I ducked back down in the fox hole. *How am I going to do this? How am I going to get away from that fetid stench and this wretched place without getting shot?* And then arose the louder and even more terrifying sonata of incoming mortars. Deep searing whistles voyaged overhead, producing an array of explosions that made land somewhere in the vicinity of two, maybe even three hundred yards to the east. They had been launched and landed with such precision that I imagined everything in the adjacent property had been annihilated.

Reverberations from the impact tremors shook the earth beneath me. Shockwaves jolted through the hollow of my bones, and, for a second or two, my fingers went numb. Panicking would only get me killed, so I sunk into the dank, dreary trench bed, trying to remain inconspicuous. All I could do was breathe dirt as I frantically prayed the bullets and bomb blasts wouldn't find me.

For those who had died that field ended up being the location that marked the end of their existence; the place that transported their souls to death's door, their final resting place, their mass grave. The damp, blood-drenched soil entombed a thousand dreams, a thousand tears, and a thousand memories of stolen lives. Friend and foe lay side-by-side as rice stalks wept into the damp earthen bed. For those who were hurt, it became their theatre of panic and pain, cries and calls out, and feral desperation. And for those like me, it became a place of transformation.

I, William Walsh, had lived a life of leisure and ease. Yes, I had struggles. My mother died three days before my ninth birthday, leaving my father's abusive tendencies as a default form of parenting. However, most of the things in my life had been handed to me. I was the prodigal child, provided a wealth of opportunities, treated well, and respected just because of the way I looked. My blonde hair, blue eyes, and Arian ancestry were my golden ticket to elite social standing. Grades were easy for me to obtain. Jobs were easy for me to obtain. Becoming a police officer was easy for me to obtain all because I had inherited traits that were conducive to being successful in a society designed by and for White men. But not that day, that day I was Otis Cleveland Merriweather. That day I experienced another transcendent journey into another man's life, and, somehow, I became reborn.

Instead of lying in wait, hoping for good fortune to rescue me, I realized I needed to react. Repositioning myself inside the foxhole, I located a gun and immediately rotated the barrel. *It's an M16! An M16 in a rice field can mean only one thing.* My gut plowed into the earthen bed as the realization crystallized.

I'm in Vietnam! I remember this war; I studied it in school. I even saw a couple of good flicks featuring my favorite movie stars. This war had one of the worst outcomes! Of the approximate three million people that died in Vietnam, 58,200 were US Military casualties. All for what????? Then came the epiphany: *What happens to me if I die here? Will I go back to another part of Otis's life, my own life, or will the demons from hell rise from beneath the soil and collect my soul.*

Lying on my mud-drenched water-soaked belly in an unknown rice field somewhere northeast of my outpost (waiting to be blown up or for help to arrive), I closed my eyes and tried to go back. I tried to go back to my life as William Walsh. I tried to go back to the rock-hard hospital mattress. I tried to go back and awaken so I could stop them from pulling the plug. *I have to save myself! I have to prevent them from killing me. Go to sleep so you can go back! Go to sleep.*

Unfortunately, I had no control over the existential circumstances. I wasn't a pilot who could steer dreams or navigate jumping in and out of someone else's life. I had no control over anything, really. I wasn't a husband or police officer; I was more of a lost soul trying to make sense of it all. And that is when – as I laid in that dark, dank, rice field in the middle of a losing battle, gagging on the wretched stench of burnt human flesh, gun smoke, and my own desperation – I learned to do something different. I didn't jump in and out of Otis's life. Instead, I found a way to tap into a channel of his memory. It felt so real. It felt like it really happened as if I were actually taken away.

I had returned. I returned to the warm and cozy ramshackle bungalow of a home that I knew so well. This time I detected the aroma of something sweet and cinnamony baking in the oven; the scent of which filled my heart with childlike anticipation and joy. Ben (or "Dad"

as I knew him) settled in his favorite captain's chair with my brother Emmitt perched on his knee. Loosening and tightening the tension of his lips, Ben demonstrated for Emmitt how to elicit various pitches on a shiny new trumpet. Emmitt attempted to follow along; however, the loud, obnoxious wails his instrument produced sounded more like a lovesick moose then actual music.

Once Emmitt completed the series of almost notes, Ben beamed with pride as he patted Emmitt's back with congratulatory approval.

"Excellent!" Ben declared with a hearty laugh, and I wondered if he needed to have his ears checked. "Perfect for a first-timer."

My mother person slid a pair of floral-patterned baking mitts onto her hands, and then she reached inside the enormous antique oven to retrieve whatever created that delicious scent. And I realized something about the moment felt special. *This isn't just an ordinary day! I can feel it. Something good is about to happen, something extraordinary.*

"Otis!" my mother person chided, "I sees them big brown eyes of yours whatchen' where's I put this here pan of apple fritters." She chuckled in a leisurely tumble of belly rumbles. "There's plenty of 'em here, and I promise one of em's gots your name on it! You don't need to be sneakin' around and trying' to gets one before they get iced. Have some patience, man-child. Have some patience!" And then she chuckled again.

"Emmitt's 'bout done with his lesson," Ben chimed in. His eyes let me know he was talking to me. "Go gets your sax, and we'll get our practice in, maybe even try that new song you like before we gets to enjoyen' your mammas cooken.'"

He looked towards Harley who sat in the chair next to mine with an assortment of silverware on his placemat and a threadbare polishing cloth in his hand.

"You too, Harley. You should have completed dem chores by now. We got's to get some rehearsing in before I leave for the club."

"Do you *have* to work tonight?" Harley groaned as he placed the last spoon into the meticulously maintained box. "Can't you take tonight off and stay with us?"

"That'd be nice," Ben chuckled. "But there's no nights off for me, and pretty soon there's gonna be no nights off for any of us. I'm hoping our little band here takes off, and we earn enough money to buy a big fancy house for my beautiful wife, your Mamma."

Emmitt blew into the trumpet, producing a cat-getting-stepped-on screech, and we all broke into a chorus of laughter.

Once the fritters had cooked to perfection, they cooled on a rectangular-shaped wire rack my mother person set on the table. She slid into the seat by Ben and Emmitt as Harley and I retrieved our saxophones. A few seconds later, we each had a chair and a musical instrument except for my mother person who held a different kind of device — a pastry ladle.

"Before we begin," Ben glanced at my mother person and smiled slyly, "we have an announcement to make."

"What!?" Harley and Emmitt straightened in their seats with faces lit with expectancy.

"Well, boys," Ben began, and then he reached for my mother person's hand and clasped his palm around her precious, flour-coated fingers.

Something about them seemed different, and I knew my suspicion had been right. My mother person beamed; she actually beamed with joy. She looked so alive and animated that her positivity resonated throughout every inch of the house.

"We have some exciting news," he declared. And then he paused for a second or two while we held our breaths with anticipation. "In a couple of months, we're gonna be having a new band member!"

"What?" Emmitt squawked while Harley and I sat speechlessly.

"A baby," my mother person intervened. "The Lord's blessed us big time. We're gonna have another member to our little family here! At my age, I wasn't sure it's possible but--"

She couldn't finish her sentence because Harley and Emmitt rushed over and wrapped their arms around her. And the next thing I knew, I had been pulled into their embrace. As she hugged the three of us – wrapping her warm, soft, maternal limbs around her three, skinny afro-headed boys, – I swam in the abyss of Otis's joy. I felt his enthusiasm for a new life and the overwhelming abundance of love he had for his family.

"What about me?" Ben gushed. "I'm gonna be a new Paw! Can I get in on some of this?'"

Slipping out of his seat, Ben huddled before us and wrapped his long, protective arms around our entire family. And for a few seconds, time serenaded my heart. What I experienced at the moment eclipsed my core of self-centeredness and narcissism. I felt contentment, true contentment; a blessing that was pure-hearted, selfless, and strangely surreal.

I reveled within the moment. I reveled in experiencing this Otis person's bond and the happiness he felt for his parents, and I reveled in the glorious scent of cinnamon-rich apple fritters and supper on the stove that was either chicken and dumplings, chicken pot pie, or some other yummy chicken concoction. Rejoicing within the moment, completely immersed in another place and time, I suddenly heard the *Psoooo. Psoooo. Boom! Boom! Boom! Boom!* of mortars and rockets. And within the wisp of an instant, the ephemeral illusion had disappeared.

Ka-BOOOOM! A bomb detonated just behind me. This one seemed larger and louder than the others. It hit close, sucker-punching mother earth's fertile farmland somewhere in the vicinity of a hundred yards to the east, maybe two. *They're closer. If I don't do something, Otis is going to be killed here and now.* Planking against the damp earthen basin, I glimpsed back just in time to see a bombardment of body parts (actual dismembered limbs and lives) raining onto the field, and I wondered if anyone could have survived such an attack.

I had to do something. I couldn't just lay there and allow this Otis person to be shot or taken hostage, not after what I had done. I had no time to think, just react. Scoping the muzzle of my M16 directly into a flashpoint of oncoming fire, I threaded my finger onto the trigger, steadied my nerves, and then I methodically pulled the trigger. Without even thinking or concentrating about what I did next, I adjusted the site towards the second flashpoint, then the third, fourth, fifth, and sixth, and it reminded me of an arcade game I played at the fair (point and pull, point and pull) only this time the only prize was the wrath of someone receiving my bullet. I'm not sure if I killed anyone or stopped them from firing back. All I knew was that I got caught up in the moment of kill or be killed, and my will to survive superseded surrendering my life.

And it was then – as I lost myself in the barrage of return fire – that I heard my radio transmit, "Betty Davis, Betty Davis 23rd Inf. 82nd airborne coming in with some hugs and kisses for them Clyde's in field 2-10 Cherry. After that go to Field 10 Echo with a helo Hail Mary on Old McDonald's farm. Make'n it a quickie. Coming in low and fast, so get your arses up and out there. Bring casualties and try not to get any more of us--"

The voracious roar of a fleet of F-4 Phantoms descending from the west drowned out the transmission. They came in fast, dipped quickly, and obliterated the attackers with a barrage of bomb blasts. And if that wasn't enough of a joyous sound, what I heard next was equivalent to a church choir. The spectacular *whump-whump, whump-whump, whump-whump* of helicopter blades let me know six or seven UH-1 copters (Huey's) sailed overhead. They buzzed by, releasing an array of smoke canisters on a neighboring farm, signaling our rendezvous.

Gotta do this! I told myself. *Gotta make it over there!*

The moment I stood, I saw twenty-five or maybe even thirty other Marines (all in the regiment of the 23rd) jump up and proceed towards the smoke funnels in a crouched position. Following their lead, I mimicked their crouching as I took off in the same direction. Somewhere to the north of me, I heard the *ra-rat-tat-tat ra-rat-tat-tat* of gunfire but couldn't tell if it was friendly fire or foe. Instead, I grasped how my boots made an unusual slopping with each step that sounded like foot farts. If it had been another time and place in my life, I might have thought it humorous and laughed to myself, but there is nothing fun or funny about running for your life.

I confess here and now that I was terrified. My thoughts flurried into moths with plucked wings while my heart pummeled my ribcage in pure panic. *Go!* I pushed myself. *Go! Go! Go!* Go! And then I reached a slight plateau before the field, and my panic and fear were eclipsed by what lay before me. A grove of tangled bodies glistened under the refraction of a thousand moonbeams. They lay sunken into the earth in varying degrees. *There's so many of them,* I kept thinking, *so many wasted lives.*

Nobody can imagine how horrifying it is to wake up like that. To wake up in the middle of a war zone, hearing and smelling and witnessing so much death. Seeing things like amputated limbs, scattered debris, burnt off faces, leeches the size of river snakes, and the wretched stench of burnt skin. Everywhere I looked, I witnessed the carnage of war.

Gotta do this! I told myself as I trekked towards the Hueys. *I have to make it!* And then – just after the first helicopter made ground, as I sprinted towards my (Otis's) salvation, – that is when I heard him.

"Over here!" someone frantically bellowed. "Please help! Help! We're over here."

I don't know if it was me that made the decision or, somehow, the residual will of the true Otis, but instead of saving myself (William Walsh) I turned around and ran back.

The guy who called out was a medic of some sort who needed help rendering aid to an unconscious Vietnamese woman. "Please," he asked desperately, "you gotta help me. I'm shot and can't get her up. Gotta get her over to—"

I wasn't sure what to do. I didn't want to get mixed up in something over my head. After all, helping a Vietnamese person in the middle of a bloody battle in the Vietnam War went against my every instinct. I just wanted to get on the Huey and get the hell out!

This is real! I kept thinking. *Somehow this is real. This isn't a dream or something from my imagination. These are real bodies. I saw them get blown up. I saw them die. I witnessed it firsthand. This is very, very real, and I'm in danger. And if I'm in danger, that means this Otis person is in...*

That is when the realization occurred. Not just any realization, what I thought of that day could only be described as immoral, if not despicable. Never in my life could I imagine fathoming such a thing, but

I did, and to this day I can't deny it. I had a temptation that could remediate my problem and fix everything. *I can keep my promise to Liz. If this Otis person dies here, then it's over. He ceases to exist and dies a hero. He won't be in the powder-blue sedan with tipped-tail lights. We won't pull him over. I won't shoot him. Riley won't stash the gun. Riley and I won't be at the intersection the moment the distracted trucker hits us. Riley will still be alive, and I won't be in a coma on the brink of death. I'll hop back into my body, learn my lesson, and move on. I can fix this. I can change the timeline and fix everything.* Then I remembered Ruby Josephine's heed, "You're on the fencepost, William Walsh. H&H!"

The woman woke long enough to cry out something in her native language. I couldn't understand what she said because her dialect and articulations seemed so foreign and strange. As a matter of fact, everything about her seemed unusual.

That is when I had the second epiphany. It was all right there. The similarities were too blatant, the message entirely too clear. The situation had somehow transpired into a parallel predicament of the day I shot O.C. I stood at the chasm of time, reliving how I reacted and what I did led to the life or death of another human being. It mirrored the day I shot O.C. with the exception that she was a small Vietnamese female instead of a large-statured Black male. This dream of mine, divine intervention, or time-warp into a parallel universe could lead to alternate realities that affect so many lives, and I was about to do it again. I almost let a preconception of race and culture taint how I reacted when in fear. After everything I had been through and all the guilt I had felt, I was about to make the same mistake. Letting her die would have been like shooting Otis all over again. And this time (for, perhaps, the first time in my life) I stowed all of my preconceived notions aside.

"Please be careful," implored the Marine who tended to her. "Get her to the Huey! She's important. She's… to the war. We need her."

If I was in my (William Walsh's) body, I don't know if I would have been able to do what I accomplished that day. Luckily, this Otis person was a mammoth of a Marine. Without saying anything, I sank to a knee and slung her over my shoulder.

"Hurry and get her over there!" the guy pleaded as he staggered to his feet. "I'll be right behind. We need to get her…" And the guy fell.

I don't know if I infused with adrenaline, fear, or a little of each, but once I had her on one shoulder, I heaved him onto the other then lifted the both of them off the ground. And then I hiked towards the pasture where the first helicopter prepared to take flight. *Please wait,* I pleaded as I trudged over a barrage of divots in the pockmarked ground. *Please don't take off without us.*

Step by step, this Otis person's boots lumbered through the blood-drenched paddy field, over ruts and rocks and uprooted stems, with legs that steeled with strength under the weight of two grown human beings. That's when I had my third epiphany. *This is crazy because it's all I ever wanted to do. As a police officer, I wanted to help people and do something heroic. I wanted to experience the glory of being a good guy. It's crazy because it's taken me a long, arduous journey to get here, but I'm actually helping people. I'm saving lives.*

The rotors quickened, indicating the Huey prepared to take flight. As I approached the whirling blades, a part of my brain feared an imaginary beheading, but I didn't have time to think or react. The door opened, and the gunner leaned out, operating an M60-D.

"Hurry!" he called to me from a packed inside. "Hurry the hell up! Get over here!"

The moment they pulled the medic and the Vietnamese woman from my shoulders, the weight of the world melted away. *I did it!* I rejoiced. *I saved them! I got them to the copter and safely inside!*

In the wisp of a blade revolution, my moment of accomplishment was taken. The instant my hand latched onto the lift rail so I could climb inside, a guy with the nametag Corporal Hughes rotated an M16 on me.

"No Can Do," Corporal Hughes ranted. "Y'all gotta move! Get down! We're past capacity. You're just too big and too--"

"Let him in!" the medic I aided called to them. "He saved my life! He saved the life of Dr. Lê. He carried us both--"

The door to the Huey remained open, enabling me to overhear Corporal Hughes' swift response as it rose from the ground. "Ain't never risked my life for no Colored person and reckon I never will!

Later, nigger."

A part of me thought about grabbing onto the cargo winch and doing something crazy like pulling myself onto the rung, but I stood frozen. Something about the irony caught me off guard. Something about the sheer racism brought me back to my life, to me, William Walsh. *Thank God, I was never like that! I'm nothing like him. I made a mistake out of fear, not racism. It was a mistake.*

Hearing the *whump-whump, whump-whump* of whirling rotors, I stood in my blood-soaked uniform, watching the helicopter rise into the air before taking off and voyaging across the skyline. The bright blinking lights and thumping rotors streamed in the direction of Khe Sanh Combat Base, and I found it odd that it reminded me of something. The *whump-whump-whump* reminded me of a foot tapping – *his* foot tapping. The tapping the day we sat at the long wooden table in the kitchen, holding instruments while reading from the ole timeworn sheet of music. We were practicing again, and Ben tapped his foot, ensuring Harley and I stayed with the beat.

As my body sank to my knees – as I knelt in the war-torn wreckage that had once been a plentiful pasture where animals grazed with leisure and ease – I disregarded the circumstances and hellishness around me as I went back. I went back into his memory of that happy night when life was simple and serene, and the apple fritters were warm, buttery crisp, and straight out of the oven.

Harley's heel smashed the top of my shoe. We sat side-by-side, holding our saxophones, harmonizing to "When the Saints Come Marching In" on page 122. Never in my life had I heard music like that or played a musical instrument, yet there I sat somehow playing the song. As this Otis person, I could decipher music on the page. It felt bizarre. I somehow knew how to fiddle my fingers and apply the correct pressure to produce notes. *I'm doing it!* I kept thinking. *I'm playing an instrument! I'm following along with the song!*

Ben commandeered his usual chair in front of us as our conductor and Dad. His foot tapped out the beat while his arms orchestrated the pitch of each note by raising and lowering his right hand.

"Harley, you're a little flat. Raise it. Uh-hm. Uh-hm. That's good. Sounds beautiful."

"O.C., you're doing fine! You got it. Hold it. Okay. Perfect!"

Before we reached the bottom of the sheet of music, Ben motioned to Emmitt, who eagerly reached his lanky little arm out and turned the page, inadvertently jabbing his elbow into Ben's ear. Ben ignored it as he smiled approvingly at Emmitt who sat up straighter, ready for his next chance for a page turn.

And while all of this was happening – as Harley and I produced harmonies that filled the ramshackle abode with the rich bluesy melody of an old-time jazz classic – my mother person settled across the table in a hand-stitched blue denim smock and colorful headwrap. Her eyes shined as she performed the unfathomably glorious task of glazing apple fritters. One by one, using a pastry bag fashioned out of a folded sheet of wax paper, she meticulously coated each fritter in whirling layers of buttercream swirls.

She glanced up and caught sight of me watching her. Instead of admonishing me to pay attention to my task at hand, she winked at me, and then she lifted the biggest apple fritter (the one I eyed with eager expectation) and pretended to take a bite.

No! my stomach screamed in panic.

Chuckling out loud, she muttered, "Lord, child," before returning it to the cooling plate.

Sitting back in my chair, I took in the moment. I took in the maternal love and the mischievous gleam in my mother person's eyes. I took in the delicious scent of freshly-prepared apple fritters. I took in the paternal pride and patriarchal affection that gleamed in every crook and crease in Ben's weather-beaten expression and gingerbread eyes. And I took in having brothers. Emmitt with his curly eyelashes that bowed at the end and Harley who – even while playing a sonata of soulful jazz melodies – still had the yearning to prank smoosh my toes like brothers sometimes do. The music we produced that day was gutsy, moody, and soulful mixed with heart. Being able to play an instrument felt like an awakening of a creative side of me that I never knew existed. It was so empowering, liberating, and stress-releasing.

The pressure on my toes intensified. The bridge of my foot began to ache. Then both feet began to ache. And then the memory started to fade as I returned to the blood-soaked mud-drenched uniform, back to kneeling in a rice field, back to running from my own demons as I returned to a lovely little nightmare called Vietnam.

No sooner had the landing skids of the second UH-1made ground when I observed a flock of fellow service members running, limping, and crawling in the direction of the open bay door. I had just reached for the pull bar and hoisted myself onto the lower rung of the ladder when my decision to seek safety somehow became overridden by the true Otis. It had to be Otis because what happened next was the last thing I wanted to do. My boots leaped off the ladder and made ground, and the next thing I knew I had taken off in the direction of my fellow service members who needed help.

What the hell? Why am I doing this? Why am I going back? This must be what really happened, and I can't stop him or alter his timeline. I have no choice but to return and help these people.

Everything warped. Going back like that marked another instance when I felt the instincts of the true Otis override my intentions. It was still me in his body, but I wasn't so much the navigator as a passenger in this part of the ordeal. I felt my legs running. I felt my feet striding over the rocks and ruts in the pasture. I felt myself stumble and almost fall. I felt breath barreling in my lungs, but it wasn't my decision. He had somehow retaken or retained control. He had somehow (either by the memory of the actual events that occurred that day or some divine intervention) made it back to help the fallen and began to render aid. And – just as he had done the time before – when I came across two badly-injured soldiers, he bent to a knee, carefully slung each of them onto my shoulders, and then rushed them back towards the Huey.

Is this guy stubborn or stupid or what? If he keeps this up, he will surely die. Here I've done everything to keep him alive to fix things the right way, and he's sabotaging my every move. Maybe I should let him. If he dies here and now, it's not my fault. I'll go back to my old life and redo the events that day. He won't be around, so there will be no shooting, no throwaway, no accident. I'll go back to being Riley's partner, and my life will return to normal. I won't be on life support attached to that Godforsaken machine.

But, frankly, the idea of intentionally letting this Otis person die didn't sit right. It felt shady. It felt wrong. So I opted to do my best and assist him in making trip after trip, rescuing injured and unconscious Marines as we loaded them onto the third UH-1 then ran back to fill up the fourth. It wasn't until all of the casualties had safely made it onto the copters that Otis permitted himself to board the very last ride.

The rotors quickened, and the Huey took flight. The whirling wind that resulted lashed my face as hundreds of microscopic particles of dust and debris battered my eyes, momentarily blinding me. Never in my life had I seen more clearly. Saving people, rescuing my fellow soldiers, assisting the wounded, bringing the fallen home (everything I had done in the short span of fewer than forty minutes) is what I had intended to do when I became a police officer. I wanted to help people. I wanted to be someone children yearned to emulate. I wanted to be a good man.

Perched on the Huey's ladder as it rose into the air, I looked down at the field and no longer saw only destruction and death; I saw how this Otis person was a good man. Without his help, dozens of soldiers wouldn't have made it home.

"Whatcha doing setting your nasty, blood and mud-stained, big-as-a-boar behind on my rack!" a pale, lanky-thin, and very disgruntled PFC grumbled after we landed.

Two minutes before, I entered the barracks, clueless as to where I should go and what I should do. This time-travel, daydream gone wrong delirium nightmare had the noodles in my brain twisted in knots. One minute I sat at a kitchen table, indulging in the sweet deliciousness of fresh-out-of-the-oven apple fritters, and the next I returned to my battlefield trench in Vietnam.

"C'mon now. If you had to flop on a cot and take ten, why didn't you sit on one that's not assigned? Why'd you have to pick the finest one here? Didn't ya sees how righteous it had been made? That spread had to be the nicest, sweetest, tightest tuck-n-bundle you'd laid eyes on since yer days in boot camp. I got talent; I'm telling you. Takes a lot of twang to make an old military cot look this good."

"Sorry," I grunted as I got up and collected my gear, "I—

As soon as I stood, the guy rushed over and frantically smoothed any wrinkles I inadvertently made in his gray wooly blanket.

"Gotta keep it clean. Gotta represent this here nice looking Arkansas stud and let everyone know that us hillbillies not only gots it in the bed making department, but we's also mighty easy on the eyes." And then he smiled, displaying a sparkling-clean set of hamster-sized teeth.

"Joe Delany." The guy in the next cot offered his hand for me to shake it. "Guys around here call me Cracker Jack Joe."

"Otis Meriweather." It felt weird saying that, actually using his name.

"Welcome to U.S. Marine garrison Khe Sanh or (as I like to call it) the royal palace with big hairy balls. Been here about eight months, so I guess I'm what you'd call one of the lucky ones. Not bad. Safe and the food's pretty good. There's a constant supply of tobacco, and I got a line on alcohol or whatever your poison is, so if you need anything just let me know."

"Okay," I said. I didn't know what else to do, so I stood there, holding my duffle, wondering how much longer I would be in this charade.

"And this here handsome hillbilly is Private Motts."

The skinny guy who made the squawk about messing his cover stood and shook my hand as if he were excited to be my new best friend. If I had to describe Motts, I would say he was a combination of Frankie (the kid with crutches from Otis's high school) and a golden retriever.

"Motts looks a lot older than he is, but he's only eighteen. And from the way he acts, you can imagine it's his first time away from home. His mamma's probably lactating as she misses him and--"

"Don't be talken' about my mamma," Motts snapped. "She's the finest mother in the whole damn state of Arkansas. Probably the whole country. And besides, I'll be nineteen at the end of the month."

"Nineteen's still young," Delany chuckled.

I chuckled too.

"Not *that* young. Once I'm nineteen Lorelei's mamma said I'd be old enough for us to get hitched. Lorelei's somethin' else. *Ooh wee*! She's a Bentonville beauty. I'm gonna go back home and marry the girl of my dreams and…" His face squished into a scarecrow swagger. "…get to making them babies!!!!"

"Making babies," Delany chuckled again. "You's thinking about the baby-making part of it and not all the work that goes with caring for a family."

"*Ahem*, if you don't mind." I tried my best not to interrupt as I waited there, shaking my duffel bag.

"Oh, yeah." "Hey Tank," he called to another Black guy, two rows over on the other side of the barracks. "You gots a new one. Fresh out of battle for your pond."

Pond? I wondered.

And then my thoughts became interrupted by the haloing silhouette of the largest, darkest man I had ever seen. Otis was big, but this guy had to be six inches taller than Otis and at least eighty pounds heavier. He took up so much space that he had to turn sideways and slide, shuffle-stepping between the narrow row of bunks.

"Don't forget if you need anything, I can hook you up," Delany prattled before I left. "Weed, smokes, uppers, downers, a blowup Bonnie. Whatever your—"

"Shoot, them dolls don't work none. My inflatable Lorelei lookalike popped the very first day. One little lip smack and she burst to smithereens. Still waiting for my refund. Besides, if you gots all that clout, why don't you end this here war so I can get home and marry the lovely Lorelei. You make it sound like you's got--"

Delany grabbed ahold of a nearby pillow and chucked it at Mott's head. "Lactating. I'm telling you. I can practically smell the milk drip."

"Over here," Tank called from three racks over. He summoned me with one hand while his other massive mitt delicately covered his chest pocket. "New spot just opened up. It's a good one, but I hear you deserve it by what happened."

As Tank led the way, his voice became drowned out by the sounds of activity inside the barracks. One guy played a rock song on his portable radio. Another listened to news from Saigon. A couple of guys huddled around a running poker game, joking and jeering and having a good time while a pack of others leaned into a cracked window, smoking *cigarettes*. And I could tell that most of the guys there seemed pretty young. Several hibernated on their cots as if beaten by the war. One guy lay so still; he practically looked dead.

"He's alive," Tank exclaimed as if he had read my mind. "Recovering. Lost half his battalion in a mishap with friendly fire. He won't talk about it, but everyone knows it's Hughes' fault."

"Corporal Hughes?" I asked, remembering the incident with the first Huey.

"Yeah. Don't know how he made rank. Seems to me he's better at getting us killed than…" Tank paused and pointed. "Right there. The one by the window with a panoramic view. Only six bunks in the dorm got luxury views like that!"

Looking out the window, I saw twenty-five yards of glorious weed-infested dirt that led to the edge of a precipice.

"You earned it after the day you had."

Someone's belongings were on the bunk (a pair of sunglasses, a box of mail, and a draped towel), indicating ownership.

"It already belongs to—"

"Beetlejuice won't be coming back. Chaplin should be here in a minute or two to collect his stuff. After that, it's all yours."

"What should I do in the meantime?"

"Don't know about you but after a day like that, I'm famished. We'll stow your stuff in an empty supply locker until we get back. Let's go to the mess hall an' rustle some grub."

Following Tank's enormous form, I wove back through the long narrow row of bunks, through the crowd of soldiers sleeping and reading and milling about towards the front of the barracks. When we neared the cot where I temporarily rested when I first walked in, Delany called out, "Hey Tank, where you two headed?"

"Just out for a stroll," Tank attempted to skirt the issue, "back in a sec."

"Chow Hall's secured," Delany sputtered. "Been closed for hours."

"What'd you mean?"

"Don't BS me. You ain't going nowhere else. You so hungry you look like a bear coming out of hibernation."

"Is that a size reference or race innuendo?"

"That's a growling stomach innuendo. I could hear your stomach rumbling from ten feet away. Besides, I'm starving too. They should let Boxer keep it open at night."

"If they did that, you'd be in there robbing it blind like you 'appropriate' all your other supplies. In the meantime, we'll be back. Gotta get a little something-something for Tater Tot." Smiling slyly, Tank patted the front pocket of his shirt. "When she gets hungry, she starts testing her lungs."

"Crap," Delany groaned, "not another stupid--"

"Never mind you and how many critters I save."

"Hey," Motts whispered secretively. He sat up with no shirt on, displaying a ribcage that resembled paper-mâché over piano strings. "Ya'all sneaky-sneaking for some grub. Can I join ya? I'm mighty hungry too! Can't let this here body go on account of Lorelei likes her men on the Herculean side."

"No!" Tank snapped.

"No!" Delany snapped.

"Herculean?" I scoffed.

Not wanting to draw any more attention to the others in the barracks, Tank silently hand-motioned the “let’s go” sign, and the four of us clandestinely crept out the door. Not even fifteen feet away, we spotted a roaming night patrol, so we ducked behind the generator box and waited for the pair of them to pass. Once the coast had cleared, the four of us journeyed into the massive sparsely-lit encampment.

Scurrying alongside buildings, we passed three structures, and a row of dumpsters before we came across a chain-link enclosure where we slipped into the back of a structure through a door labeled “Mess Hall Supply Room.” Three minutes after that, our little clique sat at a back table, feasting on a smörgåsbord of cold cuts, salami sandwiches, and an eclectic selection of leftovers.

“Boxer’s the best. He’s a cool dude. So glad he hooked us up.” Delany prattled.

We all nodded in agreement because we liked the concept of free food.

“He’s always looking’ out for us. Always letting us sneak leftovers and making sure anyone who has a birthday gets cake.”

“Lorelei's a good cook also. She cooks the best bologna sandwiches I ever had. Sometimes she puts barbecue chips in them for flavor and crunch. This’s good, but I miss Lorelei’s cooking. I miss the way she puts mayo next to my chips, so I have something for dipping.”

“Is that why you’re so skinny?” Tank scoffed in dismay. “Cause you’s been living on bologna sandwiches and chips!”

The three of us chuckled.

“I ain’t skinny. I’s what you call feisty. It’s in fashion. All the famous rock stars are built like this.”

Tank sat befuddled, shaking his head in amusement as he broke off bits of meat and fed whatever resided in his pocket.

“Lorelei tried to make fried chicken once. Burned it so bad it looked like deep-fried clumps of tar with itty bitty bones sticking out.”

“Ouch,” Tank cut in, “it should be a crime to burn fried chicken. I actually think there's some places she could go to jail."

Motts ignored him. "Hardest thing I ever did when I ate that stuff."

"You ate it!?!" Delany gasped.

"Tasted like the crud from the bottom of an oven, but 'course I ate it. I didn't want to disappoint Lorelei."

"If she can't fry chicken, what can she cook?"

"Just sandwiches, but she's good. She knows how to cut the crust off the bread and cut them into little squares."

"Oh, Lord," Tank groaned. His eyes bobbled in dismay. "You's thinking of marrying this girl who can't cook none who can only make--"

Tank's furry little friend peeked over the edge of his pocket, looked around, and then used its tiny kitten claws to climb onto his massive shoulder.

"Well," Tank announced meagerly, "I'd like to introduce you to Tater Tot!"

"It's cute now!" Delany said, "but in a week or two, that thing will be howling and crapping all over the place! Can't stand cats. They're nasty!"

Tank bowed his head. "I'll train her. She—"

"You'll train her to what? Make less stinky poops! Cat poop stank can ruin the morale of an entire—"

We heard tampering of the doorknob. Without saying a thing, we immediately silenced as we hunkered down to the floor. Tank grabbed ahold of Tater Tot, cradling her into his chest. The door to the front of the Mess Hall opened, and a flashlight of a roving patrol scanned across the room over our heads. We all remained silent. Nobody said anything. Nobody breathed. Not even Tater Tot who remained contented and safe inside Tank's protective embrace.

When we returned to the barracks, I found my cot had been cleared of the last guy's possessions. I was exhausted. Delany, Tank, and Motts were kind and welcoming, but after a day like that, I wanted nothing more than to unpack my belongings and get some shuteye (hopefully returning to my real life). However, when I reached into the last pocket of my duffle, I discovered something that had my mind spinning with intrigue. I found Otis's carefully-stacked bundle of mail.

Curiosity had me under its spell. Therefore, I spent the last twenty minutes before slumber, catching up with his life. Within the letters from his family, I ascertained another baby had been born: a little girl this time! That my mother person and Ben were over the moon while Emmit and Harley spent a good deal of time teaching her how to make bizarre animal sounds. That Ben had jumped ship from jazz and befriended a new aspiring Blues singer named "Muddy Waters," and together their band had gone out on tour on the soon to be famous Black Chitlin Circuit. And, even more awesomely, Harley had moved up a grade in preparation for college.

And then I opened the last letter in the carefully bound pack; the envelope with the swirly cursive writing that smelled like honeysuckle on a springtime afternoon.

DEAR OTIS,

THANK YOU FOR WRITING. I'M HAPPY YOU'RE DOING WELL AND CONTINUE TO PRAY FOR YOUR SAFE RETURN. THINGS AROUND HERE HAVE BEEN GOOD. I JUST GOT A JOB AT SEARS, ROEBUCK AND COMPANY AND HOPE TO WORK MY WAY TO MANAGEMENT. MY DREAM IS TO SOMEDAY OWN MY OWN LADIES BOUTIQUE. RODNEY'S DOING WELL AND SENDS HIS REGARDS, SO DO OUR OTHER FRIENDS FROM AROUND HERE. AND, NO, WE'RE NOT DATING. SOMETIMES YOU ASK THE SILLIEST QUESTIONS. MY HEART IS ALREADY SET ON SOMEONE. HURRY HOME SO YOU CAN BUY ME THAT PAIR OF SHOES YOU OWE ME.

VERY TRULY YOURS,

MISS MABEL MORRISON

P.S. MY FAVORITE FLAVOR OF ICE CREAM IS STRAWBERRY

P.S.S. JUST FINISHED *THE SOULS OF BLACK FOLK* – ABSOLUTELY AS GOOD AS YOU SAID

P.S.S.S. DEFINITELY, CHICKEN AND DUMPLINGS!

P.S.S.S.S. MY HEART IS SET ON *YOU*!

In the cold of the night whilst not even the smallest thought formed, I awoke to the electrifying commotion of an explosion and shattering glass. Amidst the turmoil of bellows and screams, the realization formed that we were under attack. The date: January 21, 1968. The time: 3:34 a.m. The place: Keh Sanh Combat Base (KSCB) Vietnam.

The front portion of the barracks took the hit. The rooftop caved in while the power went out, providing only a moonlit view of soldiers frantically rushing about the settling debris. Smoke permeated every inch of that place, reducing visibility to near zero.

Numerous events set into motion. Alarms sounded while Tank and a couple of guys dashed over to render aid to those injured in the building's destruction. Once I slipped into my boots, I used Otis's brawn to aid in removing a sizeable portion of the roof that had collapsed. What lay underneath broke my (Otis's) heart. Motts and Delany lay crushed. They were among the five or six killed upon impact. The sight of their dead disheveled forms shook me to my core. Just a few hours before, I had sat at a table with them. We laughed. We shared grub and good conversation. We talked about our dreams. They were good guys who were quirky and fun and had so much living to do. In Mott's right coat pocket, he held onto a letter from Lorelei as if it had been the last thing to course through his mind before the bombs rained.

Under the storm of additional blasts, we had no time to grieve or do anything else besides rescue the fallen. It's around then that it hit me. That is when I realized my great mistake. Not any mistake, I forgot something that could have cost me my life. When I rushed over to render aid, I inadvertently left my M16 in my locker. And I realized how stupid it was to leave something as important as a gun behind during an emergency. I didn't say anything or tell Tank of my blunder; I just headed back to my bunk and found myself more than a little relieved by the sight of my rifle stowed inside the support. But within that fleeting second (while sliding the nylon sling over my shoulder), I glimpsed through the window and spotted something that became a gut punch to my soul.

In the mayhem of death, destruction, and bombs – as Marines

amassed to await orders and defend the lives and liberties of our outpost, – I caught sight of a sole soldier riding off into the distance. Corporal Hughes! The infamous ringleader and racist sped off on a small motorized bike with an attached trailer. *He's deserting! He's abandoning his regiment, abandoning his friends, abandoning his troops! His trailer's loaded with food and supplies! He's deserting his people when we need him the most!!!!*

Then another bomb hit, and I didn't have time to go after him or out him as a traitor, too many lives were at stake. Tank had a bunch of us form a scrimmage line along the northwestern perimeter where the base had taken the brunt of the attack. We had our guns out and were told to shoot anything that approached. Another bomb hit and a splice of debris flung across the encampment and got me, knocking me to the ground.

Pandemonium ensued. Bombs burst. Bullets rang out. People got hurt. And a noise, this strange, earsplitting noise. As I lay there, trying my best just to breathe, I listened to a guy (ten or fifteen feet away) screaming his distress. And then the next thing I knew someone slid their arms underneath my torso and proceeded to drag me back to the interior of the base.

"Gotcha, Soldier!" he declared as he mustered all of his strength to save me. "Not gonna let you die! Don't give up!" he encouraged as he dragged me further and further towards safety. "Don't give up, Merriweather. We're almost there."

And it was then – as my body skidded onto the hard concrete lip of a walkway – that I looked up at my rescuer and recognized his face.

"Dad!?!" I grunted. "What are you doing here?"

He must have thought I had become delirious. It was my father, no doubt, a much younger version of the man I had known my whole life.

SECTION VI

PREPARATION

CHAPTER EIGHTEEN
MILDRED RUDDIBAKER

Clank, swish, clack, whoosh! Clank, swish, clack, whoosh! Floating in a sea of uncertainty, I awoke to the familiar clatter of the machine, ascertaining where I was before I opened my eyes. *I'm back,* I told myself. My throat hurt. My back hurt. As a matter of fact, every part of my body tormented me while my tongue marinated in the wretched flavor of bile (or something equally putrid) that had leaked from my gut, slithered up my esophagus, and soaked onto my taste buds in the tantalizing savor of gastral stew. *I'm back, back in room 242, back to being moored to myself.*

Parting my eyelids, I found Liz in her usual seat. By then, her body formed an attachment to the sturdy, blue upholstered armchair, so much so the cushion would have appeared barren without her. This time, her freshly washed locks had been gathered into a ponytail while her skin glistened without even the slightest hint of makeup. And she had changed out of the mismatched raggedy getup into a burgundy velour jogging suit and matching shoes. *She must have showered in a lavatory here. I wonder if that means she's afraid to go home. Worried if she traveled too far, I wouldn't be around upon her return.*

On the gray upholstered futon, my brother postured, tall, fit, the personification of good living and vitality. Jeremy donned the same sports shirt, same cap, same unkempt beard. Getting a better look at his beard, I could have sworn it had grayed in the short period of time I had been out.

Am I imagining this also? Am I imagining Jeremy's facial hair sprouting grays as if he's aged? Could I have missed it, or could the stress be getting to him as well? And what about these dreams or time travels? Are they figments of a fractured mind? Are they drug-induced hallucinations, or could I be experiencing another man's life? Is that his family? Does he have little brothers named Emmitt and Harley? Does he play the sax? All of the death and destruction during the war seemed so real. Each explosive concussion, the particle storm from the rotors, my stomach fluttering and falling when the Huey rapidly lifted into the air felt as if I was there. Every second of it seemed like the real thing. Had Vietnam been a figment of my imagination? Were Motts and Delany crushed to death, or could it all have been a delusion? Is my brother (Jeremy) really here, or is he back in Dallas managing his patio furniture company?

The gloom on my brother's face confirmed my suspicion. Jeremy was there; I saw it in the depths of his eyes. Those eyes, I knew every speck and nuance inside them. I knew the language they spoke. I knew their happiness, their triumph, their heartbreak, and their lies. I knew those eyes as well as I knew my own. *Stop being paranoid!* I told myself. *Jeremy's here, and even though I may have been a stubborn, hardheaded fool, I know when it comes down to it, my brother has my back. He will always have my back. Even though we've had our ups and downs, Jeremy will do what he can to protect me.*

As my brain frantically scanned iconic images (my brother, my predicament, the stench of antiseptic, and Vietnam), Liz sat slumped in her seat, clinging onto syllables of Jeremy's ramblings. *She looks terrible, beautiful, but terrible. She looks as though watching me die is killing her as well. I can actually witness her heartbreak.*

Jeremy uncrossed one leg then crossed the other. Monopolizing Liz's attention, he entertained her with glimpses from our childhood. He kept rambling and going on, so unlike the quiet, introverted, shy person I always knew. Jeremy had always been tight-lipped when it came to personal information, yet there he sat gabbing and going on as if his life were an open book. It took a moment or two before it dawned on me. This charismatic personality bit was nothing but a ploy to keep her distracted. He wanted to keep her mind occupied and away from the dilemma at hand. So he sat there, weaving one story after another as chapters of our childhood flowed into the room.

"You've always been good at that," I said even though I knew Jeremy couldn't hear me. "You're good with people, not selfish like me. You've always been the compassionate one."

That's when the realization settled over me that Liz would have been better off without me. *We have no children so she wouldn't have the burden of supporting and rearing little ones. She has a good job and is intelligent, personable, and attractive (very attractive). And she'll get my life insurance and pension. She'll be financially and emotionally set. Her family will be there to support her. My brothers and sisters on the force will be there to support her. Her friends, college girlfriends, students, and most importantly, my brother will be there to shepherd her through the dark days and grief. With Jeremy's help, Liz will weather my passing and move on.*

And then I heard a word, one simple word that rattled my senses. Jeremy said something that sounded so foreign and strange. A word we never used, discussed, or even whispered. Something we buried. He used the word "Mom."

Our mother's death overshadowed every part of our adolescence. She didn't die quickly or peacefully in her sleep. She didn't die with dignity. No, our poor mother suffered for two and a half years as she wept, screamed, and cried guttural pleas.

My attention immediately honed in on Jeremy's voice. I didn't know how much time had elapsed (it may have been as little as a minute or two), but I relaxed into myself as Jeremy took me back to a happier time when he and I were kids, our father was carefree, and our mother – our beautiful, vivacious mother – very much alive.

Jeremy spieled about our trip to Sea World and how a sea lion splashed stinky fish water all over my clothes. He told her about family picnics and how Mom and Dad used to dance to slow country songs by Waylon Owens, Guy Campbell, and Dolly Partridge. About how our father picked flowers from the garden and brought them to her covered in aphids and an assortment of other creepy crawlies. How our mother darned holes in our socks, ironed patches on torn pant legs, placed Band-Aids on scraped knees, and tucked us into bed each night after our father read nighttime tales of adventure. He told her story after story of the good times, and then he started in on the days we didn't talk about or discuss. He told her about when our mother was in the same hospital.

It had been her fourth round of chemo, and things had become pretty bleak. Mom lay in bed (barely able to talk or move), while our father remained by her side, tending to her needs. Everyone so lost themselves in taking care of our mother as she wilted and suffered and died in that bed that no one took care of Jeremy and me. Jeremy hadn't had anything to eat in a day and a half, and it got to the point that his stomach rumbles and growls could be heard over the din of Dad, attending nurses, and the hordes of visitors and praying people. So I snuck down to the cafeteria and somehow managed to wrangle a chicken salad sandwich and chips with the little bit of change that I had. That was how I remembered the day. It was just an ordinary errand during a bad time. Nothing big. Nothing phenomenal. However, the way Jeremy relayed what I did almost made me seem noble. He made me out to be selfless and caring. He made me out to be a hero brother. After all the hard times and backlash I had given him about Dad's funeral, and he practically commemorated me in return.

"I'm not a good person, Jeremy. I messed up! You won't believe what I've done! I made a horrible mistake and then helped cover it up with a--"

"Hey," she called to me.

I didn't even know she was there. Slowly opening my eyes, I turned to my bedrail, finding Ruby Josephine perched in her favorite spot with her boots on her favorite place on my blanket.

"Hey to you," I returned, feeling a bit groggy. I wanted to complain about her shoes on my spread but figured *what the heck, it doesn't matter anyway.*

"Welcome back, William Walsh! You look like you were a million miles away!"

In the fog of uncertainty, her words shattered the peace and tranquility of an awakening mind, sharpening my thoughts into focus. "How long?"

"How long what?" she chirped as she sat there, fussing with her skirt.

"How long has it been?"

"Since, when?"

"Since…" Taking a deep breath, I made a veiled attempt to

maintain my composure. Six-thirty the night before I had been given twenty-two hours; I just wanted to know how much of that twenty-two hours I had left. "How much longer do I have?"

"Oh, you mean till they…" She pantomimed a neck slice gesture.

"Yeah. How much time until they pull the plug."

"Well," her face squelched into a rotten milk gag, "I believe you have six and a half hours, but they're gonna wheel you down to surgery in around five."

"Damn, that's not long."

"You're right, William Walsh! Pretty soon they're gonna be cutten' into you and carven' out all them organs and gooey parts until half your insides are gonna be missing. You won't feel it none though on account of you'll already be…" She stuck her tongue and arms out, pantomiming a corpse.

"Thanks," I scoffed sarcastically. "Great visual!"

"Really?" she sang. "Wowzers!" She paused for a moment or two as if contemplating what she wanted to say. "Before I died, I was hotsy-totsy about a part I got in *Pygmalion* by George Bernard Shaw."

Died? I perplexed. *What does she mean?*

"Of course, you probably know it as *My Fair Lady*. I was a peasant girl, and, man-oh-man, it—"

The door swung open, and Dr. Baylor scurried into the room in his traditional doctor's smock and stethoscope. Jeremy and Liz simultaneously rose from their seats.

"Never mind that," Ruby Josephine said dismissively, "It's time you returned to the corridor."

"But I want to hear what Dr. Baylor has to--"

"You already know what he's gonna say, William Walsh." She turned and leaped off the bed rail. Instead of walking in the direction of Liz, Jeremy, and Dr. Baylor, she sauntered over to the side of the room that encompassed the floor to ceiling cabinets that contained an assortment of pillows and ordinary room supplies. Ruby pointed to a wall clock adjacent to the cupboard that I never noticed before. It could have been there all along; I just didn't remember seeing it.

"When did—"

Disregarding my attempt to ask a question, she went on with, "It's ten in the morning now." She directed my attention to the clock. "It takes 'em a while to get you prepped and ready, so they're gonna come an' collect you sometime around three." Her shoulders shrugged while her lips smooshed to the side. "That's just an assumption on my part, but it's a pretty good guess if you ask me."

Gazing up at the wall clock, I observed the second hand ticking away at my life. "Is there anything I can say or do? Any way I can stop this?"

"Naw," she goaded dismissively. "After they load you on the gurney, they're gonna wheel you down the hall here, up to the elevator, and over to the OR. It's creepy there, super crypt-like. Has lots of them newfangled machines with all these funny looking gizmos and do-dads for cutting and slicing." Her hands mimicked cutting and slicing. "Four-thirty's when they'll start the cleaning and prepping. There's a gentleman here (he's a father of three) who's gonna be prepped at the same time. He's supposed to receive your lungs. Ain't an exact match, but it's preordained he doesn't die. He can't. It's--"

"What?" I snapped. "Are you saying he is more important than me?"

"No, William Walsh. It's just that his time's not up. That's all."

"And mine is? Are you saying all of this is predetermined? That we're born with an expiration date already set? That nothing can change that? That *miracles* don't happen?"

"Of course miracles happen, William Walsh! That's a silly thing for you to say."

"Then, what?"

"What I'm saying, *Officer*, is that you really should think about getting that ginormous ego of yours out into the corridor. Time's a-wasting and you have business to attend. There's still a lot for you that happens."

"You mean the celebration?"

"Not quite yet, although you did miss the hoopla with Mrs.

Kravitz' family. Came all the way from San Mateo. Nice people, although her grandkids were a rascally crew. Rambunctious and rowdy, if you know what I mean. Two of her grandsons played hot potato with a filled urine bag."

"Nice!"

"Not nice, William Walsh, but I see you're gaining a sense of humor." She grinned, shaking her index finger. "That's a good step."

"What is so important about the corridor?"

"Think," she hinted not so subtly. Her voice squeaked as it raised an octave. "There's someone you need to see before it's too late."

"Ms. Cunningham?"

"No, William Walsh." She paused and gave me a stern scowl. "You know *who* I'm talking about."

"Okay," my eyes lowered as I replied grimly, "I know."

"It's time, William Walsh. You know what you have to do."

Sitting up from inside myself, I slid off the concrete hard mattress then sauntered over to Liz and Jeremy who were occupied listening to Dr. Baylor as he broke down how he was going to end my life with the utmost mercy and care.

"I'll be back," I relayed to the both of them. "I have an idea. I'm gonna do my best to fix everything and stop this. Somehow," I leaned down and mimicked planting a kiss on Liz's forehead, "I'm gonna make things right.

For the first time, I didn't fret about going through surfaces. Evaporating into the door's firm, wood-planked concentration, I made it to the other side as if it were simply a shadow. Once in the hallway, I found three frazzled nurses frantically trying to coax Ms. Cunningham back to her room. Ms. Cunningham stood in front of them in full theatrical makeup and festooned hair with her walker basket and side rails loaded in a dangling array of shopping bags.

"What do you mean 'I can't go?' I'm checking myself out. Didn't you hear me, dearie?"

"But, but you're not ready!" "You haven't been released yet!" "Your hip still needs to heal!" "The doctor hasn't discharged you!" "It's not time!"

"Listen," Ms. Cunningham declared obstinately, "I'm leaving whether you like it or not. I'm not missing another bridge tournament at the home. All the girls are going, and I've got to be there because Mildred is hot to trot for my Edgar. If I'm not there, she'll try an' steal him! I just found out from Ruth Fienswaugh that Mildred *Whoremonger* Ruddibaker took the courtesy shuttle to the Valley Plaza. She got her hair done and nails did, and she purchased a skin-tight romper with a zipper that goes down to her crouch!" Ms. Cunningham attempted to jostle her walker out of No-nonsense's hands. "To her crouch; I'm telling you. Such a floozy! I'm returning whether you like it or not! I've gotta keep that zipped. Gotta protect Edgar from that man-stealing…."

And then my eyes scanned past Ms. Cunningham as the nurses cajoled her back inside her room, over to the chairs that lined the passageway perimeter. That is where I saw him. He still occupied the chair on the end of the grouping next to Cheddar. I recognized him immediately. Otis Cleveland Merriweather. Otis Cleveland Merriweather encompassed the same spot. This time there was no going back or escaping the inevitable. Ruby Josephine was right: I knew what needed to be done.

"YOU!" He stood in an oversized hospital gown, pointing me out the second he saw me. "What-in-tarnation, are you doing here? How'd you get here? What do you want!?!"

"I…" I wasn't sure how I should go about this. I didn't know what I was doing or why I was there. I just knew I owed this man an apology. "I wanted to say that I'm, I'm--"

"What???" he snapped. And then his big bare feet commenced their approach. He came at me with so much fury that his eyeballs scorched part of my brain. Within seconds, he towered over me. We stood chin to chest. Me and the man I shot; the man I inadvertently shot and almost killed. It was definitely him. I knew that face, those arms, and that scar practically as well as I knew myself.

"I just wanted to say that—"

Bam! I couldn't complete what I was saying because Otis punched me. He actually punched me! It was so fast and spontaneous that I never saw it coming. That one blow knocked me out. One second I stood there trying to apologize for "inadvertently" shooting the man, and the next, I found myself sprawled out on the cold, hard, linoleum floor, nursing what felt like a cracked jaw.

"He's awake!" Ruby Josephine sang out. "Hurry! Hurry! Help him up!"

"Give him some space." Cheddar stretched out his arms. "Move away. He's dealing with a poppen' in his noggin.'"

Opening my eyes, I found the three of them gazing down at me. Otis looked like he wanted to clobber me again. Cheddar looked as though he had seen it a hundred times. While Ruby, – well, if I had to describe the way she looked – I would say she actually seemed delighted! Lying there on the floor, I attempted to collect my bearings. *I got punched!! I got punched in this transcendental journey, time travel dream thing? What could happen next?*

"Nooo, way!" Otis bellowed. "That guy's bad news. He's a racist! I did nothing wrong, and he shot me. He shot me for *no* reason. In fact, that yellow-bellied, chicken-hearted, scoundrel of a lizard pulled the trigger four times!!! Not letting him get away with it. Not letting him get away with shooting me in front of my grandbaby! He's--"

"Sorry," I groaned from the cold, linoleum floor. I'm—"

And *BONK!* He did it again. This time, his big bare foot pummeled my ribcage. I didn't hear any bones break, but I swear it felt like a flying cement truck crashed into my side.

"S,sorry," I groaned through the pain.

Nothing happened, so I looked up and saw Otis deliberating where he should clobber me next. I didn't know what else I could do, so I held my hand in the air in a feeble attempt to dissuade him.

"No!" I gushed defensively. "Please! Come on! I'm trying to—"

His leg flinched in preparation.

This is crazy. How can it hurt if I'm out of my body? Nothing makes sense. Aren't all my nerve endings and muscles back in the me on the bed?

"Shit!!!!" I grunted. "Stop! Can you stop for a minute, so I can—"

Otis smirked as he lifted his colossal, size 14 foot and gingerly balanced it on my throat. Sneering into my eyes, he taunted me, "So you can, what????"

His foot began to apply pressure, and little by little, it got to the point I could barely breathe.

"You can't just apologize for what you did! That doesn't make it right. An apology isn't a magic wand that *poof* makes gunning someone down go away. It doesn't help me. It doesn't help my family. It doesn't help all the families of innocent Black folk cops shoot for no reason. It doesn't help Charlotte and what she's endured. They're empty words. They mean--"

I thought about calling out for mercy. I thought about praying. I thought about begging Ruby Josephine and Cheddar to make him stop. My mind drifted amid a tempest of ideas while my heart knew mere words would have been feckless. I had done a terrible thing: something so awful that nothing I could do would ever make it right. And then it occurred to me.

"Emmitt!" I stammered under the pressure of his arch. "Ethan! Miss Mercy! Pastor Washington!"

"What???" Otis gasped.

The pressure intensified in every crook and crevice of my neck. *Can disembodied people get strangled with a foot? This would be a crazy way to die.*

His eyes spit venom as they bore into me.

"Ben!" The pain reached a level that had me incapacitated. "B, B, Ben… taught… you how to play the s,s, sax!"

"How'd you?"

I couldn't respond; the pain had become too much. Otis relented a fraction of his hold.

"Your m…m… "

He released a tad more pressure.

"Your mom's a good cook. No, fantastic. She makes the best chicken and dumplings, but your favorite is her fritters. Man, she made some good apple fritters."

"How'd you?"

He released his hold until the weight no longer seemed unbearable. His foot remained – ready to crush my Adams Apple at a moment's notice – but the pressure diminished to a delicate threat.

I paused, coughing and gasping for a moment or two, before continuing with, "I know Jimmy-John cornered you in the boy's restroom in high school. He put a noose around your neck, throwing the other end over the stall enclosure. They called you names as Jimmy-John attacked you with the baseball bat. That scar's from when he got your face.

Grabbing onto the back of a chair, Otis tried to maintain his balance as his expression waned.

"And Harley, such a prankster with all that Siberian Snow tiger stuff. Did he make it to college? I don't know the answer to that, but I'm curious. What about your sister? How is she?"

"Leave Maybelline out of this!" His arch stiffened while his eyes welled with anger.

"And I know about the war. I know about the Vietnamese woman you saved. I know about the attack on January 21st and how terrible you felt when the roof caved in killing Delany and Motts."

"How?" He lowered his foot to the ground. "How could you possibly know this? These are details from my life no one could possibly--"

"Remember when Tank had you work perimeter. You were all standing there with your M16's, and that damn scrawny cat crawled onto his shoulder?"

"Yeah," he uttered faintly. "I remember that! I remember that ugly orange and white kitten. What was his name??? Umm--"

"Tater Tot. The cat's name was—"

"Tater Tot," he confirmed with a smirk. By then, Otis stood disorientated. He appeared shell-shocked and confused. "I don't understand. How could you possibly know this?"

"Guys," Cheddar chipped in. "Guys, you may wanna hold off for a second. There's something you need to see!"

"What?" I groaned as I awkwardly lumbered into a stand.

"What?" Otis grumbled.

The door to Cheddar's room opened, and Granny Jin walked out, accompanied by three of Cheddar's brothers.

"Otis," Cheddar exclaimed joyfully, "This is my Granny Jin!"

"What?" I asked lost. "I don't understand. What does she have to do with this?"

"You, be quiet!" Otis snapped at me.

Watching Granny Jin as she stopped to chat with Grey-ear hair at the centralized nurse's station, I thought she resembled someone I knew. "Is she the woman Otis helped?" I cut in. "Is she the woman he carried to the helicopter? The woman he--"

"Saved," Cheddar completed the sentence. "Close, but not quite. Ruby told me about it. The woman you rescued and carried to the chopper that day was a doctor. Dr. Lê saved the lives of hundreds of people during the war, one of them," he smiled brilliantly, "being my Granny Jin."

No one said anything because no one understood where he was going.

"My Moms was in her womb at the time. If you hadn't saved Dr. Lê, my mom and I--"

"Never would have been born."

"I don't understand," Otis perplexed. "I don't understand why *he*," Otis pointed at me "knows all this stuff, and why your Granny Jin just *happened* to be here. This is too much. Too kismet-coincidental. Nothing makes sense."

"I don't understand a lot of what's going on either," I said. "Welcome to the club!"

And so we sat there. Otis and I sullenly sank into a couple of empty seats in the corridor, feeling lost, confused, and riddled with unease. We had nothing better to do, so we watched Granny Jin and the boys as they made their way to the elevator. After pressing the call button, they patiently waited for the elevator to arrive. Just then, the door to room 239 whisked open. Half a second later, Ms. Cunningham darted her Sexton Walker 396 across the hallway, directly into the elevator, just in time to catch a ride with Granny Jin and the boys.

"I'm coming for you, Mildred!" Ms. Cunningham decreed as the doors began to slide shut. "You better hold onto that zipper, cause I'm not letting you steal my—"

Once the doors secured, the four of us waited there, watching the panel tally its descent. Peace pervaded for a moment or two before Otis exasperatingly rumbled, "Now, what?"

Although he wasn't clobbering me, kicking me, or suffocating me with his jumbo-sized foot, I could tell he still harbored a lot of resentment.

"Now," Ruby chirped excitedly. "We wait for it!"

"What?" I asked. "What on earth are we waiting for?"

"A miracle, William Walsh. A rip-roaring doozy of a miracle." And then she tapped her wrist, signaling once again that time marched on as the end of my life drew near.

CHAPTER NINETEEN
MUFFLED MOTORCYCLES

Nothing much happened for the next hour or so. The four of us sat in the walkway, observing the hospital's natural ecosystem as security officers, x-ray techs, food service personnel, a respiratory therapist, sprinklings of doctors, and accumulations of nurses and other staff tended to their duties. When Otis began to get cold (a consequence of being out of body), Cheddar accommodated him with a blanket because they didn't have any robes large enough to cover someone of his size and stature. Other than that, the four of us sat in the chairs, watching the shuffle of hospital scuttle, punctuated by the occasional patient displaying crack.

"You're gonna have to talk sooner or later," Cheddar eventually chided. "Being button-mouthed like this is bogus. Don't work none. In the skateboarding realm, we come up with players all the time who snatch tricks or accidentally slay competitors with an elbow nudge or bogus knockdown, and we pick up our big boy pants and move on. That's what you gotta do. You gotta move on."

"Who does this guy think he is?" Otis asked in dismay.

"This guy," Ruby Josephine intervened, "is international skateboarding champion Hung Luu, but the world knows him as--"

"Cheddar," I cut in.

"So," Otis scoffed, "he's just a kid. Why does he think he can—"

"Actually," Ruby vetted squeamishly, "you may wanna rethink how you label people." Her face squelched. "Hasn't that kind of been an overall theme in your life? Judging people???? Ah, discrimination. For your information, Cheddar may be young, but the little skateboarding company he started in the garage will someday make an impact on the world. He's young, but he's smart. His little invention will one day be worth boocoo buccaneers."

Cheddar nodded his head in agreement.

"How?" I scoffed. "How do you know this? How can you say how much something will be worth in the future?"

"Yeah," Otis commiserated, "it's just getting more and more bizarre."

"My diagonal rods," Cheddar clarified. "Before the accident, I'd been working on a concept to improve performance, even got the forms to make a patent. Hoping someday companies will use them for everyday items."

Otis and I sat stunned and, perhaps, a little envious for a moment or two. "Okay, smart guy, I'll take the bait. Sitting here in this here hallway ain't cutting it, what do you think we should do?"

"Well for starters, I think you could, ah--"

"The nursery," Ruby cut in. "Why don't you skedaddle to the fourth floor and check out all them babies. Nothing like the miracle of birth to balance one's perspective. Marvel in new--"

"Sounds good," Otis said, and then he lumbered his large, massive frame into a stand. "Anything's better than this."

Without so much as another word or goodbye, he strode off in the direction of the elevator.

"Go, William Walsh," Ruby whisper insisted. "Don't let him leave without you. And don't think about romping. If you try and leave..." She repeated her dramatic neck slice gesture.

As I silently lagged behind Otis, I glanced back and saw Ruby and Cheddar animatedly immersed in conversation. They stopped talking for a second, and Ruby tapped her wrist again in her "time's a-ticking'" reminder.

♫ ♪♪♪

Not knowing and, quite frankly, not caring that much for babies, I stood in front of the thick plate of glass and pretended to take in the scenery. The nursery at St. Ann's had nine incubators lined in rows of three; however, only four of the small plexi cubes harbored occupants.

"This here one. Now, that's one handsome baby!" Otis declared assuredly. "Strong. Proud. Very machismo! I imagine someday he'll grow up to be a football stud or a—"

"Mother," I cut in as I pointed out the name placard. "Your little machismo football player's a girl. Her name's Lilith."

"Oh," Otis relayed with a squeamish squelch. "Lilith. Well, I guess no ones gonna pick on her! Good for her."

Otis stood there for a second or two, marveling at the miracle of new life. "Look at that one over there," he said, pointing to the baby in the largest incubator. "He's so tiny! Fight on, little buddy. Fight on--"

"Poindexter," I read his name from his birth chart.

"Poindexter? Ohhh! Now, what kind of mamma's going to name her son something like that! She's just asking for him to get--"

A young woman in a hospital gown entered the nursery, looking confused and maybe even feeble for a moment or two. Then she found her newborn baby girl, and her face warmed with relief. Her hands trembled as she reached into the incubator and picked up her precious petite newborn. She stood clutching onto her beautiful baby girl as a river of grief streamed from her eyes. The sight of this mother and child became so confusing and heart-wrenching. I couldn't understand why she seemed so sad. Turning to Otis, I discovered tears streamed from his eyes as well.

"Why are you crying?"

"The mother's dying," his voice cracked. "She has the cancer."

"How do you know that? You're psychic now? You're able to predict the future?"

"See that patch below her collarbone and the one on her arm?"

"Yeah."

"Those are the same patches they put on my Mabel. One's for chemo, the other's for pain."

My heart quickened. *Mabel's dead? Mabel died of cancer?*

"The purple one's the patch they administered three days before she passed."

Two nurses came in and coaxed the mother out of the nursery. It was an uncomfortable scene in that I felt like a voyeur eavesdropping on the private circumstances of someone else's life. *Isn't that what I've been doing? Eavesdropping on Otis's life? Experiencing his struggles? Being him?* And then the breadth and reach of the circumstances consumed the thought.

They're real! I thought they might have been dreams. I assumed they might have been delusional episodes brought on as a result of the accident or maybe even the medications injected into my veins. Yes, I had my doubts. Yes, I had my suspicions. Everything felt real, but nothing made sense. However, now he's confirmed it. Otis confirmed everything I experienced was real. All of it (his brother's rehearsing, his mother's apple fritters, the events in Vietnam) happened. What does this mean? Has my mind crawled into an old episode of the Twilight Zone? Or could all this be the result of having my brain bashed in or bloated? I'm stuck in bed. I'm on life support. I'm dying. I'm running along a field. Perhaps, this is the process of my neurons fading out.

"Code Blue, Room 242!" an announcement sounded over the public address system. "Code Blue, Room 242!"

It took a split-second for it to sink in. "That's my room!" I gushed before tearing off down the hallway. Otis tore off after me, and within seconds we stood in the enclosed cramped elevator as it descended to the 2nd floor.

"Strange," Otis perplexed, "I feel like this is really happening. I feel my breath when I breathe, the elevator's descent in my belly, and the grated-metal plating of the doorplate on my feet." Otis looked down at his bare feet. "Well, now it's linoleum." He shook his head and scowled at the faux marbled pattern. "I feel it also. I feel the texture, how cold it is, and the tiny particles of grit beneath my toes." His face leveled as he gaged me in the eye. "I've never had a dream that felt like this. I feel myself breathing, my heart's frenzied beat, my thoughts coursing through my mind. Nonetheless, I know none of this is happening. That stuff you said about knowing my family and life details, confirmed it. I'm probably on some newfangled pain killer that's got me messed up."

As soon as the elevator came to a rest, the doors opened, and Otis and I hurried down the corridor; my butt covered by the warm fuzzy robe that adorned me, Otis's mostly by the blanket draping his tall, husky form. Standing outside the threshold of 242, Ruby Josephine and Cheddar frantically motioned us inside. And the next thing I knew, I entered the bustling flock of medical personnel, including doctors Baylor and Skeets who vigilantly tended to the me on the bed as my limbs spasm and trembled. Next to my gurney, I saw the harrowed expression of my wife's face and Jeremy's eyes, and my heart saddened for them. The machine sounded a voracious alarm while my nostrils frothed a funny yellowish-brown substance.

"Man-oh-man, William Walsh," Ruby chirped over the chaos, "that looks gross!"

Otis squeezed his massive frame into the pocket of space by the supply cabinet. He took one look at the me in the bed and became sickened. "What on earth happened?"

Otis and I stood on opposite sides of the bed, dumbfounded and confused, as we watched the slew of doctors and nurses frantically working at saving my body. One of the nurses injected a medication into my IV, and the spasms and frothing dissipated. And then, finally, the shrill rings of the machine became silent.

Liz almost collapsed to the floor. Jeremy braced her shoulders as he carefully guided her back to the blue padded armchair.

"That your family?" Otis noted. "They—"

And it was then that the sound of a muffled motorcycle chuckle could be heard from the adjacent hospital room. Not 240 or 244. No, the distinctive chuckling emanated from the wall behind the machine.

"What the?" Otis gasped in astonishment.

I know that laugh! I've heard it before. There's something about the roguish, almost mischievous pattern that sounds familiar.

And the next thing I knew, Otis walked over to the wall behind the machine and slipped through it. He journeyed into the barrier of plaster, cords, and wall sockets and evaporated into the surface.

This has to stop! Every minute there is a new twist. I can't keep up. I'm floating. I'm dying. I'm getting the daylights beat out of me. Ruby Josephine warns me one minute then seems to be mocking me the next. And Otis, he appears to be going through the same thing (not the time-travel experience into another person's life part of it), but he's out of his body and just as confused as me. Nothing makes sense.

And then I did something that even surprised myself. Instead of remaining in my room with the real me on the bed (instead of consoling Liz and Jeremy, kicking Dr. Skeets in the nether regions, or trying to find the diode to adjust the volume of the machine), I did something unlike me. I walked over to the wall where Otis evaporated into the adjoining chamber and followed him through it.

Otis stood over himself, nodding in disbelief. He had no machine, gizmo, or ventilation tube, indicating he was on life support. Instead, he appeared at peace as he snored from atop his mattress.

"You're not in a coma?" I asked astounded. "You didn't receive a brain trauma or catastrophic event that brought you out of your body?"

"No," Otis declared despairingly, "nothing like that. Had my surgery – what – six, seven days ago. Doc said it all went fine. Supposed to be discharged late tomorrow. Think I'm just taking a nap."

His body looked good; I couldn't understand why Otis seemed so glum.

"Weird," I gasped. "Cheddar said he and I received brain injuries. I thought it was the same situation for you, but…"

I stopped when I realized Otis paid no attention. He resigned to staring at the crowd of guests gathered around his bed. Having overlooked them when I first entered the room, I realized that I knew some of them. They were Otis's family (an older, much taller version of the brothers I encountered through time).

Otis's youngest brother Emmitt sat in a blue upholstered armchair, identical to the chair in my room. *Oh my Gosh, oh my gosh, it's really you! You look the same, older, but the same. I still see the cute cobbled-toed kid I carried over to the restroom; the kid who feared Siberian Snow Tigers, spiders, and the impending slither of poisonous snakes. It's you! It's really you!"*

Emmitt had the same face (same eyes, same curly eyelashes, the same mischievous smile) only decades matured. On his lap, he balanced a matching set of girls who donned similar smiles.

And look! Next to him, that's Harley. I knew I'd heard that laugh. That's Harley's family. Wow, his middle daughter looks so much like my mother person!

She's so bright and cheery. Her happiness imbues the room with joy!

"It's hard," Otis exclaimed remorsefully. "Seeing 'em here like this. My brothers. Some of their grandkids. My best friend."

That's Ethan! That's Ethan, same freckles, same coppery hair.

"Seeing 'em like this leaves me humbled. I just wish…" His eyes welled with sorrow.

"Mabel?"

He nodded in affirmation. "Jackson's a captain in the Air Force, gotta heap of respect for that boy. Two of his brothers followed him into service. Don't see 'em much but they is good boys. Proud of all of 'em. Only had one daughter. Handful growing up that one, but today she's with the Secret Service in Washington, D.C. Still hasn't slipped any Intel, but I hear she's good at her job. That right there's my fourth son."

Otis chin-pointed to the thinly-statured man with waist-length dreadlocks who leaned against the wall, conversing with a nurse. "Abraham's different. That boy started his own computer company when he was just a youngen. Hard worker and smart, always been smart that one. Now, he makes more than anyone I know." He beamed proudly. "Those beads are from his last trip to Tanzania. Kid has so much money; he travels the world for fun."

"Okay?" I cut in, not sure where he was leading.

"Just, hurts." His eyes cast somberly. "Hurts to see 'em like this without her. Every moment aches without the love of my life. Music doesn't even sound the same."

"A little dramatic, don't you think?"

"Maybe. Mable always said I was a big old softy." He looked down as he contemplatively shuffled his feet. "I just… I miss her so much. Ain't easy missing the love of my life."

"How long were you married?"

"Spiritually or legally?"

"What?"

Otis chuckled. "Legally, we got married two years after I returned from the war, but spiritually--"

Otis's response became drowned out by a buzzing inside my ears.

And the next thing I knew, pinpricks of static prickled my skin. I began to feel dizzy, and then my vision faded as I lost sight of Emmitt holding onto his daughters. Before everything went blank, I remember gracefully settling into my body. As I lay inside myself, evaporating into a nonentity of non-thinking, I couldn't talk or see anything. The world around me fizzled as it faded away. And then I heard a voice. Not Liz. Not my brother. Not a heavenly welcoming or the wretched howling from the shadows of death. No, it was Dr. Skeets.

"Sorry, Mrs. Walsh," he abruptly proclaimed, "his heart's having trouble. We must move up the surgery. His organs won't be viable much longer. It's time. Gotta tell them to prep the OR!"

CHAPTER TWENTY
THE SIXTH EVENT

I awoke in a stale reception area of some sort. It may have been a waiting room or lobby; I couldn't be sure. Scents of musk, evergreens, and ocean water permeated every inch of the place, and I found myself choking on an assortment of artificially-enhanced aftershaves and cheap cologne. In the thirty to forty seats that surrounded me, a hodgepodge of different sized and statured men donned business attire; they appeared to be waiting for something. And then I saw a pair of dark well-manicured hands threaded through a briefcase handle on my lap, confirming my suspicion. *I'm back!* A thousand pinpricks bristled my feet. *Back to living another man's life.*

The door to an adjacent room *clicked* and abruptly opened. Everyone in the lobby spontaneously quietened while a lady in linen wide-legged trousers and a cowl-necked shirt positioned herself in the doorway. After she slid on glasses, she ensured she had everyone's attention before calling three names from a clipboard in her hand. Three applicants anxiously rose from their seats then accompanied her into the passageway that led to the innermost portion of the building. Once the door closed behind them, everyone returned to hobnobbing while drinking their coffee and reading newspapers. I had nothing better to do, so I opened the briefcase on my lap and combed through the contents in an attempt to garner where I was and what on earth I was supposed to be doing. Inside, I found Otis's résumé, a facsimile copy of his honorable discharge from the military, personal and business references, an accreditation from an energy institute, and a crumpled sheet of newspaper. That newspaper page (crudely torn from the classified section) ended up being an incremental clue.

Otis is applying for a job. He circled a power company ad seeking applicants for a variety of full and part-time positions. The ad offers training, decent compensation, and flexible benefits. The power company, that's perfect for you. You would be good at that. You're a good worker; I think. Well, I imagine. At least I know you've got the smarts, especially with all the research you put into that paper.

The door opened again, and the cowl-necked woman summoned three additional applicants. The three of them practically flew out of their seats then animatedly accompanied her into the sanctum that I assumed must have been personnel. Once the door secured behind them, I decided to get up and stroll towards a magazine stand. I didn't necessarily want to read anything as much as I needed to get blood circulating into my feet. I feared if I didn't get up and move around, I wouldn't be able to walk right. I sure as heck didn't want to stumble into an interview and ruin the opportunity for the real Otis.

After sauntering by the magazine rack, I made my way over to the water fountain where I partook in a generous drink. And it was then – as I meandered about the place and then back to my seat, – that I appraised my surroundings and the thirty to thirty-five fellow applicants, realizing they were all the same. They were all like the real me. There was no racial or gender disparity. They were an army of all White males.

No, no, no, no, no, not another race thing. Why am I dreaming this or time-traveling here? It's not me, NOT my battle. Besides, I need to go back to being myself. Dr. Skeets wanted to move up the surgery. Any second now, they could--

"Excuse me," asked a stranger in slightly rumpled business attire, "mind if I sit here?" He stood by my chair, gesturing to the vacant seat next to mine.

The guy was another man of color, although he stood five or six inches shorter than Otis and was significantly lighter complected. His eyes were knowing and kind while his skin glistened with a shimmer of wellbeing. The guy had no wrinkles, no discolorations, no knurled scars. He waited for my response while trying to catch his breath.

Once I nodded affirmatively, the guy slid into the chair next to mine, meticulously draping his coat over his lap. His brow had a trace of sweat, so I handed him a handkerchief from Otis's briefcase. As he patted his forehead, he smiled and shook his head as if we knew each other.

"Ride failed to show," he chuckled in disbelief. "Called for service three hours ago, and it never arrived. You know how they is with us sometimes. Here I was showered and spiffy, wearing my Sunday finest for this interview. Cab doesn't show, and I gotta bust a move all the way here. Must have looked like I was running from the KKK, the way I was hauling through the hood in this here suit and all."

Chuckling to himself, he folded the handkerchief and returned it to me. I didn't know what else I should do, so I stuffed it back into the front fold of Otis's briefcase.

"Jim Carter," he introduced himself, extending his hand for me to shake it. "Folks call me 'Jimbo.'"

And it was then – in the brief wisp of time that I shook this man's hand – that I sensed a shift in the room's atmosphere. No one said anything, at least not out loud and not to our faces. However, a sudden negativity – this unknown, unexplainable, force of hostility – seemed to brew and seep into the very air we breathed. And then I witnessed it in their body language. The other applicants prattled with disgust. They stared at us. They leered and sneered and gawked as they remained in their seats with coiled lips and eyes badgered with disdain. As Jimbo sat smiling at me, the entire room tilted with ill will and animosity.

No! That can't be me! It's obvious, so blatantly ridiculously obvious. Of course, I noticed skin color. Everyone notices skin color, but did I stare? Did I don dirty looks? Was I that much of an idiot? Is this the separatist outlook that led to the shooting? Oh, God! Oh, God! The shooting! Suppress that thought! Suppress what happened!

The door swooshed open again, and everyone expectantly silenced. But this time it wasn't the cowl-necked woman or someone from company personnel but rather a gruff-faced custodian pushing a utility cart. Ushering the cart through the sea of faces nodding their approval, he headed over to the drinking fountain where he commenced to scrubbing the apparatus, occasionally sneering my way with flustered scorn.

"Make sure you don't forget the button!" someone commented.

He scowled in my direction, relaying his disgust.

"Get the nozzle twice," another person commented, "germs can stick around and make one of us sick."

Two more trips to the drinking fountain and two disinfectant treatments later, Jimbo and I still waited in our seats. We ended up spending the entire afternoon in that small stale reception area. And then, finally, Cowl-neck opened the door and read off the last two names. Even though we didn't know each other beforehand, lived in different sections of town, and arrived at different times, we were called in together as if having the same skin color made us akin.

The round-bellied, burley-browed man in the captain's chair behind the desk undoubtedly dismissed us before we even strolled through the door. He didn't ask about college or training. He didn't request copies of our references or ask about experience. He didn't even look us in the eyes. He simply provided an insincere, trite, better-luck-next-time statement about how the positions had been filled and how Jimbo and I would receive a call "if anything became available."

"Sir, please," Jimbo practically pleaded, "this is my twenty-seventh interview this month. I need this. Please, I just need a break. I got a family. Promise I'll show up on time. I'll work hard. I'll…"

Just as it probably happened the twenty-six previous times, it didn't matter how much Jimbo pleaded or persuaded. The color of his skin negated equal consideration. It was horrifying to witness Jimbo grovel like that. In our conversation beforehand, he had been so optimistic about attaining a position. He seemed like a good guy who just wanted to do right by his family.

"I'll work through lunch. I can apprentice. I have references and…"

As Jimbo continued his rant, I accessed Otis's work history, recalling how hard he had sought work after the war. Job after job, interview after interview, Otis had been denied one opportunity after the next for *one* apparent reason.

I never realized how difficult it was for these people. Every job I went for I received. Every promotion I requested I got – not because I was better qualified or had some crazy great work ethic – because of the way I looked. My skin color, my ethnicity, has been my golden ticket. I was the first person called into every interview.

I was the first person offered every job. Even as a car salesman when some of the other applicants had prior experience in retail and sales, I was immediately given the position. Was I wrong to overlook something so obvious? Was I wrong to accept opportunities based upon skin color and race? Should I have said or done something differently?

Jimbo and I walked out of there, feeling discouraged.

"Man," he groaned disappointedly, "I was hoping they'd give us a chance, but you know what it's like for us Brothers. Gotta hit the pavement ten times harder."

And then he said something I found peculiar. He didn't complain. He didn't call the company out for blatant biases and discriminatory practices. In fact, he didn't resort to any form of negativity at all. Instead, he quipped, "Good luck, Ole' Boy!" as he took off, walking down the sidewalk. "Sure I'll see your jive-styling beady little head out there sometime soon!"

I stood there for a moment or two – observing Jimbo's perfectly-sculpted head bob and weave through the bustling throng of pedestrian traffic – baffled and confused by the circumstances. Otis had been through forty different interviews and rejected forty different times; it seemed like a lot. Therefore, I made the determination to do something about it. Turning around, I decided to head back into the office of Southeastern Rim Power. With Otis's briefcase in hand, I marched through the door into the inner sanctum, by the desk with the woman in the cowl-neck shirt, and then back into the office of the director of personnel.

"What do you think you're--"

"Before you call security and kick me out, you may want to open that closed-off mind of yours and listen to what I have to say!"

I awoke again. This time my thoughts disjointed as if a disconnect of some sort occurred from the last transcendental memory experience. This time, I came to in the driver's seat of a fire engine red 1973 Chevy Chevelle. Matching stripes draped the massive elongated hood, producing an impact of boldness, bravado, and swag while the interior gleamed with not even a speck of dust. The car was new, no doubt about it; it even had that new car smell. Unable to recognize the street or any of the buildings, I determined it must have been an alleyway or some back road squashed in-between teetering rows of seedy-looking establishments.

As the skyline simmered in swaths of purples and a skirting of orange, I began to feel stuffy. The windows were up, and the air within the compartment riddled with traces of stale cigar smoke and cheap booze. The situation became unfathomable, however, when I discovered what I had on. *What the hell*?! I gasped, shocked, stunned, and more than a little outraged. *What on earth is this!?!*

Inside that magnificent car with the magnificent passenger compartment, I found myself in black, silk, bellbottom pants, a grape-toned shirt, and – the most outrageous part of it all – a pinstriped, silver and pink vest flocked in ruffles! The vest didn't just have a row of ruffles; the entire bodice encompassed layers upon layers of crazed rippled frills. The vest was something my Great-uncle Milt might have worn as part of a Halloween costume. I couldn't understand it. *Why's Otis dressed like this? I look like an overly dressed penguin or one of them sophisticates from George Washington days minus a wig, tights, and heels.* Then I looked down at my feet and saw platforms and about had a heart attack!

The sun crested the horizon. The sky brightened, and I experienced a sudden urgency that I needed to be somewhere. Not me (William Walsh), the Otis me. I had fallen asleep in the floozy penguin outfit outside some seedy honkey-tonk when I should have gone home. *Shoot, after working all day and playing sax at Dirty Dan's, I must have dozed off instead of heading to the house.*

And it all came to me. Mabel and I had gotten married. I was late to my wedding because I purchased a brand new car as a wedding gift for my bride. *The Chevelle, that's when I bought the Chevelle!* I used most of the nest egg saved from the military as a down payment on a small three-bedroom cottage. The little I had left, I scraped together with my salary to buy the car. *I got the job at the power company!?! Wait a minute, how did I get the job at the power company when I remember storming back there and demanding equal consideration?*

Then I remembered getting kicked out. I collected the memory of angular-faced security guards strong-arming me into the lobby while calling me a slew of racially offensive terms. I recollected being threatened with a restraining order and the smug indifference on Cowl-neck's face when she peeked out her office window. Then I remembered sauntering over to the drinking fountain and rubbing my hands on all of the knobs before scurrying out the door.

Shoot! I said to myself. *It's Sunday! I can't sit here and unravel memories now. I gotta get out of here! I gotta get home and take Mabel to church!!!*

I don't know how I did it. I don't know if it was me steering the way, Otis, or a blind combination of both, but once I turned the key in the ignition and slipped the Chevelle into gear, I somehow acquired the ability to drive stick. I had never driven a stick before, but that day, my left foot gained the knack for depressing the clutch while my right hand operated the gearshift. I also knew which roads to take and what direction to go, even though I had no clue what city I was in, let alone if I was in the same part of the country. I just knew I couldn't be late for church because I couldn't fathom disappointing my Mable.

So many oddities came with time-traveling into another person. My feelings for Mabel weren't my own; they were his. But I experienced the whole-hearted joy he felt for her. That's the pull that had me driving a strange car down a strange street, wearing a flamboyantly-strange getup. One high-heeled purple suede platform remained steady on the gas pedal while my eyes stayed vigilant to the world around me.

Sixteen minutes later, I guided the Chevelle down a narrow cobbled street into the driveway of a blue-toned house with peeling paint, a weather-beaten roof, and ramshackle window shutters. Soil filled planter boxes adorned a matching set of window panes while the front door was simply planked pinewood with an attached knob. After parking and exiting the car, I remembered to collect my saxophone from the trunk before walking up to and entering the small humble abode. And then (this is the part that warmed my heart and let me know I was in the right place) I heard the sweetest sound in the world of Mable calling for me from somewhere inside the kitchen.

"Blue," she summoned in her singsongy voice bristled with bossiness, "hang your coat and them grime-coated boots in the closet; I don't want them smelly, smoke-soaked belongings in my nice, clean, purdy house. Wash your hands and get in here. You's got to be starving after working all day and playen' all night. And by the way…" She walked through the swinging door then over to me by the closet where she helped me stow my vest on the hook she tenderly indicated. "Missed you, bunches."

She wrapped her arms around me, and I inhaled scents of something sweet and fruity, something creamy, and definitely something hickory in the bacon or sausage family.

"But I ain't allowing your lateness to get in our way of making it to service!" Her eyes scanned over to the wall clock then back at me. "You got forty-six minutes, to eat, get dressed, and gets out of here. I know you're tired, but them pearly gates don't stay open for those who live by the devil's time."

I honestly didn't have the energy to figure what she meant. I was hungry. Actually, I was more than hungry and became even more so as the smorgasbord of delicious aromas emanated from the other room. My stomach pitched. My mouth watered. My mind practically performed summersaults in anticipation of a home-cooked feast. So instead of questioning her or making a fuss, I nodded obediently, and then I let my nose lead the way to a soul food connoisseur's paradise. Once I sat at the kitchen table, I scooped forkful after heavenly forkful of sweet potato pancakes, freshly grilled sausage, and eggs scrambled with leftover mac and cheese. Mabel sat next to me, and something about the experience of sitting there like that (in front of a plateful of scrumptious deliciousness) felt like home.

This time I awoke on a church pew, donning my Sunday best while my middle back throbbed from the unrelenting surface of the backrest. Pastor Jeremiah Langston Washington stood behind the pulpit, rousting everyone with a lively sermon on virtue.

"Holding onto grudges or any form of resentment will fill your soul with wasted space. It will debride your life of happiness. It will eat away what is good and decent and leave an empty husk of sorrow." He scanned the faces of his congregation. "Can I get an Amen?"

"AMEN!" the people in the pews energetically replied.

"That means learning to forgive yourself as well as learning to forgive others! Can I get an Amen?"

"AMEN!" the people in the pews choired a little more energetically.

"Whether it's something you've done and are sorry for or something someone else has done to you, do *not* hold onto that negative energy. It'll strangle you. It'll make you sick. It'll rob your life of quality. Anger is a disease that steals the ability to love and be loved. Instead of all that, y'all need to fill your souls with the healing power of mercy." He held up a thick black book with ornate, bright golden lettering. "The Good Book shows…"

Having never been a church person, it felt odd to be there. It was my first experience in the house of worship, where I felt something besides an abyss of nerve-wracking boredom. The churches I had experienced as a kid were the kind I had to sit down, sit still, and – God forbid – not say anything. This place was different. People shouted their praise. They belted out songs that radiated positivity. Some even danced in place, clapping and quick-stepping in their pews. It was surreal. Everyone seemed happy.

Floating within the sweetest of slumbers, I found myself in the pleasantest of dreams as vibrant, gritty melodies drifted through my mind. I was in a happy place – cheerful and contented – until I heard a persistent *tack, tack, tack* on my driver's side window. My eyes opened peacefully, and I discovered myself in a predicament that encompassed several things at once.

I had fallen asleep in the Chevelle again after another long night at the club.

This time I donned a fuchsia velour pantsuit (bell-bottoms, of course) with four-inches of metallic fringe embellishing the collar, all the way down the front seam, and the inseams of each sleeve.

And lastly – and probably the most significant circumstance at the time, – a pair of police officers stood outside my driver's side door, donning agitated expressions and snarled grins.

The taller one, Officer Riggs, repeatedly smacked his baton off the palm of his free hand, and I immediately ascertained I (Otis) was in a heap of trouble.

"Massey," he goaded angrily. "Getta gander at what's going on in here! This monkey thinks he's Elvis or something. Ain't them curtains he's wearing?"

"Holy moly!" Officer Massey crooned his astonishment. "Now, I seen it all." He stood there in his 1970's era dress blues, shaking his head in bemusement. "Ain't that a peculiar sight. Betcha he sings and dances if you play the accordion. Betcha if we give him peanuts, he'll do the hokey pokey and poop his pants."

"Officers," I calmly intervened while raising my hands in full sight. (I do not know why I held up my hands like that; I never behaved like that for any police officer as the Caucasian me.) "What seems to be the problem?"

"The problem," Massey snarled, still smacking and grasping his baton, "is we got ourselves a funny looken' nigger who's a car thief."

Riggs got ahold of my driver's side door handle and attempted to open it, but it was locked.

"OUT!" he snapped, staring at me as if I were a flea-infested stray dog with a leaky bladder. "Unlock your door and exit the automobile."

As I reached over and unlocked the door, Massey added, "And don't try no monkey business!"

They cracked up at the pun.

"I'm not a thief," I attested earnestly. "This is my car."

They cracked up again. The pair of them cackled so hard and with so much enthusiasm that for a second there, they reminded me of Riley and me. Not the snide racial insults, the fact that they clowned around and had fun while on duty. And then I wondered how many of the times Riley and I joked around had been at the expense of a minority.

"No, seriously," I attested again, "this *is* my car."

That part, I was sure. Gaining access to Otis's memories, I recounted the events behind purchasing the automobile and how excited he had been to give it to Mabel as a wedding present even though Otis used it most of the time.

"Yeah," Massey grunted sarcastically, "as soon as you stole it, it became yours. Sorry little monkey turd, but you ain't pullin' no fast-talk flim-flam. You's going to jail. Jigaboos around here don't got no money like that. This here's a sweet little ride. Expensive. Hell, I been with the force twelve years, and I couldn't afford a car this nice. Don't insult me."

"Yeah," Riggs agreed. "Don't insult us, jigaboo jungle bunny. The most Coloreds around here can afford is a donkey, or maybe if you's a hard-working, good, little niglet, you can get yourself a fine bicycle. Ya hear me, nigger?"

They laughed again. And then they reached in through the window, opened the door, and shoved me down to the asphalt. As I lay on the hot, filthy surface, I felt infuriated. And then somewhere from another life and time, the following words drifted into my mind: *Rings like a bad dude. Black as hell. Seems like trouble. Just look at him; he has to have a gun! The guy had to be Black, African American, Negro, or whatever they called themselves or was politically correct in them days. The guy was a beast. Almost snout-like nostrils. Darkest skin I had ever seen.*

One of them handcuffed my wrists while the other collected my wallet, helping himself to the eighty-eight dollars in earnings from the previous night. Then they took turns kicking me while laughing. It was the same hardcore belly cackle I heard throughout the entire arrest. They had so much fun kicking me and cracking up that pretty soon a crowd of spectators formed. Some recognized me as Otis. They knew the car was mine and that I worked at the club, but none of them bothered to say anything. No one dared say anything because no one trusted the police. And the next thing I knew, I had been shackled, dragged over to the police cruiser, and secured inside the back seat.

As I sat there with a busted lip and black eye, I saw one of their cop cohorts take off in my beautiful Chevelle. All the way over to the station then all the way over to jail, I remained numb as the pair of them cackled their pompous decrees about how dumb jungle bunnies are, how jungle bunnies can never amount to anything, couldn't drive, and sure as hell would never be able to purchase their own cars. No decent, God-fearing car salesman would dare allow something like that.

This time I came to while steering the Chevelle into the narrow cobbled strip of a single car drive. One second I'm out, and the next I found my hands clasped around a finger-molded steering wheel of a slow-moving automobile. Immediately sensing the danger of almost colliding into the garage, I quickly applied the brake then shifted into neutral before setting the emergency brake. Upon exiting the vehicle, I found myself in jeans and a uniform shirt embroidered with a company logo, recollecting how they paid pretty well but still make jest of Otis's "lame-brained" aspirations that an HVAC company should branch into alternative forms of energy.

While walking up to the house, I saw that the roof had been re-shingled, the shutters had been sanded and painted, and the planter boxes hosted a variety of flowers in various stages of bloom.

"Otis!" Mable dashed out the front door. "Otis! Otis! Otis! You won't believe it!" She had on a white shirt, blue knit pants, and her hair twisted in swirls. The surprising thing, however, is that she was barefoot. Mable, the dust phobic clean freak, had hurried out of the house disregarding her shoes. "Come, come, come, come," she chirped as she practically pulled me onto the porch, "I can't wait to tell you!!!!"

"What?" I asked curiously. It wasn't like Mable to be this over-the-top excited about something and not immediately share the news.

She didn't answer while I followed her into the living room. She still didn't answer when she offered me a chrome-hooked wooden hanger to store my coat. Her mischievous silence continued when she led me to the kitchen table, where a feast awaited of delicious foods. No, she squirmed in her seat as the two of us dined on homemade chicken pot pies with oven-roasted green beans and sliced baked pears for dessert.

It was weird – really, really weird – because I knew I was not there. I knew I lay in a bed in a hospital far, far away in another time. I was not Black, and Mable was not my wife, yet indulging in the experience felt purposeful and, somehow, significant. So I ate up every second of it, literally and figuratively, until my plate sat empty and Mable was ready to share her news.

"Otis Cleveland Merriweather," she crooned impatiently. "I've got a surprise!"

"A what?" I responded. Otis did *not* like surprises; he preferred to ruminate on matters, taking his sweet time to formulate a decision that best suited their needs. I felt his keen sense of unease.

"Well," she started, "before we be getting' to making babies, I've decided it's time for us to get a, a…. Well," she stuttered squeamishly, "a dog." Putting her hands on her hips, she braced for my response.

"A what? I don't like—"

"Lordy, lordy, lordy, Blue," she placated. "You've had a bit of struggles since you came back. It's not your fault; I know it was brutal out there. You saw a lot, and a lot of your friends didn't make it. I just think a little doggie will help with the moving on. Once you've learned how to deal with caring for a small animal and all the attention they need, well, then we can talk about having one of them babies you keep--"

Someone rang the doorbell. Mabel got up and dashed over to answer it. A minute or two later, she returned to the kitchen, cradling a straggly, foul-smelling, matted-haired mutt that appeared to be part poodle, part warthog.

"That is the ugliest, grossest—"

"Miss Allyson found her in the garbage bin behind Mac's Market. She's got no place to live. As soon as we get her cleaned up, we can make her a good home."

Mable brought the ugly ball of matted, stinky fur clumps over to me and placed her on my lap. The poor little critter actually reeked like a garbage bin. As I held her – straight-armed and away from my face, – I felt her tiny little bones quivering. She had two sad, weltering pools of eyes that stared up and into me with complete terror. And then somehow, someway, for some reason, I wasn't grossed out and disgusted by the creature's ugly appearance and putrid odor. Instead, I felt a spark of compassion.

"Dolly," I uttered out of the blue.

"What," Mabel mouthed with a hint of bemusement.

"I think I'll name her Dolly. She's the ugliest creature I've ever seen, but those humungous doll eyes have the ability to melt hearts."

I awoke on stage in front of a large crowd. I'm with the band, sax in hand, playing a jazzy funk-filled ditty while the audience gyrated to the beat. An ambiance exuded that was joyful, sensual, vibrant, and loud – very, very loud. And then I caught sight of a large-statured man staring back at me from the metallic backside of the amplifier. *What the hell?* I gulped when I saw myself (Otis). *What's he got on now?*

In the amplifier's reflection, Otis blissfully played the saxophone, wearing a glitter-embellished golden jumpsuit. Not just any shade of gold – tailored from the lightest, brightest tissue lamé that refracted all forms of light, – this jumpsuit lit up like the sun. Otis looked like a glow-in-the-dark trophy. And if that wasn't bad enough, on top of his head (the pièce de résistance of the trophy costume), Otis sported a bright golden top hat adorned with an array of feathers that appeared to have been plucked from an ostrich's butt. *What's with this guy's sense of fashion? This outfit is, is… It's ridiculous! This is bad! Really bad! Wait, I know this song. I somehow…*

Notes swirled then encapsulated me as I melted into the moment. I played music, beautiful music: foot-stomping, funk-filled ditties that transcended what I was wearing, who I was, and even time. I felt the grit, gravy, and grime of each tune. My saxophone wasn't just an instrument producing tones; it was an attachment of my being. My spirit rejoiced as music unshackled my soul. Song after song, beat by beat, I felt the audience's jubilation, the power of tone, and the liberation of groove.

Shaken awake, I found myself crammed into a passenger seat of a crowded commuter bus unsure of the destination or how I had gotten there. Every part of my body ached while something stank, perhaps the soiled diaper of the nearby toddler who vehemently objected to being constrained. Mable's elbow sank into my abdomen while her head rested on my shoulder. Throughout the entire racket (the bus's engine, the animated woman gossiping in the third row, and the continuous squeaking of the shocks as the bus jostled down the network of rut-riddled roads and highways) and that woman slept like an angel. She didn't snore or drool or talk in her sleep like I did.

Running away like that must have been trying for a woman who had spent her entire life forging friendships and ties. As I sat on that backbreaking, metal bus seat, Otis's memory traced it out for me.

Everything began on a typical church day. Mabel and Otis walked through the door then greeted everyone like usual. She guided them into their customary row (second from the front on the northwest side) while Pastor Jeremiah Langston Washington stood at the pulpit in a starch-pressed suit and dapper tie. Everyone looked their dandiest as they did every Sunday at service. The Holloman sisters wore colorful Afrocentric ensembles accentuated with wide-brimmed hats flocked with feathers and bows. The elderly Steelers fan wore pants so high on his waist that his spindly ankles displayed the full logo of his favorite sports-themed socks. And the Singleton family (the entire flock of noble-faced women and men, boys and girls) filled a little over two rows, wearing an array of bright colors and pastels complemented by freshly-polished shoes. Everyone seemed snappy and clean. Everyone seemed jovial. The choir started a lively version of "When I Rose This Morning," and the entire congregation stood in their pews and joined in a communal celebration.

Everything was perfect and holy, just like usual.

After the hymn and opening prayer, that is when Otis casually glanced over his shoulder and inadvertently caught sight of a familiar silhouette two people over in the row behind him. His breath stuck. His heart froze. His brain fumed with uncertainty. *What the?* he frantically wondered. *How? How is this possible? How could this be happening?* Disregarding all forms of church etiquette, Otis impulsively snapped, "What Are *You* Doing Here?"

The Holloman sisters looked in his direction and gasped. Pastor Washington looked in his direction and struggled to continue. While each one of the Singletons stopped their praying and praising while turning in his direction with flustered concern.

It's him! It's him! It's actually him! Otis's memories screamed. *Jimmy-John!!! The racist who tormented my childhood! He's here! He's in the pew behind me!!! He belittled my mother. He tormented me for years. He and his friends almost killed me!*

"Brother Merriweather," Pastor Washington called from the pulpit, "is there a problem?"

"Why, why, yes," Otis proclaimed loud enough so every person there could here. "This here *racist* has no business being here." Otis felt his blood run cold. "He's a bad seed and a--"

"Brother Merriweather," Pastor attempted to cut in.

"… liar and a thief. He cost my mom her--"

"Mr. Merriweather," Pastor attempted to cut in again.

By then, the entire congregation stood steeled with tilted ears.

"… job!" Otis spat between gritted teeth. He wasn't just mad: he was furious. He wanted to hit Jimmy-John. He wanted to lay him out, but couldn't because of all of the lessons his mother and Ben instilled regarding public perception. "He's a thief, and he's, he's—"

"Here to give a speech on the importance of compassion. He's today's speaker. Yes, I understand he's had some problems. Yes, I understand he grew up around you and probably stirred up a ruckus or two. And yes, I understand you may have had problems with him in the past as, I imagine, is the case with nearly everyone here."

A rumble of uncomfortable gurgles emanated from various pews.

"However, Mr. Anderson has gotten into a bind, and in lieu of going to state prison, he's performing community service in minority-based municipals and establishments. His reputation preceded him, so no one else would afford him that chance. But I believe everyone deserves a chance in the house of worship; therefore, I've invited him to give testimony and share--"

"Testimony???" Otis scoffed. "What could someone like *that* know about—"

"Enough!" Pastor Washington commanded. "There's no room for antagonism here!"

Jimmy-John appeared taken aback. The Singleton family appeared taken aback. In fact, the entire congregation mumbled and grumbled in their pews. Mabel attempted to grab ahold of his hand, but Otis jerked it away without thinking.

"Now if everyone will turn to page 117 of their prayer books," Pastor Washington endeavored to proceed with the service, "I think we'll get started with..."

Otis tried his best to listen to the sermon. He tried to stand still and resist the urge to look back but kept getting tempted. *Don't look back there! Don't look at him! Keep your face forward and listen to Pastor Washington.*

But he couldn't help it. Eleven minutes of temptation and torment later, he may have unconsciously peered over his shoulder and saw his arch-nemesis respond with a wink! Otis was so disgusted and infuriated that he supposedly started to growl.

The Holloman sisters clutched their hearts. The elderly Steelers fan sped his spindly chicken legs up the aisle in case they needed someone to intervene while the matriarch of the Singleton's fanned herself with disapproval.

And then he saw it. The real Jimmy-John reared his mean, spiteful ways underneath his fake finely-glossed exterior. Delicately rubbing his pristine left brow (indicating the precise location he had clobbered Otis with the baseball bat), Jimmy-John taunted Otis with a magnanimous sneer. Not only did Jimmy-John's malice show his ugly ways, but he ridiculed Otis in a manner that no one else understood.

I can't hit him! Otis kept repeating. *Can't disappoint my mother or my wife. I have to remember all the lessons Ben taught me about a Colored man's personification of dignity and respect. Can't perpetuate society's perception that Black men are prone to violence.* Every single vein, every single molecule, even the space between Otis's molecules ignited with frustration and rage, but he remained motionless.

"Mr. Merriweather," Pastor Washington patiently proclaimed, "you need to turn around and..."

Otis did not hear him. He didn't hear Mable, the elderly Steelers fan, or either of the Holloman's. Jimmy-John sniggered at him and ever so subtly mouthed the word "nigger." And the next thing Otis knew, his right fist may have inadvertently hurled through the air in the immediate vicinity of Jimmy-John's left eye, resulting in the neighborhood supremacist and bully taking a much-needed catnap in the envelope of space by the knee rest.

Embarrassed out of her wits, Mable collected her purse and prayer book and abruptly fled down the aisle. Otis couldn't allow his pregnant wife to leave without him, so he took off after her.

"Otis. Cleveland. Merriweather!!!" Mable chided from the passenger seat on their way home. "I swear I's mad at you! I'm so mad, I'm... *Errr*! Why'd you do that? How could you hit him in church? Why couldn't you just forgive the man? Why'd you do that in front of the entire congregation! Everyone we know! All our friends. I swear! On my Mamma's grave, I swear sometimes your stubbornness; it's, it's..."

She sat quietly with her hands clasped on her lap, contemplating the depth of the situation and what she wanted to say. A moment or so later, she continued with, "Listen, it's gonna take something big to get over this. The Good Lord will forgive you, but it's gonna take something mighty big, something mighty fine, something stupendous. It's gonna take something grand."

Otis steered the car as it navigated a left onto Apple Blossom.

"A miracle."

Otis steered the car passed a three-story condominium complex where two little girls played on a wood-framed swing set.

"It's not just gonna take *one* miracle. It's, it's gonna take… five! It's gonna take you *five* miracles to get into heaven, Otis Cleveland Merriweather. I swear as I live and breathe; it's gonna take *five* of 'em miracles to make up for them hardheaded stubborn-minded ways. Socking someone in front of Pastor Washington and the entire congregation, how could you? Mrs. Singleton practically had a heart attack. I've never been so embarrassed. And lordy, lordy, lordy, poor Etta May Ellison. That woman, bless her heart, is close to ninety years old. She didn't need to see all that! What were you thinking? Six!!! Otis Cleveland Merriweather, it's gonna take *six* miracles. You hear me? *SIX* of 'em for you to step on through them purdy pearly gates!"

Relaxing on my lounge chair on the front porch of our new southwest Bakersfield home, I awakened to a slight breeze caressing my skin and found myself feeling comfortable. In the chair next to me, Mable sat with her feet propped onto an ottoman and an Agatha Christie balanced on her round, protruding belly. She gasped while clutching her heart, and I presumed she had gotten to another tantalizing twist in the story. And I wondered if the baby followed along with the plot. The experience lasted only for a moment or two. It was a short, crisp glimpse into Otis's life. Mable patted my knee as she turned a page without saying anything. My eyes closed. I lay there, contented, relaxed, and at peace as I returned to the land of dreams.

The next time I awaken, I sat in a chair directly outside Mable's hospital room.

"*Ahhhhhhhhhhh!*" I heard her scream.

My insides twisted while my nerves tightened into steel. *Oh, God! Oh, God! She's in labor. Mable's in labor! She's having my--*

"Mr. Merriweather!!!" A pin-faced nurse with a turkey-gobbler jowl summoned from the open doorway. Somehow I knew this was her third time trying to coax me back into the room.

"It's time!" she barked, eyeing me impatiently while pointing to the inside of the room. "Now that you've 'caught your breath,' I think it's best you return to your wife's side. She needs you."

No! No, no, no, no, no! I don't want to be here. I don't want to be in a hospital. And I especially don't want to witness anybody giving birth!

"*Ahhhhhhhhh*!" Mabel screamed a little louder. The desperation in her wail became a cement mixer stirring my brain.

"She's all the way dilated, and the baby will be here any second."

I have to do this! Gotta go in there and play the part.

"Oooootis! Cleveland! Merriweather!" Mabel groaned between bouts of huffing. "You big ole scaredy-cat! Stop being like that and get in here! Get in here and support me. I's hurten' like crazy but promise I won't bite your head off no more!"

I didn't answer because I wasn't exactly sure how much of this time travel birth fiasco I wished to experience.

"*Ahhhhh, owww*!" she groaned again. "Otis, get in here right now and support me or I ain't cooking for you for a year! You hear me? You'll be skin and bone!"

Rushing to the doorway, I saw my beautiful Mabel (Otis's beautiful Mabel) laying on a gurney under a tenting of sheets, with her feet in odd-looking stirrup contraptions. When she saw me peeking from the threshold, she looked more than a little irritated.

"Gets your big fraidy cat behind in here. Come on in, and let's pray! I wanna make sure this baby comes out nice and healthy and doesn't have a long cone head and floppy ears like your Uncle Thaddeus. He looks like he's wearing a, a, a, *ahhhhhh*!"

"Breathe," I tried my best to relax her once I made my way to her side. "Just breathe and—"

"Why are you telling me to breathe? Ooof course, I'm breathing. I'm alive, so I'm breathing! You trying to tell me something? You implying I look—"

"You look amazing," I cut her off. "I'm just implying you need to relax."

"*Implying* for me to breathe isn't relaxing. It's stressing me the heck *Owww*! Ow! Ow! Ow! Ow! Ow! Ow!"

"It's here! It's here!" Dr. Lightfoot proclaimed excitedly. "I almost see the crown!" And then the good doctor glanced my way, nodding her head as if confirming the significance of her statement.

"Relax, Mabel," Dr. Lightfoot soothed. "One or two more contractions, at the most. It's almost time to push."

"See, Blue!" Mable looked over at me. "If you had just told me to relax and not *breathe*, this baby would be, be, be--"

"Push!" Dr. Lightfoot cut her off. "It's time, Mable. Time to push. Oh, yes. Yes. Yes. Good job. That's, that's perfect. Keep on. Almost there. I see. I see. I see a crown. It's coming. It's coming. It's almost out. Okay, the head's out. The head is out. And now all we need is another... Push! Okay, it's time to push again. One last time. Just, push. Yes. Yes. It's a... It's a... It's a boy! He's out! He's out!" Dr. Lightfoot proclaimed jubilantly. "He's perfect!"

The room spun. I saw a tiny, pudgy naked baby boy lifted into the air, coated in a layer of mucus and slimy birthing gook. And I saw Mable's beautiful worn tired eyes glimmer with joy.

"Lordy, lordy, lordy, Blue," she started to say. "He's perfect. We did..."

The spinning increased, and the next thing I knew, I was out again.

Mable and I were walking. Pushing stroller's side-by-side, we sauntered along a suburban sidewalk on a bustling autumn afternoon. We had just left service at our new church and decided to walk home for no particular reason. I glanced over at her, our eyes meet, and she smiled at me. My heart fluttered like a puppy dog tail, much like when we were kids, right before I vomited all over her Mary Jane shoes. The leaves of the trees rustled their song. The air streamed brisk and clean. I felt happy.

I had just walked in from playing at the club. This time I found myself in a Jack-o-lantern orange cape, denim bell-bottoms with rhinestone seams, and boots with see-through heels. I didn't care because it was three-something in the morning and I was exhausted from working all day at Penny Save Energy then playing the sax at Moonshine Easy's. After grubbing on the tuna casserole and broccoli Mable had left, I crept into our room and found her nursing our newest little one. I couldn't remember if this one was a boy or girl, only that he or she went to town nursing on the ruffle-protected mound of Mable's chest. It looked poetic, peaceful, and serene.

Somewhere far off in the background, I occasionally heard the *rattles*, *beeps*, and *clanks* of the machine, but they were far, far away in another reality. And then, the time-traveling transitions quickened in pace as Otis's real-life occurrences flashed as quickly as a shuffling of cards. There was an experience of having another baby. Changing diapers and retching from the stench. Buying a bigger house. Getting a promotion at work as an incentive for educating his boss to the intricacies of solar power (with the promise of becoming partners) then getting finagled out of the concept, finding himself out of a job. Otis teaching his sons to catch a football. Doctor visits, dance lessons, karate lessons, visits to the dentist, and Saturday morning chores. Breakfast with the family. Police pulling him over and placing him in a line-up. Going through the interview process again. Months go by, and Otis was still looking for a job. Having to sell off household furnishings to pay the mortgage. Mabel getting a cashier position at a local paper supply. His new band cutting their first album then finding most of his cut eaten by the record label. Emmitt has his first child. They go home and visit the family. Playing music together for the first time in years, Ben's eyes brim with admiration and pride. Police pull him over for no reason and insist upon going through his car. An old friend supplies a lead to a job opening at a new HVAC company. Mabel's father dies. Mabel and Otis dance in the kitchen. One son gets a broken arm from falling out of a tree, another gets his tooth knocked out skating down a staircase. His daughter goes to prom. The kids' graduate. Mabel and Otis go on their first cruise. He hears a commercial that his old company amassed wealth specializing in solar power. His grandmother dies in her sleep. He goes to funeral after funeral and birth after birth as life pressed on. The time travels passed so quickly that I'm not sure if I'm experiencing all of them in time or memory. They flip by as Otis's life trickles through my mind. And then Mable gets sick. She has leukemia, and I harbored the wrath of pain Otis experienced watching the love of his life wither away. I experience his suffering. I experience the endless breadth and depth of his infinite love. She dies, and I experience Otis selecting a dress for her to be buried. I experience his heart's fracture when he stood on the altar and gave a long rambling eulogy that would have only made sense to her. And then I experience his extreme emptiness when he cast dirt upon his beautiful wife's grave. The kids were grown and gone, and Otis finds himself alone in the house. He tries to hold his head up while drowning in an ocean of despair. Tears stream down my face as I experience this. His heart's fracture felt true. Loneliness consumed me.

And then I awaken, and I'm glad I no longer inhabited the heartbroken, hallowed form of the man who roamed the earth, spending his time tending to others. I had returned to 242, being myself. As I lay in the bed, listening to the infuriating commotion of the machine, I cradled happier memories of Otis's love for his children, music, that ugly, crusty-eyed dog, and his beloved Mable. Something about holding onto that joy just seemed right. It gave me a glimpse of contentment as I returned to the misery of me.

SECTION VII

TRANSCENDENCE

CHAPTER TWENTY-ONE
ARRIVEDERCI!

My back hurt. My neck crooked at an unforgiving angle while my jaw burned from being braced for so long. And then I heard the familiar *clank*, *swish*, *clack-clack-clack* and the aggravating *whoosh* sound, and that's when I realized how much I despised this stage of my life.

"Hey, William Walsh!"

My eyes remained closed, yet I distinctly heard Ruby Josephine's squeak-riddled voice from her usual perch on my bed rail.

"Geeze Louise, we almost lost you for a second there. Ain't much time left, that's for sure."

I didn't move. I didn't flinch. And I sure as heck didn't open my eyes. Instead, I tried to go back. Keeping my eyelids closed and concentrating, I tried to go back to being the childhood version of Otis where I could run in fields, swim in creek beds, climb trees, and gorge to my heart's content on all those delicious dishes and treats my mother person made.

"Okay, be like that!" Ruby proclaimed. "You're still hardheaded an' stubborn, even after all them lessons you learned. Give up then. Go ahead and die like that. Check on out! Close your eyes an' greet the reaper! Don't say I didn't warn--"

"What!?" I sat up from inside myself. By then, I had become flustered and confused from all the hurdles this girl had put me through. "What do you expect me to do?"

She said nothing.

"How can I change this?"

She said nothing.

I pointed to the horde of doctors, nurses, and medical staff conglomerated in the room. "How can I stop them from divvying up my body?"

"Wellllllll," she trepidatiously sputtered, "for starters, you can join us in the corridor. Everyone's set for the celebration. Its gonna be peachy. I mean it; it's bound to be—"

"A really big show," I cut in unenthusiastically. "You already told me that. I don't see how…"

My thoughts trailed when Ruby hopped off the bedrail then squeezed herself through the brigade of medical staff, over to the blue chair where Liz sat in the same burgundy jogging suit, looking sullen and distraught. Jeremy sat next to her with their hands clasped as torrents of heartbreak streamed from their eyes.

"Liz," I said to my wife, "What's up with the—"

"Have some decency!" Ruby Josephine snipped. "They're saying goodbye! Could you show some respect and be quiet! If you wanna sit here and miss out on everything, that's up to you. You're choice. Sayonara! Arrivederci! Later alligator! Adios amigo! But you're gonna have to be quiet."

"No!" I hopped out of myself and off the bed. Standing there with my heart fracturing into a million see-through pieces, I took one last look at Liz and Jeremy and said my goodbyes.

"Sorry, Babe. Sorry for being a jackass. You've been good to me while I put myself and my needs first. We should have had kids; you're right about that. You were right all along. I think if we had kids, it would have made me a better person. Perhaps, if we had adopted, none of this would have happened. Thank you for everything you've ever done. You're the world's greatest wife. Mr. Pickle and I will always love you."

Feeling a little choked up, I turned to my brother. "Sorry, Bubba." Calling him "Bubba" brought back a lot of pent up emotion. It's the endearment our mother used throughout his early years. Not wanting to cry, I tried my best to hold in the tears.

"You've always been a big-hearted feisty little dude. And brave. Man, I used to give you some crazy dares, and you trooped through all of them with the resilience of a caveman. Remember the time I dared you to eat a spoonful of peanut butter with ants crawling on top, and you did it then asked for seconds." Shaking my head, I chuckled at the recollection. "You've always looked up to me, but it should have been the other way around. You're the strong one. Sorry for not standing up for you, but I've learned a lot lately. The man who raised us had a mental illness. You may not remember much because you were young, but Dad used to be a decent person. People liked him; he was popular and accepting of others. He even made cake. If I had known his behavior was a red flag that he battled depression, I think I could have made it better. Maybe if I had talked to his doctor, he wouldn't have taken all of his problems out on--"

The door to the room swished open, and I caught sight of something remarkable and unexpected in the hallway. Directly outside the door, a row of perfectly-statured police officers stood in their dress blues. The vision of police blue struck me with awe. I only got a glimpse of three or four of their faces, but there was no mistaking Bettencourt and Doyle as they leaned against the wall, looking distinguished and distraught. Seeing them like that stole my breath.

CHAPTER TWENTY-TWO
END OF WATCH

Exiting the room, I stumbled into the hallway. My heart bloomed when I realized that it wasn't just four or five of my friends and fellow police officers, but an entire army. The complete length of the passageway (from one end of the hospital wing to the other) overflowed with men and women from my department as well as departments from neighboring communities. Within the small space of the nurse's station, there must have been thirty or forty of them, squashed in so tightly that I couldn't make out everyone's faces. Behind the janitor's closet and the adjoining corridor, additional armies amassed of my brothers and sisters from the force. All of them donned their dress blues with polished badges and freshly-shined shoes.

And then I discerned a few civilians amongst the ocean of police officers. I recognized Deserie and a couple of other dispatchers, a secretary, and even the janitor who always took the time to greet everyone. I also saw Jeff Brittles in his postman's uniform. Something about seeing everyone lined up like that let me know something spectacular was about to happen.

Not even a minute later, a pair of orderlies transported my gurney out of the room. On top of the padded mat, I saw a gray-skinned gaunt-faced version of myself as I lay unconscious with my body bloated and emaciated at the same time. No-nonsense leaned over me, monitoring a portable breathing apparatus that enabled my body to breathe.

I'm off the machine! I'm off the machine! I triumphantly rejoiced. *I'm so fricken glad to be away from all that noise!*

The moment my gurney rolled into the corridor, the entire spectacle of police officers and civilians snapped to attention. And then I had to catch up with myself as they wheeled me in-between rows of perfectly-statured columns of blue, by rooms 244, 246, and then 248, while officers raised their right hand and saluted. One by one, every single officer and civilian there hailed salutations as a form of respect for their fallen comrade. Even though I dreaded the concept of being taken to the OR so that my organs could be replanted, the pomp and circumstance of being paraded like that remained spectacular.

"Hey!" Otis called to me from a spot he procured on top of the nurse's counter, next to Ruby Josephine and Cheddar. "Wanted to apologize for knocking you around. Shouldn't have done that. Just got mad and kinda lost it on account of you shooting me and all." He grimaced and shook his head. "Still not happy with that, but this…" Opening his hands, he gestured to the crowd of officers dutifully lined in the hallway. "… is something else. Look, even the nurses are lining up. Oh! Oh! There's Flapjack. Good ole Flapjack's standing in this here hallway, flapping them johnnycakes to show her respect!"

Escorting my body, I followed along as the gurney rolled towards the elevator, passing Fuzzy-ear hair who trembled with heartbreak and remorse. The public address system came on, and with a background composition of *Taps*, a female voice announced, "God's speed, Officer William Sebastian Walsh. Thank you for your service to God and country. We want to ask everyone to take the time to salute our fallen hero who leaves behind a wife and grieving family as he's escorted to the OR for his final call of duty and end of watch."

Glancing over at Otis, I was surprised to see that he, too, had become misty-eyed.

CHAPTER TWENTY-THREE FAREWELL

As we waited for the elevator to arrive, Commander Bennett pinned my badge onto my sheet, directly above my heart. His fingers trembled while a tear streamed from his eyes. Everyone in the corridor remained silent, almost as if the moment held a sacred significance. And then, out of the blue in the middle of this truly significant moment in time, I heard an unusual ringing and the dynamic flair of Cheddar gushing, "Chippity-chop!"

"Code Blue, Room 222!" the announcement blared over the public address system. "Code Blue, Room 222!"

As nurses and medical personnel suddenly ran off down the hallway, it took a second or two for it to click in. *222? Wait, that's Otis's room!* And then I saw them negotiate the bend at the end of the corridor, turning out of sight. Otis hopped off the counter and took off after them. Ruby Josephine and Cheddar took off after Otis. And I stood there beside myself, feeling dumbfounded. Part of me wanted to go with them, but I didn't want to leave myself as they escorted me to the OR.

The elevator doors mechanically opened, and Fire Captain Cal Akeman and a cluster of his firefighter friends poignantly filed into the hallway.

"Sorry, I'm late," Captain Akeman exclaimed as he pinned a fireman's badge next to the collection that adorned the top of my fresh hospital spread, "was out on a call. Rushed back because I didn't want to miss this."

Accompanying the orderlies and No-nonsense, I followed the gurney inside the elevator's small, claustrophobic cubicle. And there, standing beside myself, I looked out upon the hundred or so uniformed and ununiformed personnel who had come to show their respect and bid me farewell.

"Thanks," I quipped even though I knew they couldn't hear me, "but I don't deserve this; I don't deserve anyone's respect or sympathy."

"Gonna miss you," Captain Akeman proclaimed (a man I only met the day of the shooting). "You'll forever be remembered as a hero and a good friend."

CHAPTER TWENTY-FOUR
A FEW HUNDRED YEARS

When the elevator closed its doors, my heart thundered in terror. No-nonsense and the other medical personnel who stoically stood by my side would never have imagined that the braindead patient they were about to sacrifice, stood by the gurney, worrying about a million different circumstances at the same time. *Maybe I should see what's happening in Otis's room? I hope he's okay. I wonder how they're gonna do this? Wonder what it will feel like when they knock me out? Wonder if the demons will rise from the earth and collect my soul as they did Riley's?*

And it was then – as the elevator commenced its slow, steady ascent to the fifth floor – that those millions of circumstances frayed or, somehow, short-circuited my mind. That's the only way I can describe it. Instead of going back into Otis's time and having one of his life experiences, I crawled into chapters in the life of his father, his father's father, the father before that, and so on. Within the eleven and a half seconds it took the elevator to climb to the fifth floor, I experienced real-life synopses from three hundred years of oppression and torture. Three hundred years of hell.

I awoke in the dank, mildew-rotted hull of a large cargo ship. Fifty to sixty of us lay side-by-side, emaciated and naked, shackled in metal collars attached to filthy wooden planks. Stenches of fecal matter, urine, and body odor permeated every inch of the place, and it became apparent by the number of bugs and rodents that feasted on his bloated, ashen carcass that the guy next to me had been dead for quite some time. The ship swayed with the tide, and my stomach wrenched. It felt like I would puke again, and I feared if I did, I would receive another lashing. I didn't know why I had been abducted, where they were taking me, or how much time had elapsed. All I knew is that I worried about my family, who had also been taken and held hostage. *Please*, I prayed. *Don't hurt them none. Don't hurt my sisters. Don't let them have their way with them.* By then, I had seen so much evil, so much suffering, so much torture, and death. *How?* I kept asking myself. *How can this happen?*

A man with wood-covered teeth and a high topped hat led me up a set of stairs onto a raised platform where I stood naked in front of a crowd that made jest and mocked me while checking my bone structure, musculature, teeth, and eyes.

The three of us purchased by Master Farmington, were chained to one another because we possessed "spunk." I didn't know what that meant. I didn't know his language, nor the words of the others to whom I was bound; all I knew was my family didn't come with me. I never knew if they made it off the boat or had been discarded over the edge of the ship and fed to the sea. So many strangers and fellow tribesmen were dumped into the water like trash.

Later that night, we arrived on the Farmington plantation. It was a grand place with massive fields and a house so tall that the roof stood higher than the trees. I had never seen anything so striking in my life. They led us around the structure, down a path, and out back to a smoldering fire pit where several men unlocked and released our chains. The tallest of the three of us was forced onto a tree stump where his arm was strapped to the surface so that it couldn't be moved. Then a fat, red-faced, porky man grabbed a red hot poker from the most scorching coals in the fire pit and directed it onto his arm, branding him with the Farmington symbol. As the stench of singed skin assaulted my senses, the third guy in our assembly attempted to take off. Five or six of Master Farmington's men surrounded him, beat him with their whips and lashes, and brought him back. After he had been branded, he was strung up and hanged upside down as an example to not "misbehave." I took my branding and spent the rest of that long lonely night peering through a loose board in the wall at the "dumbshit" who didn't know how to behave, wondering if I should risk the attempt of rescuing him or keep myself safe by watching him die.

I awoke and found myself to be a different man, a man who felt special. A man sired from a father and mother who didn't know each other but produced a strong, productive offspring who would do well. My mother died shortly after that from the cough while my father was shot for stealing an apple off a tree limb then fed to the pigs as repayment for his sin. At 3:00 a.m. I am eager to work. I am eager to be a good Christian and do my job well because I doesn't want to be fed to the pigs or allow Master Farmington's savior to send me to hell.

Two weeks shy of my twentieth birthday, I receive my third set of lashings, accused of looking at a white woman. She is bigger than a boar, equally pig-headed, and much less attractive. I couldn't fathom anyone looking at her let alone me. The girl picks her nose, spits on the ground, and waddles about the place, calling us demeaning names like "spook," "bluegum," and "mule boy." If she lies again, I'd be strung up and killed. The only thing left for me to do is try and make a run for it.

My daughter, my beautiful, quirky, sparkly daughter, was ripped from her mother's arms so she could be taken to a nearby tobacco plantation. At eight years of age, she's too young to be someone's bed keep, but Mr. Ledbetter had eyes on her for quite some time now. Part of me felt relieved her hands would never be cut up and calloused from fieldwork, her back wouldn't stoop from the wear, but my heart fractured and broke because I missed her. I missed her so much. To me, she would always be my baby girl. I weep into the field I plow. So many tears in this soil, so many bad days. I have to stop making daughters for Master Farmington to sell.

Master Tacket is at it again. We do our best to ignore his unusual propensities because none of us wants to be flogged or receive another lashing. Master Tacket is my fourth boss-man, and, by far, one of the most peculiar people I have ever seen. Instead of bedding his wife, who longs for his company, yearning to bear a child, Master Tacket spends an extraordinary amount of time with the animals, a certain goat in particular. He grooms this goat and brushes her fur, assuring it is free of tangles and always tidy. Frequently, we see him sneaking into the barn bearing gifts of freshly picked carrots and, perhaps, a turnip from time to time. As Master Tacket has secret rendezvous with his beloved pet, his wife spends an exurbanite amount of time with his brother.

Lady Tacket doesn't care how many of us see her when she swims naked with her husband's brother in the stream, when she rides the iron plow naked with her husband's brother in the wheat field, or when she and her husband's brother lay naked beneath the whispering almond trees out yonder as they wrestle upon the ground, pretending to ride horses. Ever since Lady Tacket bought her husband that silly irresistible goat, she seems to become less and less distraught that he ignores her.

To scare us last week, Master McWilliams installed a set of torture boxes and contraptions where we would be contained and publicly scorned for the wrongdoings of our wicked ways. One of the contraptions is a large wooden box with a hole in the top, just big enough for a human neck so that whoever is being disciplined will be in the box with his or her head on top for everyone to bear witness. Of course, there's no place for the urine or the excrement, so I expect by mid-spring those boxes will be pretty ripe and riddled with flies and other insects. Master McWilliams also conjured up a way to make concrete shoes, so it is difficult to run off when someone is working in the southeastern field. I don't know how he intends for the concrete shoes to come off, but imagine Master McWilliams has an ingenious idea for that also. When we was youngens, all of us kids used to be best friends. We spent our days running around, fishing, riding horses, climbing trees, and making up stories and adventures about when we grew up. In none of Master McWilliams' tales did I imagine him growing up and torturing, maiming, and beheading the rest of us.

Years, maybe even a century later, I found myself plowing the field behind an old, hard-working mare when I see a fast-footed silhouette scurry across the freshly tilled soil. My stomach plundered. My bowels plummeted to the ground. *He's doing it! Jodeth's making a run for it, joining the forces to fight in the war. He yearns to make a difference, but what difference does winning a war make to a dead man?* As the mare turns and commences the next row, I realize I would never see my son again. I would go too, but I already had an ear cut off, and the next piece of me on the chopping block was my testicles. As a man tilling the field, I fill already castrated, but I still want to spread my seed.

CHAPTER TWENTY-FIVE ELEVEN AND A HALF SECONDS

The elevator slowed to a stop, the doors parted open, and I returned to the safety and security of being transported along the corridor towards my death. Everything that transpired during the elevator's ascent – the entire transcendental passage into the shackles of slavery – had taken a smidge over eleven seconds of actual time. In my mind, I had experienced dozens of events from hundreds of years of a hellishness no human being is meant to endure. Never in my life had I given Black history or slavery a second guess. Living it, experiencing the horror firsthand, proved to be eye-opening as well as unfathomably grim. No-nonsense rested her hand on my shoulder. She and the rest of the crew scuttled alongside my gurney as we traveled the final stretch towards the OR.

"William Walsh," Ruby Josephine appeared on the gurney's lower railing, "gotta confession to make. I know I made gest of it, but to tell you the truth, I don't like any of that blood-n-guts stuff. Never liked it, never will. So goey an'gross! There's a couple of minutes left before they…" She pantomimed the neck slice gesture.

When we got to the staging area in the center of the OR, No-nonsense and a couple of orderlies carefully transferred my body from the padded transportation gurney to a stainless steel table. Overhead, a series of flat-faced spotlights shined down on me while the large-grated floor drain patiently waited to collect my bodily fluids. As they taped my eyes open and prepared the IV, I began to feel dizzy.

"Come, William Walsh!" Ruby Josephine announced excitedly. After hopping off the gurney, she officiously stepped over the drain. "There's something you've gotta see!"

"But, but I'm--"

"I know. I know. You're about to croak! Never mind that. Come, come, come, come, the celebration's about to begin!"

"What?" I asked perplexed, "but I thought--"

Without warning, she grabbed ahold of my forearm. One second, I stood in the OR with Doctors Baylor and Skeets, and the next thing I knew, I appeared in the threshold of Otis's room.

CHAPTER TWENTY-SIX
MARCHING IN

An alarm sounded. Nurses and medical staff frantically scurried about, tending to some sort of emergency. So many people were there. As more and more medical staff shuffled in, Otis's family and friends were instructed to exit the room and wait in the corridor.

Amongst the shuffle and chaos, I got a look at Otis's body on the hospital bed and immediately felt numb.

"Oh, my God," I gushed, "what's going on? Save him! Save him! Don't let him die! If he dies now, it'll be my fault, and I'll be a--"

Otis stood beside himself, looking flustered. "I don't understand," he said perplexed. "They said I was gonna be fine. Bullets didn't get any vital organs or anything that would kill me. Doc said so herself. I'm supposed to be discharged in a couple of hours."

"Yeah," Ruby Josephine squealed squeamishly. "About that—"

"Don't die, Otis!" I shouted at the top of my lungs. "Don't die!"

A tall-haired nurse whisked through us as she ushered the last of the family members out of the room. Otis's brothers seemed shell-shocked and dismayed as they stood on the other side of the doorway.

"Sorry," Nurse Tall-hair placated, "family's gotta stay out. We need the room."

One of Otis's aunts attempted to return for her purse.

"No!" nurse Tall-hair snapped. "No, no, no, no, no! No getting anything. You have to clear the area. This is—"

"What's going on?" I asked Otis.

"Don't know," he said dumbfounded. "Thought I was just out for a nap, and now--"

"Some things are preordained," Ruby Josephine calmly intervened. "This more-or-less falls into the category of fate. You see; every once in a while brain aneurysms happen. Nothing to do with the shooting, it's just his time."

"NO!" I screamed, gripping my temples. "I DON'T want him to die!"

Looking over at Otis, I pleaded, "You can't die! You can't!"

"Yeah," Cheddar scoffed from the doorway. "If he dies, that slims your chances of getting into heaven."

"NO!" I snapped, cutting him off. "It's not that. I don't care about me. I messed up, and I'm taking accountability for my actions. I feel horrible. Seriously, I'm sorry for what happened."

No one said anything in response, so I continued. "I've been a terrible husband, a terrible police officer, and the worst possible brother. All I ever thought about was myself, but Otis…" Stepping over to the Otis on the bed, I reached over and clutched onto his forearm while the real Otis stood in bewilderment, staring at me in his persnickety stubborn way. "Please, Otis. Please. You're a good man, and you're kind to people. Yeah, you have outlandish taste in clothes. And shoes. Man, I despise your shoe collection. And, yeah, you've had some lame-brained predicaments by working too much and sleeping in your car. Other than that, you're a good person 87% of the time. From what I know, your main downfall is your inability to forgive.

Otis's expression flattened.

Turning to Ruby Josephine and Cheddar, I elaborated. "He's a little blockheaded when it comes to holding a grudge. He even moved halfway across the country because he couldn't pardon the man who gave him that scar."

"Otis." As I pleaded, a slow, subtle melody emanated from somewhere I couldn't identify. "Please forgive me! I don't care what happens to me; it's you I care about. I don't want you to disappoint yourself. Please forgive me, Otis. Tell me everything's going to be…"

The music seemed to grow louder. Inside the varying levels of percussion and strings, I heard a faraway choir of uplifted souls.

As the doctors and medical staff worked on the Otis in the bed, his body tremored for a moment or two then suddenly went limp and began to pale. When his pulse monitor registered a straight line, surrounding medical personnel performed a sequence of lifesaving maneuvers. And while all this occurred, the background sympathy began to brew louder.

"Okay." Otis looked at his sad, forsaken body and then back to me. "I forgive you."

"Wowsers!" Ruby Josephine gasped. She ran to the foot of the gurney and excitedly hugged him. "Repeat that! Say it again! Say it louder so *everyone* can hear!"

As the machine continued to flatline, medical personnel frantically attempted to bring him back to life.

Otis smiled at Ruby Josephine. "Thanks," he said sincerely. "Thank you for the company and the encouragement."

"Geeze Louise," she relayed. "Flattered that at a time like this, you'd think of little ole' me!"

"You too," he directed his attention to Cheddar. "Hope you wake up soon and win a thousand championships." They shook hands. "Take care of Granny Jin!"

And then he directed his attention to me. "You didn't set out to hunt me down. I know you shot me because you were afraid of my skin color. You saw me only by our differences, not by the many things we share in common. I don't like and can't accept cops murdering people like this. No one deserves to die like that. It's wrong. It's racist. And it's murder."

"Doesn't sound much like an apology acceptance," Cheddar interjected.

The music rose in volume, filling the room with an uplifting melody. Something about the rhythm flowed through my form, bringing joy into my heart.

"But I believe you!" Otis proclaimed. "I believe you've learned something. Don't like what you did, but I believe it when you say you're sorry, and…" Looking at his lifeless form on the hospital bed, he disregarded the implication. "I accept your apology."

My heart swelled with humility. I felt humbled and grateful and human again. I actually felt human.

"Otis Cleveland Merriweather," a woman's buttery-smooth voice summoned from the doorway.

Turning towards the door, I saw the most surprising person in the world. Mable. This is the part where it gets a little murky because I knew Mable had died many years before. Nevertheless, she stood there in a long colorful dress with a group of men and women who sang the beautiful music that echoed and flowed all around.

"Dad!" Otis gasped when he recognized the bright shiny face of the man who had raised him. "Auntie Luann!"

The choir entered the room and surrounded Otis. He started hugging and greeting them as they rejoiced in the happy, harmonious reunion.

"Thanks," Mable quipped as she turned and winked at me. "Don't know what I'd do without this big ball of handsome man here. Thank you for bringing my Blue to his senses."

Cheddar, Ruby Josephine, and I followed the group of them as they accompanied Otis down the corridor towards an open doorway that I had never seen before. They clapped and sang and danced and cheered as Otis and his happy family of angels, spirits, or whatever they were walked into a vast beautifully-adorned room. A second before they faded from sight, the ceiling appeared to open, and then I saw Ben reach his arm around Otis's back as he and Mable shepherded him into the clouds.

"Proud of you, William Walsh!" Ruby Josephine exclaimed as she elbowed my thigh. "You did well. At first, I didn't think you had it in you." She shook her head, chuckling to herself. "You proved me wrong. You proved that even the most stubborn, pig-headed, lame-brained, silly people can--"

"Is this supposed to be a compliment?"

"Yeah," Cheddar budded in. "What about me? When's it my turn to walk the walk and join the celebration of song?"

"Not everyone gets the same passage, silly! That'd be so blasé, and, quite frankly, rather discriminatory! There are people from all over the world from all types of cultural backgrounds and religions. Each person receives transport that best suit their needs. Some people get a light; some get stairs, some get a temple or St Peter in front of a gate. I've heard of angels, winged horses, and wooden canoes. I even heard of a little girl from Tibet who got a pink dragon once. The possibilities are endless. It all has to do with personal preferences."

"Another donor!" Dr. Baylor anxiously sputtered as he rushed through the group of us.

"Can you at least tell me if I'm going to wake from my coma or die soon?"

"For you, you're gonna wake up, but it's gonna be different. You'll be happy, though. Anticipate your career taking off and using the proceeds to help others."

Looking back at the room, I wanted to get one last glimpse of Otis before he disappeared and saw that it had somehow transformed into a small, enclosed janitors closet.

"And me?" I asked feebly. "Who's gonna come and collect me? I've got about ten seconds until they stop my heart. Will it be the ghoulish apparitions of demons, or will it be my Mom with my Great-uncle Milt in his favorite sparkly shoes?"

Ruby laughed without answering me, and then her eyes spanned over at the clock.

Glancing at the wall clock, I saw my end drawing near.

"Well, William Walsh," she finally injected. Once again, she placed her hands on my back, giving me a sharp shove. "I guess you'll have plenty of time to find out!"

CHAPTER TWENTY-SEVEN WRONG PEG

In a dark, dark place, a zap of energy electrified my every nerve. Startled into consciousness, I gasped. Breath filled my lungs as I choked on the oxygen, taking in the succulence of life. Slowly opening my eyes, I found Dr. Skeets standing over me with his knife (or whatever doctors called their splicing instrument) perched above my sternum.

"What the!?" Dr. Skeets blurted. "No! No way!"

"*Ahhhhhhhhhhhhh*!" The nurse tending the instrument tray shrieked at the top of her lungs.

"Stop! Dr. Skeets, stop!" No-nonsense snapped. "The patient's come to!" Grabbing ahold of his hand, she jerked it away at the precise instant the blade made contact with my skin.

They all stood there (my entire team of transplant specialists), frozen and dismayed, as I stretched out my arms and inhaled deeply.

"Sorry," I groaned, focusing my attention on Dr. Skeets, "but I think I'd like to hold off on the transplant thing and keep my innards for now."

Having a patient sit up and speak like that must have been a real doozy and shocker of all shockers. The nurses, doctors, and medical professionals looked at me as if I'd been possessed by a deranged clown. None of them had ever seen or witnessed anything so bizarre. And it was then that No-nonsense did something entirely out of character by passing out and collapsing onto the floor.

"Dang," I quipped as I stared at her sprawled out in her latex gloves and paper jumpsuit. "Had you pegged wrong the whole time!"

SECTION VIII

INCLUSION

CHAPTER TWENTY-EIGHT
ELEVEN YEARS LATER

The thing about comas, sometimes it isn't a smooth transition back to your old life. That is what happened in my case. Doctors Baylor and Skeets still haven't provided a reasonable explanation that makes sense, either than coming-to like that must have been some sort of freak incident or phenomenon. A couple of nurses told Liz it was a miracle, and getting a second chance at life must have been divinely orchestrated. I don't know it if was a phenomenon, fluke, or a miracle from above; all I know is that the road hasn't been easy and that nothing about me or my life will ever be the same. And I owe one person for all of the turmoil and change. Ruby.

Experiencing the life of a Black person made a dramatic impact on who I am. No longer blinded by seeing the world from a solitary perspective, I guess I would say I'm reborn on a sociological level. Today, I recognize the compartmentalization of cultural differences hones a propensity for discrimination and hate. It's an age-old dilemma. Hitler thought that way. So did the Hindus, Egyptians, Incas, Spaniards, and a gazillion other people, leading up to the colonialists who murdered millions of indigenous people then imprisoned millions of dark-skinned people as slaves. It is an age-old dilemma that has infected, perhaps, every civilization throughout time.

I know not why. Perhaps it is a defect in our genetic makeup, some sort of mutated chromosome in our DNA. If that is the case, maybe it is part of our purpose. Why we exist and why we are here in the first place. The meaning of life could very well be overcoming our predisposition to judge others. That is, I guess, the biggest takeaway from my do-over. I used to be self-absorbed. I knew history existed. I knew racism existed. I knew races and cultures of people treated each other better than others. I just thought nothing of it. Preferring to live in my bubble where everything was handed to me on silver platters and spoons, I grew up complacent.

Being Black and experiencing life from the perspective of another race made a profound impact on the way I view others. I am not the same person. Actually, little about me is the same. Today, I can confidently say William Walsh is a transformed man. I'm not perfect. God, no. Believe me; I'm still knuckleheaded from time to time and still make mistakes. Nevertheless, each day, I try my best to amend the sins of my past. Nothing can right the wrongs that I've done (it would take a hundred thousand lifetimes to do that), but as I live and breathe and walk in these shoes, I try my best to do better.

After the coma, my dutiful wife took time off work to nurse me back to health. It started well but quickly transitioned into a turbulent fold in our lives. I had a lot going on in my head because I refused to tell her what happened. All that tension led to a short fuse and the inevitable foot in my mouth syndrome. Liz put up with me, time and time again, but it got old and led to frequent disagreements. We quarreled so much that we almost parted ways. Divorce lingered over each conversation while we both began to visualize a life free from the baggage of this marital bliss.

That is when my brother stepped in and insisted we go to church. I didn't want to do anything spiritual like that; I preferred to stay home and hide in my little world, wallowing in a pit of self-loathing. But he wouldn't give up. He kept pushing and pressing that it got to the point that I finally broke and accompanied Jeremy and Liz only out of resentment. Sitting in the very back pew, I existed. I didn't pray. I didn't sing. I didn't even hold hands when it was time for the community prayer. Still, God found a way into my heart.

I didn't say anything in church or after the service. I didn't say anything on the way home. However, once we returned to the solace of our small, safe little abode, I sat them down and confessed everything. I told Liz and Jeremy the truth about the shooting, the setup afterward, and the dreamlike events that happened during my coma. That confession led to the first steps in repairing my life and finding happiness.

May 17, 1993, seventy and a half days after the shooting, I walked into the Bakersfield River Police Station and turned myself in. Providing Commander Bennett with a sworn, signed affidavit, I recounted the events behind the shooting, detailing everything that happened as it did. My report concisely relayed the fact I had shot out of fear, and that I shouldn't have been intimidated by Otis's appearance and the color of his skin. I also conveyed how Riley had come up with the throwaway and staged the scene to make the use of deadly force appear warranted, and that coming forward had been crucial in clearing Otis's name.

When I drove in that morning, wearing a pale-blue, long-sleeved, dress shirt, I didn't think I would ever see the inside of my house again. My wardrobe had been stored, paperwork put away, affairs tidied. I thought I would be arrested and remanded to custody. I truly believed my signed statement sealed the deal. Instead, the decision making honchos sent me home so they could confer with legal and determine an appropriate course of action.

Two weeks later, I received a letter in the mail from the city's attorney. An official notice informing me, my initial statement had been deemed correct, and any accounts and/or revisions made after the fact – whether or not they *appeared* real in my head – would only be considered the construed meanderings of an altered mind. Going into detail about the extent of the frontal lobe damage I had incurred, they told me they felt sorry for me and to "have a nice day." I tried, again and again, to make things right; the city merely placated me with counseling appointments and awards for meritorious service and heroism.

I don't know if it was Commander Bennett, Sergeant Fleckman, Sergeant Morrey (or someone else close to the investigation), but copies of my affidavit somehow made it into the hands of almost everyone in the department. And then arose the storm of retaliatory backlash as Liz and I became inundated with harassing phone calls, a slashed tire, a busted window, and a slew of hate mail from my *brothers* and *sisters* on the force. They turned on me. Terming me a "traitor" and a "farce," they ranted and raged and name-called as they tarnished me in every way possible, and a couple of ways that were anatomically quite misleading.

Here's the ironic thing. No one was up in arms about the shooting. No one called, yelling and screaming because an innocent Black man had been shot in front of his granddaughter. No one freaked out that a cover-up had been exposed. None of that mattered to them. What mattered, what had everyone agitated and irate, what *terrified* them was a singular word: justification. In my affidavit, I elaborated the need to redefine the parameters in *justifiable* police shootings.

You see, in California, simple "fear" substantiates probable cause in nearly every police officer shooting. "I saw a cell phone and thought it was a gun." "The suspect reached for his wallet; I thought it might have been a weapon." "The suspect moved in a threatening way." All an officer has to do is express a *supposed threat,* and his actions (whether conscionable or unconscionable) would be perceived "reasonable" under the broad blanket of the law.

This is the part for me where it is tough because I understand what it is like to be a police officer. I know the sick feeling in your gut when you roll up on a domestic because you never know who or what you will come across. I know how your veins gel when you're dealing with agitated parolees or drugged up gang members because they tend to turn into walking time bombs. I know how bystanders like to jump in and instigate trouble. I know how monsters abuse kids. I know how they drive drunk and mow over pedestrians then run off, leaving their wounded suffering in the middle of a hot road with intestines splayed onto the asphalt. I know hate and drug-induced rage.

Those stressors lead to quick trigger fingers and rash decisions. Police officers deal with dangerous people at the most critical time in their lives. They deal with society at its breaking point. Having that kind of pressure can morph an officer's good, sound, judgment and transform them into someone cold-hearted and corrupt, or even worse – as in my case – someone in fear. Then that corrupted officer or fearful officer responds to minor traffic violations (a cracked tail light, unlit license plate frame, an object such as a rabbit's foot dangling from the rearview mirror obstructing vision) with their guns drawn and loaded trigger fingers, and innocent people get gunned down for no reason. No life should be that expendable. No child should be gunned down because police officers train with Old West tactics that put the probability of chance (what *could* happen) before the sanctity and value of human life.

Today, I head a nonprofit that sets out to clean up the verbiage used in the laws that oversee incidents of law enforcement shootings. We want to move away from vague terms as "perceived fear" and what a "reasonable" officer would do because written that way even the rashest officer (such as me) will be found innocent in a court of law. It's a simple change that will force departments to adopt a less-than-lethal approach to policing, saving thousands of lives while bringing nobility back into law enforcement. I still get flack every once and a while from some of my hard-headed former compatriots, but I can't help but think of little Charlotte's expression in the backseat of the car. Her heartbreak, her terror, fuels my drive.

If I lived another hundred years, I don't know if I can right the wrongs of my past. Guilt consumes me; it writhes in my bones, my skin, and my eyes. Sometimes when I am sleeping, the shadow person sneaks in and attacks me. I am punched awake and discover only a vacant room. I am not sure who or what it is, although I have begun to suspect it is my own conscious: my fed up inner self subjecting me to the retribution I deserve.

I'd ask God to help out, but I don't know if everything really happened or if it was all a figment of my imagination like most seem to think. All I know is that I have been blessed with a second chance, and I am going to do my best to get it right this time. I suppose that's all I can do. Perhaps that is why I'm telling you this story. It's the final step of my redemption, not only proving what a great man Otis Cleveland Merriweather was to me and so many people, but in writing this textual account, I can show how horrifically remorseful I am for what I've done. I can't make things right. I'll never be able to make things right. But I can take this experience and do what I can to nurture the vines of tolerance to bring about a harvest of acceptance and inclusion in the world.

One huge step in bettering myself happened two and a half years into my recovery when Liz and I adopted our first child. Then we adopted our second, third, and (yes) fourth. That is four times the craziness, spilled milk, homework assignments, and mess. Our home has become a beacon of madness, and my beautiful, loyal, very patient wife shines through it all.

Liz still rocks blue suede pumps and red chiffon dresses, but only every once in a while on that rare special occasion when we go out. These days, my beautiful wife wears jeans with holes in the knees, faded t-shirts, and boring tennis shoes riddled with mom stains. It doesn't matter what she looks like to everyone else. To me, she will always be my beautiful bride.

As more and more time passed, I immersed myself in my new life, no longer dwelling on every single factor that happened to me while in the coma. It was still there (all of the events remained a significant part of my being), but I shelved the memory in a place in my mind so that it was safe, allowing me to cope with day to day life. It was the subtlest occurrence that dredged up a clue I may have overlooked, and the next thing I knew, I had a tangible lead that would help me determine whether or not everything was real or only a figment of my imagination.

While driving my eldest daughter to her dentist office for a routine cleaning, we passed a young boy skateboarding in the bike lane, and a slew of memories filtered into my mind as if a door unlocked and a vital clue walked into my head and knocked on my brain. Hung Luu. If he had come out of his coma, I could talk to him and confirm – for once and for all – if everything really happened or if it was all some sort of bizarre dream. So I set out tracking anything I could find on the infamous skateboarding legend. Of course, I wouldn't admit it to anyone else, but there was a place in my heart that thought we would share the same memories and bond over the circumstances. Unfortunately, that's not the way it went down.

My computer skills were pretty weak back then; however, after some research, I discovered an ad featuring the Luu brothers in a street league skateboarding demonstration sponsored by a popular energy drink. The date of the show was a few months away at a park near Santa Monica; therefore, I made the determination I would bring the family for a weekend of fresh air and beach activities and see if I would run into my old friend.

When the day arrived, Liz and I packed the kids and the car, making it just in time to see the introduction. Sitting on the bench like that, I actually began to feel nervous. I don't think I was as worried about seeing Hung Luu as much as I fretted having everything proved false.

So we're sitting on a bench in this beautiful place on this beautiful day and lol and behold, Hung Luu walked onto the staging platform and took a seat at the judge's table. Sitting there with my insides twisting and turning, I became a nervous wreck. *He's real! He's real! He's an actual person. He was right about skateboarding and being a legend.*

Hung Luu's eyes scanned past me as he looked into the audience. While I sat in the front row, they scanned by me again and again with no hint of recognition. So I stood and waved, and he still didn't recognize me. After five or seven frantic calls out, he had security personnel ensure the overly-zealous fan blocking the television monitors take a seat or leave.

The music came on, and the announcer started the show by introducing the judges. Feeling sad and discouraged, I slumped in my seat, sullenly waiting for the stunts to begin. When he got to the third person sitting at the judge's table, he said, "For our third judge, we have the infamous Cheddar, who's famous for Pro-Am Board tour circuit and back-to-back championships in the International Skateboarding World

Tour."

As the audience clapped their applause, Hung leaned into the microphone and charismatically chirped, "Chippity-chop, y'all!"

Leaning into the back of my bench, I relaxed and contentedly sighed. And then I chuckled to myself as Liz, the kids, and I enjoyed an incredible demonstration.

As I look back, I realize these past ten or eleven years have brought about so many transitions and change. The most significant change, however, is something that came out of the blue and completely unexpected. Something I never, not in my wildest imagination, dreamed could happen. It all began one ordinary Monday when I set out on my usual morning trek to pick up some coffee. I remember that day as if it's embedded in my brain.

Having just turned onto Gosford, I inadvertently adjusted the station on my radio. I intended to focus on an NPR discussion on reforming social security when I accidentally caught the tail end of an old jazz number with a heart-pounding beat. My attention frenzied for a moment or two because not only did I recognize the song, I remembered that I liked it. Surprisingly, I liked it! I liked the rhythm, and the beat, and the way it flowed throughout the car. Listening to the melody felt so bizarre and unexpected. Then I recognized the next song and the song after that as if the tones, rhythms, and cords had imprinted on my being.

Instead of going home, I immediately did a roundabout, heading over to Optimal Music on 19th Street. There, on a velvet-lined shelf in the middle of the store, I found it. Shining with so much improvisation and spunk, it nearly took my breath away.

"Would you care for some assistance?" the gangly-thin salesclerk who worked there prudently inquired.

"I guess," I uttered hesitantly, mustering my composure. "Is that a saxophone?"

"Why, yes," he answered, eying the hefty price tag.

"And they play jazz, blues, rock, and—"

"Saxophones can play anything. They're pretty adaptable." He eyed me skeptically. "Would you like to see it?"

"I, I guess." I couldn't understand my pull to the instrument. Otis had played one, but it would take me over a decade and thousands of hours of practice to master a musical instrument as he did.

"Are you thinking of purchasing this for yourself, or do you have a son or daughter in mind?" When I didn't say anything, he clarified with, "We offer a student discount."

"Myself," I muttered meekly, eyeing the instrument while he guided it into my hands.

And then, without warning or reason, I mysteriously positioned the body of the instrument. I knew how to hold it in my hands, how to situate and place my fingers, and the way I needed to glide my thumb onto the middle of the rest under the octave key. Without any warning or thinking about it, I blew into the mouthpiece, procuring my first note.

"Wow!" he gushed. "Okay, pretty good for your first time."

That is when the miraculous event happened. I had never had a music lesson. I certainly never held a saxophone in my hands when I was me. But I somehow knew the correct way to adjust pressure into the mouthpiece. Without even looking at a sheet of music, I somehow began *When the Saints Go Marching In.*

"You're, you're… Good! Really good." He stood dumbfounded and a bit flustered. "I thought you said you couldn't…"

Closing my eyes, I belted out a glitzy version of that song, then another one after that, and then another. Tunes I had never heard before as me but knew very well as the Otis me. One of them was the famous Blues number his band recorded for their first album, and the other, the funk-filled ditty I'd played in the club. Something about performing those songs brought my heart home.

Three months later, I stood on stage, playing in a seedy grit-filled establishment to a gathering of jazz aficionados, funk lovers, blues connoisseurs, and a tipsy consortium of music lovers with mad crazy beat.

I don't know how it happened. I don't know if it was Ben's doing when he patiently showed me the basics or if Otis's skill had somehow imprinted on my mind. All I know is that besides coming back to life, the ability to play the sax is one of the greatest gifts that has happened to me. Now, I am the only blondie in an all-Black band. They accept me as one of the brothers in our group. They love me not because of the way I look and dress (okay, I may have adopted a new perspective for Otis's quirky style); they like the fact that I play from heart. Music has transformed me. Now, I'm the guy with rhinestone belts and gold-fringed sleeves, belting out notes that transcend moods.

Besides my new outlook, mission in life, the open-minded way I treat people, and the miraculous ability to play the sax, there's an additional area in my life that has seen substantial change — my diet. Two and a half days into my recovery, all I could think about was food. Real food, not tapioca pudding, not broth, and certainly not the fish fricassee the cafeteria concocted. No, I wanted something delicious, something with savor, zip, pizazz, and crunch – gotta have that crunch! I craved dishes that made my taste buds whip and flip with glee; meals that celebrated textures, flavors, and spice. I wanted the foods of my dreams.

On the way home from the hospital, Liz suggested we stop at a neighborhood wellness cafe I had always likened as one of our favorites. Little did she know, I wouldn't be fancying tofu bacon, turkey soup, or soy stroganoff ever again. I still chuckle when I remember the shock on her face when we stopped at a local pancake house, and I ordered fried chicken and waffles dripping in blueberry syrup topped in swirling peaks of real whipped cream.

That's how I have been ever since. It is like the dial on my palate went from cardboard cruelty to scrumptious deliciousness. Yeah, I'll eat something healthy every once in a while, but I prefer real food. I prefer good old-fashioned soul food and southern style cooking with a finger-licking flair. Instead of steamed potatoes and kale, I'm having me some black-eyed peas, collard greens, grits, mashed potatoes drowning in gravy, tangy coleslaw, baked beans, and meat (fried, baked, smoked, slow-cooked, roasted, and barbequed). Yeah, I may have packed on a few pounds since back in the day. That's okay because the new me thinks life is lip-smacking delicious.

So what, you may ask, is the *seventh* miracle of Mr. Otis Cleveland Merriweather? Mable alluded to six; I don't know if all six happened the way she prophesized, but I do know Otis's first miracle was saving nine-year-old Mable that day on the tracks. Whether or not I was there – vomiting on her Mary Janes and making a big gooey mess of it all – Otis is the one who risked his health and safety to save the life of a friend in need.

The second miracle happened the day Ben proposed to his mother; the day his mother nearly lost her life in the factory. You see, when Pastor Washington lectured Otis about the struggle, he mentioned that his mother wasn't allowed to use "their" facility, drink "their" water, or eat "their" food, and that she took her breaks "on an ole' wood crate behind the coal barn." Otis decided to borrow a bicycle and bring his mother a fresh container of well water and a slice of her homemade cornbread lovingly wrapped in a blue linen cloth. Leaving it on the crate, he simply wanted to kindle her heart. When the factory blew up, she was taking her break out back, being inspired by her son's generous act of kindness. Otis's humble gesture saved his mother from the great bodily harm of being burned.

Otis's third miracle happened during his hospitalization after being attacked in the boys' restroom in school. Overwhelmingly remorseful for his perceived participation in the ordeal, Frankie (the boy with the cast on his leg) visited Otis in his hospital room and sincerely apologized. They forged a friendship that changed the course of Frankie's journey wherein he would go on to become Senator Frank Gallagher, an honest and moral politician dedicated to issues of racial equality, including desegregated education, an end to police profiling, and initiating legislation to resolve practices that unjustly incarcerate minorities.

Otis's fourth miracle – now, that's an easy one. Risking his life, time and time again, he saved countless others in the battle in the rice field and then again during the attack at U.S. Marine garrison Khe Sanh in Vietnam. That was just one day of a seventeen-month tour wherein Private First Class Otis C. Merriweather heroically saved the lives of hundreds of soldiers and civilians while proudly serving his country as a United States Marine.

Otis's fifth miracle is something he never knew he did. You see, Otis played a significant role in societies' acceptance of solar power as an alternative form of energy, saving billions of dollars while protecting the health of our planet. Beginning with his report in high school, he went job to job and place to place promoting the benefits of harnessing the sun's energy. Every time he touted solar energy, he planted a seed. Eventually, power companies, HVAC companies, people from school, and people he met on the street began to take heed. Word spread and Otis (whether he knew it or not) had a significant impact in illuminating the importance of saving our planet via the use of solar power and alternative forms of energy. He didn't invent solar power: the great Alexandre Edmond Becquerel did that in 1839. However, many of the applications of solar power today were born from the imagination of a skinny African-American schoolboy who spent his afternoons sitting at a small wooden desk in his bedroom, conceptualizing dreams.

His sixth miracle was a biggie in that learning to forgive people seemed to have been a reoccurring theme in his life. Forgiveness (something Pastor Washington regularly touted in Sunday sermons) is necessary for bridging the weather of life's storms. Otis had a temper. And when that temper flared, he had a tendency of sometimes throwing a punch or stepping on people's Adams Apples. His mother tried to teach him. Ben tried to teach him. Pastor Washington tried to teach him. Otis still ended up resolving a few of life's differences with a reckless fist. However, Otis's big heart worked at the right time because he was able to forgive the person who wronged him the most. When Otis forgave me, it released him of the shackles of bitterness and harbored hate, securing a sweet passage to a heavenly ever after.

And his seventh miracle – well, that is, perhaps, the most

magnanimous miracle of all. Otis saw people for who they are by looking past stereotypes and preconceptions. Otis knew the importance of family and friendship, and he loved being a dad. He knew how to enjoy a meal instead of just ingesting it. And he learned forgiveness. Living through him transformed everything in my world. He brought music and so many valuable lessons into my life. He made me a better man, and I am a thousand times richer because of him. I am humbled. I do not deserve such grace. However, this is the way the events really happened. Otis took a sinner and a loser, and showed him a better life while filling his palate with friends, family, funky beats, and fresh out of the oven apple fritters. The seventh miracle of O.C. Merriweather is me.

the end

Made in the USA
Columbia, SC
22 August 2019